Dear Reader,

I loved writing about Sadie Speers, an independent and unique woman who loves antiques, her family and friends, and the gorgeous surroundings of Colorado. Her hometown of Silver Peak was inspired by Leadville, Colorado, a place rich in history. One of the buildings mentioned in this book, *Nobody's Safe*, is the Silver Peak Opera House. I modeled it after the Tabor Opera House in Leadville. Learning more about its history revealed wonderful stories of past events. John L. Sullivan boxed on its stage, and Harry Houdini performed there as well. In fact, there is still a trap door on the stage that was installed by Houdini to assist in one of his famous magic tricks. Reading about the opera house certainly helped to ignite my imagination.

As a lover of antiques, as well as a collector, I was able to use my knowledge to add some interesting aspects to *Nobody's Safe*. However, before I began writing, I realized I had no real experience with antique safes, one of the key elements in the book. Although I do a lot of online research, whenever I can, I like to talk to real people. In my opinion, human feedback can add depth to an author's story. I spent almost an hour on the phone with the leading expert on antique safes in the country. His information helped to shape my plot.

I hope you'll love meeting Sadie and visiting all the captivating things in Silver Peak, including the opera house!

God bless you,
Nancy Mehl
writing as Carole Jefferson

Mysteries of Silver Peak

MYSTERIES
of SILVER PEAK

Nobody's Safe

CAROLE JEFFERSON

Guideposts
New York

Published by Guideposts Books & Inspirational Media
110 William Street
New York, NY 10038
Guideposts.org

Acknowledgments

Every attempt has been made to credit the sources of copyrighted material used in this book. If any such acknowledgment has been inadvertently omitted or miscredited, receipt of such information would be appreciated.

Scripture quotations marked (NIV) are taken from *The Holy Bible, New International Version*. Copyright © 1973, 1978, 1984, 2011 by Biblica, Inc. Used by permission of Zondervan. All rights reserved worldwide. www.zondervan.com

Cover and interior design by Müllerhaus
Cover art by Greg Copeland represented by Deborah Wolfe, Ltd.
Typeset by Aptara, Inc.

Printed and bound in the United States of America
10 9 8 7 6 5 4 3 2 1

Prologue

HIS HANDS SHOOK AS HE PLACED THE ITEMS ONE BY ONE INTO THE safe. A noise from behind caused him to drop the Bible. Although he tried to catch it, he failed. The book landed on the floor with a thump. He slowly got to his feet, peering into the darkness beyond the room where he stood, bathed in soft light from the lamp on the floor next to him. Barely moving, he reached for the lamp and turned it off with a *click*. He remained motionless, hidden in blackness, wondering if he would be exposed. As he waited, he realized he would spend the rest of his life hiding in the dark, guarding his awful secret from the light of discovery. After what seemed like an hour but could have only been a few minutes, he turned the lamp back on and went about completing his private act. Once everything was inside the safe, he carefully closed the door and turned the lock, covering his sins with plaster.

"Dear God," he prayed quietly, "please forgive me. Please wash away my transgressions. I can't change the past. I can only try to recompense those I've hurt so deeply. I pray my sin will stay hidden as long as I live. Should the day come when someone uncovers my offense, please show them that I was not an evil man. Have mercy and allow me to be remembered with compassion."

He began to cover up the hole in the wall, sweat dripping down his face like tears. When it was finished, he gathered his tools and his lamp and walked out of the building, never once looking back at the place where truth waited for the day it would finally be revealed.

1

"DON'T KNOW IF WE NEED A MAN SO CITIFIED TO BE OUR MAYOR," A voice called out. "You don't look like anyone who lives in Silver Peak."

Sadie Speers turned her head and searched through the crowd packed into Arbuckle's Coffee. The popular shop was filled to the brim with residents wanting to hear why they should vote for Edwin Marshall as their mayor. There was only one person on their feet besides Edwin. Sadie frowned at Marge Ruxton. It pained Sadie to admit that Marge was somewhat of a busybody, the type of person who seemed to have an opinion about almost everything and everyone. Sadie tried hard to like her, to give her the benefit of the doubt, but sometimes it was difficult. She looked back at Edwin. How would he handle her critical comment?

Edwin looked very distinguished in his oxford shirt and flat-front Dockers. At Sadie's urging, he'd left his usual sweater vest at home, which for him was a big step toward making his appearance more casual. He was a large, well-built man with silver hair and steel-blue eyes that hinted at intelligence and kindness. At only five foot four, Sadie felt small when she stood next to him. And she liked that. Edwin had been her steady boyfriend in high school until he left Silver Peak to go to college. He'd spent many years as a circuit judge in Chicago before moving back to Silver Peak after his wife died. A lot of time had passed since those days, yet when Sadie looked at him, she could still see the handsome young boy she'd been so crazy about.

Edwin smiled at the sharp-faced woman. His deep baritone voice boomed with confidence. "You're right, Marge. As a judge, I grew used to dressing rather formally. If it brings you any comfort, my friends are working on me." He looked over at Sadie and gave her a quick wink before turning his attention back to Marge. "Be assured that I am fully committed to Silver Peak. I grew up here, and my roots are firmly planted in its soil. I love this town, and I intend to represent you the best I can."

Sadie felt a surge of emotion as she watched Edwin. Although they were just friends, more and more she'd felt drawn to him, especially as his attraction to her became more obvious. Even though her husband, T.R., had been gone for several years, in many ways she still felt like his wife. They'd had a wonderful marriage, and Sadie wasn't sure she was ready to imagine herself with anyone else.

She shook herself out of her reverie and refocused her attention back on the meeting. She smiled as Marge, who wasn't used to being told she was right about anything, looked flummoxed for a moment, then shrugged and sat down, seemingly satisfied.

Another hand shot up. Edwin nodded at Doc Conroy, Sadie's physician. Doc was a longtime Silver Peak resident. He'd delivered Sadie's daughter, Alice, along with a lot of the people gathered inside Arbuckle's. Doc was seventy years old but had the energy of someone twenty years younger. The gray-haired doctor stood.

"I think it's safe to say that all of us are committed to making Silver Peak better, but most of the folks who live here aren't interested in changing the personality of this town. Your opponent has some ideas that might give us a more modern appearance, but I'm not sure that's what we want." The fine lines by his eyes crinkled with humor. "I guess some of my esteemed colleagues in the medical profession would say we might be in need of a face-lift, but we don't want to end up looking like some Hollywood starlet who's had one procedure too many." Doc paused until the laughter over his comment died down. "I suppose what I'm trying to say is that we want to make Silver Peak the best it can be without losing what makes us unique. So what are your plans for our future, Edwin?"

Doc sat down to a round of applause.

Edwin's opponent was James Morgan. Manager of the local bank, James was a respected member of the community. Originally, a third candidate, Jared Marley, had planned to run too, but a lack of campaign resources had forced him to back out, leaving the race with two very different but excellent candidates. Still, Sadie honestly thought Edwin would make a better mayor, in part because she agreed with his position on maintaining the traditions of the town and avoiding too much new development. Edwin brought to Silver Peak a perfect combination of big-city savvy and small-town sensibility. But also she knew the kind of man Edwin was, how much integrity he had. Still, she supposed it was better to have two good candidates instead of two poor choices.

Edwin smiled. "I completely agree with you, Doc. For one thing, the Silver Peak Historic Preservation Council is working hard to restore the fine old buildings in our town. I'm proud to be a part of that." His eyes swept the group. "As many of you know, we've been approached by several developers interested in Silver Peak. Unfortunately, their plans for us aren't in line with our vision."

"And what is our vision?" someone called out. Sadie couldn't see who spoke, but it sounded like Doc's receptionist, Rita Dodd.

"To maintain and preserve our heritage." Edwin responded instantly. "We're blessed to live in a special town that is nestled in some of the most beautiful country in the United States. Silver Peak has a rich history. We should work hard to protect that." He swept his hand across the crowded room. "I also have to mention our many wonderful businesses." He pointed at Hector Vidal, who owned Arbuckle's Coffee Shop where the meeting was being held. "Arbuckle's serves some of the best coffee and pastries in Colorado." His gaze moved to Sadie, and he smiled. "The Antique Mine carries fascinating antiques, many of them from the early days of Colorado. We also have lots of unique shops on Main Street, along with several great restaurants."

Another hand went up. This time it was Jeanne Sweeting. Jeanne was married to the pastor of Campfire Chapel and was an active volunteer around town. She also taught piano in her home. Sadie's granddaughter, Sara, took lessons from her.

"I agree with you, Edwin. But there are some residents who believe an influx of financing from big corporations would help us to undertake larger projects that would bring in more tourists. What do you say to them?"

"I've heard that too, Jeanne. It sounds reasonable, but we already have a fine tourist trade. If we take money from corporations, wouldn't they want a say-so in our way of operating? What if their ideas don't line up with ours?" He shook his head. "I'd rather keep our residents in control of our future, wouldn't you?"

Another wave of applause broke out, and Jeanne nodded her agreement. Sadie was pleased to see that her friends and neighbors supported Edwin and his ideas. She glanced at her watch. The meeting had already gone twenty minutes longer than scheduled. Edwin had handled his speech with amazing composure, skillfully managing all the inquiries put to him by the residents of Silver Peak. She needed to get back to work and hoped the discussion was finally coming to a close.

"Any other questions?" Edwin asked, gazing around the packed room.

No one responded to his query, so Jesse Wilson, Edwin's campaign manager, jumped to his feet. Sadie wondered if Jesse's buttoned-down, conservative appearance and hipster attitude would sit well with some of the older people in Silver Peak. So far, no one seemed to mind.

"Thank you all for coming," Jesse said. "Before you leave, I'm supposed to remind you that the Antique Mine has just gotten in some beautiful handmade quilts from all over the state. Stop by and take a look before you leave. And please see me for handouts you can pass around to your friends and neighbors." He flashed a practiced smile at the assembled group. "I also have buttons and flyers that will help to get the word out about our next mayor, Edwin Marshall."

Sadie glanced at her second cousin, Laura Finch, who sat next to her, and smiled. Laura, who had experience in managing political candidates, had helped Jesse create the handouts, and she'd done a fine job. Laura had originally come to town partly to learn about her family history, and partly because of a controlling man who'd tried to take advantage of that history. Thankfully, the man was now out of Laura's life. She'd left her job in campaign management in Boston to move to Silver Peak and now lived in an apartment on the third floor above the Antique Mine. For now, she'd decided to step away from politics and use her professional skills to help local businesses with promotional work.

Laura was a petite woman, about ten years younger than Sadie, with light brown hair and hazel eyes. Sadie was pleased to see her cousin looking more relaxed and happy as she began to gain distance from her troubled past and settle in to life in Silver Peak.

After one more enthusiastic bout of applause, conversation broke out all over the room. Some folks were content to stay seated and visit with their friends, while others stood to their feet and made their way over to greet someone sitting at another table. Sadie was pleased to see a line forming in front of Jesse, who was handing out campaign buttons and flyers.

"I'm going back to work," she told Laura.

"Think I'll stick around a bit," Laura said. "See if I can help Jesse."

"You've already done a wonderful job," Sadie said with a smile. "I know he appreciates it."

"I've enjoyed it. Edwin will make a wonderful mayor."

"I agree." Sadie stood up and patted her cousin on the back. "I'll see you later." She began to make her way toward the door that joined Arbuckle's and the Antique Mine. She'd only gone a few feet when someone put a hand on her arm. She turned around to find Jerry Remington standing behind her.

Jerry and his wife, Jane, owned Silver Peak Bed-and-Breakfast, a charming inn housed in a renovated Victorian home owned by one of Silver Peak's early residents. Jerry reminded Sadie of Harrison Ford. Not only was his coloring the same, he had a sideways smile that was an almost perfect match to the well-known actor.

"Hi, Jerry," Sadie said. "I'm happy you and Jane could come today."

"We are too." He smiled. "We're so glad Edwin is running. He seems to really understand Silver Peak."

Sadie pointed at the people lined up near Jesse. "Looks like a lot of people agree with you."

She noticed Jane having an animated conversation with Edwin. Always the picture of elegance, Jane wore her silver hair tucked into a smart-looking white wool hat with gray fur trim. Her coat matched her hat, and the outfit was set off by black leather boots that came to just below her knees. Jane was tall and slender and carried herself like a model. Even though she was in her seventies, she could easily pass for a woman twenty years younger. However, one of the things Sadie loved most about Jane was that she didn't seem to realize how beautiful she was.

Jerry laughed. "Jane's determined to get the word out. She's very vocal about her support for Edwin."

"I'm glad."

"I hope you and Edwin still endorse our goal for establishing a dinner theater in the old opera house," Jerry said.

The Silver Peak Opera House was undergoing extensive renovations, and a lot of people had ideas about what to do with it when the work was done. Jerry, the chairman of the historic preservation committee, had suggested the idea of a local dinner theater made up of Silver Peak residents. In the same manner of the plays that had once graced the opera house, Jerry and Jane had suggested the troupe act out stories about the early days of Silver Peak. The plays would not only be entertaining, they would be educational, helping to preserve Silver Peak's history. Edwin and Sadie, who both served on the committee, loved the idea. But there was one holdout. Luz Vidal, the co-owner of Arbuckle's, felt they would do better if they brought in nationally known entertainers. Sadie and Edwin were certain the cost would be prohibitive. They wanted ticket prices to stay low enough so everyone would be able to attend the shows, but so far Luz was holding firm to her opinion. The committee could outvote her, but before doing that, an attempt would be made to see if they could all come into unanimous agreement.

"We're still excited about it, Jerry. I wouldn't worry. Luz is a very reasonable woman. I think she'll come around. I hope you and Jane are still willing to head up the troupe. You're the only couple we know with acting experience."

Jerry laughed. "That's true, but it's been a long time since those high school plays, Sadie. Not sure my skills are what they used to be."

"I'm sure you'd be wonderful."

"I appreciate the vote of confidence. Jane and I truly believe it would add an entertaining and unique feature to Silver Peak." He grinned widely. "Besides, it would be a lot of fun, as well."

"I think it would too."

Jerry raised his arm in the air and signaled to Jane, who was waving at him. "Well, it looks like my wife wants me. I'd better get over there."

After saying good-bye to Jerry, once again Sadie headed toward the door that led to her shop. She glanced back at Edwin, but he was in a deep conversation with a man she didn't recognize. As she tried to place him, the man turned his head and looked right at her. He was a small man, who wore large glasses that made his eyes look too big. He smiled at her as if he knew her. She returned his smile but still couldn't figure out who he was. Turning her attention away, she continued to wend her way through the crowd. She stopped several more times to greet friends. Eventually she made it through the door and into her shop, which was already crowded with people checking out the new quilts. But there were other displays that also attracted attention, just as Sadie had hoped. She pulled the door closed behind her and gazed lovingly at her shop. Every time she entered her unique store, a feeling of contentment filled her. From the high pressed-tin ceiling, the polished wooden shelves that held all her beautiful antiques, to the rich mahogany desk that helped to make up her front counter, the Antique Mine had a charm that most antique shops didn't possess. Every item in the store was displayed with pride, and nothing was ever allowed to gather dust or grime. Sadie treated her treasures with the respect she believed they deserved. Antiques were a part of history, and Sadie, a retired history teacher, treasured the past.

The cozy ambience of the Antique Mine was enhanced by a new acquisition. An old black potbellied stove sat in a corner not far from her desk. The wood inside crackled as it spread its warmth throughout the room.

Sadie's assistant, Julie Pearson, smiled as Sadie approached the front of the store. Julie was tall, with an athletic build that came from long-distance running. With long blonde hair and green eyes, she not only looked like her twin boys, she was almost as active. Julie worked at the Antique Mine part-time while her sons were in school. Besides her job with Sadie and taking care of her husband and children, Julie was also interested in interior design. Sadie thought of herself as a busy person, but Julie's energy and accomplishments continually amazed her.

With the shop already bustling, people drifting in from Arbuckle's to see the quilt display made things hectic.

"Do you need help, Sadie?"

Sadie looked up to see her best friend, Rosalind Putnam, standing in front of her. Rosalind, whose nickname was Roz, stared at Sadie through large bejeweled eyeglasses, her gray bob framing an intelligent face. Like Sadie, Roz was a retired teacher.

"I think we'll be fine, Roz," Sadie said with a smile. "But thank you for asking."

"Well, if you change your mind, let me know." She nodded her head toward several customers perusing the quilt display. "Looks like you're going to sell some of those quilts today."

"I think we will," Sadie said. "Aren't they beautiful?"

Roz nodded. "I've got my eye on that Native American Star Quilt. If someone doesn't buy it soon, I think it will have to come home with me."

Sadie smiled at her tall friend. Roz was decked out in her usual bohemian style. A long-sleeved cream-colored peasant-styled blouse was tucked into her long turquoise skirt, and ankle-length fringed boots peeked out from underneath her skirt's scalloped edge.

"I know I said we'd try to have lunch today," Sadie said. "But it might be too busy for me to get away."

Roz waved her hand at her friend. "Not a problem. I'll stop by and check with you before we leave. If you can't go, we'll do it another time."

Sadie smiled. "Thanks, Roz."

Roz scooted off to check on the star quilt while Sadie helped a customer who had a question about a sterling-silver candle snuffer. They were discussing price when the phone rang. Sadie looked around for Julie, but she was talking to a couple interested in a large wedding quilt.

"I'm sorry," she told the woman. "Do you mind if I take this call? I promise I'll be quick."

"Not at all." The woman put the candle snuffer down on the counter. "I also wanted to check out your collection of teapots. I'll meet you back here in a few minutes."

"Thank you so much." Sadie grabbed the phone as the woman walked away. "The Antique Mine," she said loudly, trying to be heard over all the chatter around her.

"Sadie, is that you?" a man said. "It's Ardis. Ardis Fleagle."

Ardis Fleagle was the contractor in charge of the renovations at the Silver Peak Opera House. Although Sadie was on the Historic Preservation Council, Jerry Remington was the chairman and was overseeing the work. "Are you looking for Jerry?" Sadie asked.

"No, I'm looking for you, although you might want to let Jerry and the rest of the council know what I found over here."

"What you found?"

"What did you say?" Ardis asked. "Sounds pretty noisy over there."

Sadie took a deep breath, then cupped a hand around the receiver to block the sounds of her busy shop. "Yes, we're very busy. I'm sorry, but did you say you found something?"

"Yes. We started tearing down an old wall and discovered something inside that I think you might be interested in."

Something inside a wall? What in the world could be inside a wall that had anything to do with her?

"It's a safe, Sadie. And it looks very old."

2

Sadie worked another hour until the number of customers dwindled to a manageable level. After telling Julie she was going across the street to the opera house, Sadie pulled on her coat and checked out her reflection in the store's window. She wore her salt-and-pepper hair short, but it was so thick and wavy sometimes it was hard to manage. Thankfully, it seemed to be holding its shape. She wrapped her scarf around her neck. "I'm on my way," she called out to Julie. "Be back soon."

Julie nodded at her and waved.

Sadie opened the front door of the Antique Mine to a brisk October day. The thick clouds above her certainly looked full of snow. Perched at almost ten thousand feet, the town was no stranger to flakes and flurries as early as September. However, it was certain they'd get measurable snow by the end of October that would generally last until April or May. If Sadie was right, that October snow would be here today or tomorrow.

As she glanced into Arbuckle's she could see it was still busy although the crowd had dwindled somewhat. She looked to see if Edwin was still there, but she couldn't spot him.

The lights were also off at Spike Harris's small music store near the opera house. He was a wonderful musician who could play several instruments and regularly toured with a successful band, the Skylarks.

As Sadie stepped outside her shop door, she couldn't help but pause for a moment to breathe in the crisp, thin mountain air and glance around at her beloved hometown. She never ceased to find new things to appreciate about its charm. Each season gave the town a new look, a new feeling, and Sadie never tired of it. The old buildings echoed the town's rich history. The silver mines that had once made Silver Peak prosperous were gone now, but the enchantment of the past remained. The owners of the shops on Main Street emphasized the historical influence of the original architecture while still expressing their unique personalities through their own decorative touches. The sidewalks were kept clean, and Victorian-styled streetlights gave the street a homey, cozy feeling. The town managed to combine small-town appeal and rustic western ambience in a perfect blend. Sadie sighed happily as she gazed around her. There truly was nowhere else in the world she'd rather live. She wondered how many people could say that about the place they called home.

She crossed the street and hurried to the opera house. The majestic Victorian structure sat in the middle of the block like a regal old queen overseeing her subjects. Being able to watch the building being restored to its former magnificence was exciting. A lot of the outside work was already done. The grand lady was three stories high with arched windows and decorative cornices. Over the windows on the second floor the words *Silver Peak Opera House* stood out from the redbrick facade. Cut in stone, they had been cleaned and restored to their original glory. Of course, there was still a lot to do inside the building. As it stood now, it would be several months before the restoration was complete. Taking care not to destroy any of the historic elements took a special contractor, and they'd hit the jackpot with Ardis Fleagle. His love of history almost rivaled hers, which was really saying something.

Ardis and his wife, Mabel, were newcomers to Silver Peak. He'd come to Colorado from Kansas after selling his construction company. The Fleagles had always loved Colorado and had yearned to enjoy the mountains.

Sadie liked the Fleagles and was grateful when Ardis offered his services to the council. They were saving thousands of dollars because Ardis kept his prices low and employed the help of local residents who'd donated their time for the work.

Sadie climbed the steps of the opera house and opened the front door. After entering, a small foyer that held the old ticket booth was the first thing to greet her eyes. Sadie climbed the stairs to the main theater. Looking around, she was impressed with the progress Ardis and his crew had made. Much of the crumbling and cracked plaster had already been removed. It would be covered with a new kind of plaster that would maintain the original look but would be much more durable. The oak floors had been sanded to remove layers of paint and shellac built up over the years. The wood was gorgeous, the decorative grain distinctive and interesting. The main traffic area was protected with a series of plastic tarps, and Sadie was careful to stay on the path laid out for anyone walking through the building. The old theater seats had been removed and were being restored and recovered. The huge room with its high ceilings lay bare and desolate but would soon be redressed in its original finery. Sadie tried to imagine how the hall would look when it was completed. The image in her mind made her smile with anticipation. The theater, where a host of luminaries such as Harry Houdini had performed and John L. Sullivan had once boxed, would soon bring enjoyment to a whole new generation of visitors.

Although the renovations had started out within budget, a few unanticipated problems had cropped up that threatened to run the final costs over the amount the board had set aside. She hoped Ardis could figure out how to overcome any obstacles.

"Hello?" she called out. "Ardis, are you here?"

"There you are, Sadie." Ardis waved her over to the far wall on the west side of the building. "We didn't want to touch it until we knew what you wanted us to do."

Sadie stepped cautiously on the tarps, being watchful not to catch her foot and trip. When she finally reached Ardis, he didn't say anything, just pointed at the large hole in the wall.

Sadie peered into the jagged opening. "That looks like an antique pedestal safe. I haven't seen a lot of them except in pictures." The safe was covered with grime, but Sadie could see the black lacquer peeking through. Color paintings graced each side, although their colors were muted and the picture was hard to make out because of the dust that covered them. Gold piping circled each painting and continued onto other parts of the safe. Sadie thought she could see painted flowers on the top of the safe, but again, it was difficult to see clearly. The safe was probably about a foot wide and a foot deep. It sat on a pedestal leg that made it a little over four feet tall.

"We stopped working as soon as we discovered it," Ardis said. "Didn't want to move it until the Antique Lady saw it."

Sadie smiled at the mention of her nickname but secretly wished she could be called something that didn't make her feel quite so elderly.

"I've knocked down a lot of walls in my time," Ardis said, grinning, "but I've never seen anything like this before."

"It's certainly unusual," Sadie agreed. "I wonder how long it's been hiding in there. Could it have been put there when the opera house was built?"

Ardis shook his head. "This area's been patched before. They used a different type of plaster."

"Perhaps it was walled up during the renovations in the forties," Sadie said.

Ardis nodded. "It could have been done some time after that, but we've found this kind of repair in several other places. The plaster is the same, and all that work was done in the forties."

"But why would someone do this?" She was talking more to herself than to Ardis.

He chuckled. "Well, it's a mystery, that's for sure. I can hardly wait to see what's inside. I thought about trying to open it but decided I'd better wait for you."

"I'm sorry, but if it's locked, I doubt I'll be able to open it."

The wiry little man looked at her in surprise.

"I know you're curious," she said. "Believe me, I am too. But I think this safe might be very valuable. As you can see, it's got a combination lock. If it's locked we'll need an expert who can open it without causing damage."

"How much do you think it's worth, Sadie?"

She leaned in closer to study the safe. She was almost certain it was a Herring and Company pedestal safe, but she couldn't be positive. She straightened up and met Ardis's gaze. "Off the top of my head, this safe could sell for as much as seven thousand dollars."

"Oh my," he said somberly. "So what do you want us to do? We need to finish our work on this wall."

"Can you carefully remove it and bring it to my store? I'd like to find out more about it and give it a good cleaning."

He nodded. "Not a problem. I'll round up some help to get it out. We'll be very careful with it, Sadie. We should have it to you in about an hour. Will that work?"

"That's fine. Thank you, Ardis." Sadie relaxed, knowing he would be as cautious as she would with the valuable safe.

After saying good-bye, Sadie followed the plastic sheeting trail back to the stairs. Then she hurried downstairs and left through the front entrance. She was thinking about the safe as she crossed the street to the Antique Mine. She noticed that the temperature seemed to have dropped even more while she was inside the opera house. Silver Peak Octobers could vary widely, but clearly this one was shaping up to be a cold one.

As she neared the store, she noticed a piece of yellow paper fluttering on the windshield of her red Chevy Tahoe. She wondered if it was trash blown by the wind or if it was one of the flyers Jesse had passed out. She walked quickly toward her shop, anticipating a cup of chai latte from Arbuckle's to warm her up. When she reached her car, she removed the folded piece of paper from under her windshield wiper and opened it up. She read the note twice before she could believe her eyes. Scrawled in large block letters, it read:

Don't open that safe or you'll be sorry!

3

SADIE'S HEART RACED AS SHE GLANCED AROUND HER AND SLID the yellow-lined paper into her purse. Why would someone send her a message like that? She opened the door to her shop and saw that there were several customers waiting to be helped. Julie looked a little overwhelmed so Sadie pushed her concerns about the note aside while she helped them.

Within the hour, the safe was delivered to the store. It was carefully wrapped in soft tarps and strapped to a large dolly so it wouldn't move or accidentally get dropped. Sadie had Ardis's men put the safe in the store's back room so she could clean it. It was filthy from all its years of hiding in the opera house wall, but as far as she could tell, it was in almost-perfect condition. Even through the layers of dust, the finish seemed intact. It was clear the small painted scenes on each side were in good shape although they were also covered with grime.

While Julie took care of a customer who was interested in a French Castle trunk from the 1700s, Sadie looked over the safe carefully. She had an idea what it was, but wanting to be certain, she scurried over to a long bookshelf behind the counter. Making a clicking sound with her tongue, she perused the books until she exclaimed, "Here it is!" She grabbed a large volume and brought it over to the counter near the spot where the safe sat.

It only took her a moment to find the page she was looking for. Sadie's love of antiques had caused her to memorize almost every page of the books she used for research. Sadie found a picture that was close to an exact match to the safe from the opera house. She looked from the page back to the safe in front of her. As she suspected, it was a Herring and Company pedestal safe. Called boudoir safes because of their beauty and attention to detail, they were usually kept in the bedroom like a piece of furniture. And as she expected, it was worth several thousand dollars based on its condition.

Sadie studied the safe. Its black lacquer finish was decorated with gold highlights, and the carved pedestal had four legs that supported the safe's weight. Each side of the safe had hand-painted designs in each corner. Although Sadie couldn't see details on the grime-covered safe, she was able to check the picture in the book to see what the safe should look like once it was cleaned. The paintings on each side of the safe depicted gentle landscapes edged in gold. One picture was of a small, charming cottage next to a creek. The other was a meadow of bright-red poppies. Sadie admired the wonderful detail in the pictures and could hardly wait to clean the safe to see if all the qualities of the safe in her book would be found on the safe that sat in front of her. Once again, she peered closely at the sides of the safe and was thrilled to see colors peeping through the dust that matched the pictures in her book. She studied the front of the safe. It held a combination lock. Although it was hard to see, the round dial seemed to be gold colored with black numbers, and to its left sat a gold knob used to open the safe once the correct combination had been entered. Her love for antiques drew her to the lovely handcrafted safe. Sadie went back to her book and checked the safe's value. As she suspected, it was worth between six thousand and eight thousand dollars based on condition.

After finishing with her customer, Julie came into the back room to look at the safe herself. "It's beautiful," she said. "Or at least it will be when it's cleaned up."

"Yes, it is," Sadie said.

"But who would hide something so beautiful inside a wall?"

"Actually, I've heard of it before. Many years ago, some parents walled up fortunes meant for their children. Hiding them in a place where no one would think to look was their way of keeping their inheritance protected. During the Depression, banks weren't considered safe, you know."

Julie frowned. "What if the parents died before they had a chance to tell their children about their secret legacy?"

Sadie nodded. "It's happened. Home owners doing renovations in old houses have made some very surprising discoveries."

"But that explanation doesn't seem to fit this situation," Julie said. "I wonder what could be inside this safe that made hiding it so important."

"That's a very good question," Sadie said. "I honestly have no idea."

"Maybe the owners of the opera house concealed a fortune inside."

Sadie smiled at her. "I would imagine they needed the money to cover expenses. Running a business, especially during the Depression, couldn't have been a very lucrative venture."

"That makes sense," Julie said. "Still, I wonder what's inside. Have you tried to open it?"

"I turned the handle, but it wouldn't budge. Without the combination, there's no way to get it open."

A deep voice boomed out, "Why would you need the combination?" Sadie turned to see Roscoe Putnam, Roz's husband, walking toward them. "Ardis stopped by for supplies and told me about the safe he found in the opera house," he said. "Had to come by and see it."

Roz followed Roscoe over to where Sadie and Julie stood. "If anyone can open this safe, Roscoe can."

Roscoe owned Putnam & Sons Hardware Store, the shop just on the other side of the Antique Mine. He had a reputation for being able to fix anything. He was also a skilled carpenter and helped repair some of the items Sadie bought from yard sales and secondhand stores. Heavyset and balding, Roscoe always played Santa at the church's yearly Christmas party. But it wasn't just because he was the only one who could fill out the church's Santa suit. Roscoe embodied the spirit of the jolly old man all year round.

He ambled up next to Sadie and peered at the old safe. "I can drill a hole next to the lock," he said. "Then I'll put a small lens inside so I can clearly see the levers fall into place. We'll have it open in no time."

Sadie shook her head. "Thank you, Roscoe. But drilling a hole will devalue the safe, and I don't want to do that. If I can't open it, I'll have to call a manipulator."

Roz straightened up, her brown eyes peering through her glasses. "A what?"

"A manipulator is someone who can open the safe just by listening to it. Believe it or not, it's much harder than it seems.

There are only about one hundred and fifty people in the country who can do it. Thankfully, there's a man in Denver I can hire to come here and help us. I have a friend who owns a shop there. She highly recommends his services."

"How much does this manipulator cost?" Julie asked.

"Somewhere around five hundred dollars." She paused with a twinkle in her eye. "But maybe I can get him to manipulate his price, as well." Sadie let out a boisterous laugh and her friends laughed along with her.

"Just remember, you've got someone standing right here who offered to do it for free," Roscoe said when the laugher died down.

Roz patted her husband on the back. "I know you'd love to help, honey, but let Sadie try this other way first. If that doesn't work, I know she'll call on you."

"Just let me know, Sadie. Anything I can do…"

"Thanks," Sadie said with a smile. "I really appreciate that."

"Are you ready for lunch, dear?" Roz said.

Roscoe patted his stomach. "I'm always ready to eat. Let's go to the Depot. I'm in the mood for spaghetti." The Depot was a favorite spot in Silver Peak. The former train station had been turned into a combination ice cream parlor and family restaurant.

"I know you said you might be too busy, but I wanted to make sure you couldn't go before we took off without you," Roz said to Sadie.

"I wish I could, but I think I'll stay here. Alice called and said she'd bring lunch." She looked at Julie. "You can go if you want to."

"Are you sure?" Julie asked.

Sadie nodded. "Things have slowed down a bit, and if we get busy again, Alice will be here to help."

She waved good-bye to Roz, Roscoe, and Julie as they left, and then she went back to reading the information in her book. The safe was manufactured in 1872 so it could have been owned by one of Silver Peak's earliest settlers. Herring and Company merged with the Marvin Safe Company and Hall's Safe and Lock Company in 1892 to form Herring-Hall-Marvin Safe Company. They were acquired by Diebold in 1959 but that company closed down around 1964. As Sadie suspected, parts for the safe were no longer available. It meant that if the safe was damaged, finding original pieces to repair it could be very difficult. Parts could be re-created, but they were expensive and could lower the safe's value. Thankfully, it appeared to be in remarkable condition. Sadie was fairly certain a good cleaning would bring back its beauty. She would have to be very careful to preserve the patina, but once she was done, the safe should look almost as good as new.

Sadie had only been alone a few minutes when the door opened again and her daughter, Alice Macomb, walked in. She greeted her mother as she carried a large brown paper sack over to the counter.

"I picked up sandwiches from the café at the Market," she said. "I know you love their Reubens."

More and more, Sadie could see T.R. in Alice. She was taller than her mother, with her father's auburn hair and green eyes. Sadie was happy to have Alice and her grandchildren, Theo and Sara, living in Silver Peak even though the move was the result of a divorce. Sadie got along well with her former son-in-law but she felt bad about the breakup. Cliff and Alice grew apart when his work as a dentist seemed to take over his life, not leaving much time for his family. At least the relationship between Alice and Cliff was amicable.

"I want to show you something, Alice," Sadie said softly, after Alice took off her coat, "but promise me you'll keep this to yourself for now. And try not to worry. I'm sure it's just a silly prank."

Alice's eyes widened. "Worry about what? Is something wrong, Mom?"

Sadie reached into her pocket and took out the note she'd found. Then she handed it to her daughter. "I discovered this on my car when I got back from the opera house."

Alice scanned it quickly, then looked up at Sadie, concern etched on her face. "What does this mean?" She handed the note to her mother, who slid it back into her pocket.

"I have no idea. Who could know what's in a safe that's been sealed up since renovations to the opera house in the forties?" Sadie shook her head. "It's certainly puzzling."

Alice walked over to the door that led to the back room and opened it. She peered inside and stared at the safe. "It's gorgeous. I've never seen a safe like that before."

"There aren't a lot of them. Especially in that condition," Sadie agreed.

"Why would it have to happen during renovations?" Alice came back and removed their sandwiches from the sack. "I mean, knocking open a wall and re-covering it with plaster isn't brain surgery."

"But someone probably would have noticed. I'd think whoever hid this safe would pick a time when a newly plastered wall wouldn't draw much attention. Besides, Ardis says the plaster that covered the wall the safe was found in was the same plaster used during the renovations in the forties."

Alice handed her mother a sandwich and a bag of chips. "I guess that does narrow it down."

"I know a lot about the opera house's history," Sadie said, "but nothing that explains this. I'd really like to get a look inside that safe."

Alice frowned at her. "Are you sure you shouldn't take that note seriously, Mom? Maybe you should leave it alone."

Sadie sighed and plopped down on a chair behind the counter. "I'm not too worried. Besides, if I could open the safe, the contents would possibly tell me who it belongs to. It should be returned to its owner."

"What if you can't find the owner?"

Sadie took a bite of her sandwich. "If the owner can't be found, it's possible we could sell it and donate the proceeds to the opera house."

"I thought the committee raised all the money needed for renovations."

"We did. But there have been a few unpleasant surprises. Water damage behind the walls and a problem with some of the plumbing. The sale of the safe could cover those costs." She shook her head. "Perhaps whatever's inside is valuable, as well."

Alice grinned. "Maybe it's stuffed full of money."

Sadie smiled at her daughter. "Julie said the same thing, but I doubt that will happen. As I told her, if the safe belonged to the opera house, I can't imagine why they would hide money they would have likely needed to stay in business."

Alice took another bite, then chewed and swallowed it. "Look, Mom. Keep me in the loop, okay? The note might be a prank, but if anything else happens, if any more notes show up, I think we need to call Sheriff Slattery."

"If it starts to feel serious, we'll definitely contact the sheriff. For now let's keep the note between us." She shook her head.

"You know, I've been wondering how the writer of this note found out about the safe in the first place. He or she could have over-heard my phone conversation with Ardis, which means they may have been inside the shop earlier today."

"You think?"

"I mean, how else would anyone know about the safe? The only person I talked to about it was Ardis, and as far as I know he was alone at the opera house. Seems to me the only time the safe was mentioned when there were people around was when I took Ardis's call."

"Well, someone could have overheard your phone call and told someone else," Alice said. "Or maybe Ardis spilled the beans before you got there."

"Yes, I suppose that's true. He did mention it to Roscoe when he went to the hardware store for supplies. That was after I got the note, but maybe he told other people before that."

Soon, Sadie and Alice were enjoying their meal in compan-ionable silence. Sadie loved spending time with her daughter and her grandchildren. Alice was a busy elementary school teacher so getting to share a quick lunch with her on a weekday was a real treat. Of course, Alice helped out at the Antique Mine on week-ends, but Sadie could really never get enough of her daughter.

By the time Julie returned, it was time for Alice to get back to her class. After their busy morning, Julie and Sadie were happy to spend a rather quiet afternoon that only included two customers. One woman was looking for a Jadeite Fire King cup to complete her set. Sadie was able to sell her the exact cup she was looking for. A local resident came in to sell an old Roseville vase, and Sadie offered the woman a price that made her smile.

Julie left a little after four, and Sadie closed up. But before she went home, she turned on her laptop and did some research about opening safes. After reading an article about what to listen for when trying to open a combination lock, she grabbed an old stethoscope she had on a shelf that highlighted old medical paraphernalia and decided to give the dial a try. She turned the dial this way and that for over an hour but eventually had to give up. She heard at least one click from the old lock, but in the end, she realized she was in over her head.

At five o'clock, Sadie closed the store and drove to her house, which stood at the edge of a forest on an expansive hillside, just a few miles from Main Street. She smiled as her stone-and-log farmhouse came into view. Although her family had been forced to sell off most of the surrounding land during the Great Depression, two acres remained in the family. Sadie couldn't imagine living anywhere else. She, T.R., and Alice had spent many happy years within its walls. Now Theo and Sara were also able to spend time enjoying their family's homestead.

She drove her Tahoe up the long driveway lined with evergreen trees and parked. As a celebration of fall she'd decorated her wide porch with gleaming copper tubs full of pumpkins and colorful autumn-colored gourds. On one side of the porch two patio rockers sat with a small round table between them. On the other side a white wooden swing hung from the roof. Sadie loved to sit in her swing in the evenings and watch the sun go down behind the mountains, the Colorado sky ablaze with color. In the fall and winter, ice crystals in the air helped to create magnificent sunsets only rivaled by the incredible sunrises that graced the sky every morning.

When she walked in the door, she was greeted enthusiastically by Hank, her golden retriever. After giving him a big hug and receiving a doggy kiss on the cheek, Sadie rounded up his leash and headed outside for a quick stroll before dinner. She loved walking with Hank through the mountains that surrounded her property. Winter kept their excursions shorter and closer to home, but unless the weather completely prohibited their routine, Sadie tried to take him out at least once a day. She needed the exercise as much as he did. Their walks helped to keep both of them limber.

As she and Hank strolled down the road in front of her house, as usual, she was moved by the grandeur of her home state. Even though she was close to town, she was still able to escape into wide-open spaces adorned with fir trees and framed by picturesque snowcapped mountains in the distance. There was even a beautiful lake within walking distance. In the summer, Hank loved to romp in the warm water of Crystal Lake. Sadie didn't mind because the sun almost always dried his fur by the time they returned home.

Tall pine trees dotted the land, and the raw, natural scenery gave Sadie a sense of peace. She appreciated the blessings of technology as much as anyone, but in her heart, she preferred the wild, untouched beauty of Colorado.

As she and Hank walked, Sadie could see the lights on in the house of her closest neighbor, Milo Henderson. A gentle and friendly man, Milo owned a very successful ranch where he boarded horses, including Sadie's horse, a five-year-old gelding named Scout. Milo also boarded Alice's horse as well as her grandson Theo's horse, Bronco, and her granddaughter Sara's horse, Daisy. Unfortunately, with the weather turning so cold, there wouldn't be much riding. Sadie loved winter in Colorado, but she would miss long walks with Hank and leisurely horseback rides through the mountains with her family.

"We need to head back, Hank," she said to the retriever after about twenty minutes. The sun had nearly gone down, taking with it its golden warmth, and Sadie felt the chill despite her brisk pace. Even though she knew he wanted to keep going, he stopped and turned around. His reluctance was obvious. "I feel the same way you do, boy," Sadie said gently, "but I'm afraid it's getting too cold for us."

When they reached the house, Sadie took Hank off his leash and fed him. After making herself a cup of tea, something she did almost every evening, she heated up some stew left over from the night before. Then she carried her bowl and cup into the living room and put them down on the massive coffee table made from Colorado pine that Josh Ralston, a local woodworker, had crafted for her. Josh was a talented artisan who sold his work all over the country. Some of his creations were on display in the Antique Mine. Sadie took orders for several of his pieces, including his beautiful Adirondack chairs. Josh, who had short brown hair and blue eyes, was over six feet tall, with broad shoulders and an athletic build. Sadie and Julie liked to tease him about being Silver Peak's number-one eligible bachelor. So far, however, he hadn't found anyone he was really serious about.

Sadie started a fire in her fireplace and settled down on the couch to eat. Although she loved spending time in the Antique Mine, her house was still her favorite place to be. The huge living room included a massive stone fireplace surrounded by polished pine bookshelves that reached to the ceiling. Sadie's books included all kinds of volumes about Colorado history, including everything she could find about Silver Peak. Pine beams stretched across the high ceiling, and pine logs decorated the sides and tops of the ceiling-to-floor windows that looked out on the mountains.

After finishing her stew, she picked up her tea and covered herself with the warm, thick blanket she kept on her big leather couch. Hank jumped up next to her, and she stroked his soft head. As she stared out her windows, she noticed the moon darting in and out from behind clouds that danced quickly across the sky. While she sat there, she thought back to the note she'd found on her car. What was in that safe that someone didn't want her to see? Instead of causing her concern, the note had only ignited her curiosity, making her determined to find out what kind of secrets the old safe held.

4

———

THE NEXT DAY SADIE BEGAN THE LONG AND TEDIOUS PROCESS of cleaning the grimy safe. Since it was so delicately painted, she'd use only the gentlest cleanser, along with a very soft cloth. Over the years she'd even developed her own cleaning solution with olive oil, distilled white vinegar, lemon juice, and rosemary essential oil. It never loosened the lacquer or the paint on furniture the way some cleaners could. Alice had told her more than once that she could probably sell her homemade solution and make a lot of money, but Sadie's heart was in the fun of antique restoring. She wasn't in the antique business to build a product empire.

When it came to the paintings on the sides of the safe, and the gold accents, Sadie could only carefully dust them. Applying anything wet could cause the paint or gilding to soften and flake off. It took her several hours to complete her task, but when she was done, she was pleased with the results. The black lacquer shone brilliantly, and the gold highlights sparkled with new life. The paintings were clearly visible, their colors, she imagined, as vivid as the day they'd been painted. Sadie was happy to see that the safe looked just like the one in her book. The oil paintings on the sides were just as she'd seen them, but she had not anticipated the touch of gilding that lent a sparkle of color to the image. The azure blue of the stream matched the cerulean sky, and the little white cottage with the thatched roof looked like someplace Sadie would like to visit. The red poppies in the other painting were brilliant against a green field, and the sun overhead bathed them in a warm glow. The white lilies on the top of the safe were so delicate and lovely, Sadie could almost smell their sweet scent.

"Oh, Sadie," Julie said as she looked in through the open door of the back room. "It's so beautiful. I love seeing old things come back to life. Seems almost impossible that something that old and dirty could turn out like this."

Sadie grinned. "It's funny. I was thinking as I was cleaning the safe about how the first safe was invented by a cop and a robber."

"Is that so?" Julie said.

"Yep. It was quite the combination."

Julie laughed. "Oh, Sadie. Really. Your puns are the worst. Or the best? I still haven't decided."

"I'll hope for the best." Sadie laughed and then set to work cleaning up her supplies. After the room was tidied, she ate lunch and then called her friend in Colorado Springs who had the number of the manipulator she'd used when she'd needed an old safe opened. After talking to him, she hung up the phone with a sigh of frustration.

"What's wrong?" Julie asked.

"I found someone to open the safe," she said, "but he can't come for another three weeks."

Julie's shoulders sank a bit, and she smiled compassionately at Sadie. "It's only three weeks. It will go by quickly."

Sadie shook her head. "I doubt it." She pointed to the open door of the back room toward the safe as if it were her nemesis instead of an inanimate object. "I *will* open you," she said pointedly.

Julie laughed. "I'm betting on you, Sadie."

"That's very generous of you, but given my limited experience opening safes, I'm betting on the manipulator." She headed to her desk at the front of the shop, where she set to work on some inventory statements. After a few minutes, the bell above the door jingled and Sadie looked up to see Jerry Remington walk in.

"Hi, Jerry," she said with a smile. "Doing some solo shopping today?"

He smiled back. "Something like that. Jane's busy at the B and B, and I've been tasked with finding something for the table in our hallway," he said. "Jane kept a ruby red vase there, but we found it broken this morning. Any ideas?"

Sadie could picture the piece of furniture and knew the red vase Jerry was talking about. She did a mental scan of her inventory for what might best suit the table. "Have you considered a lamp? It could brighten up the hall a little. A lamp would not only be decorative, it would also be functional."

Jerry rubbed his chin. "A lamp. That's a good idea."

"What happened to the vase?"

"We're not sure," Jerry said. "We're thinking maybe a guest accidentally bumped into the table. Maybe they couldn't see it well enough. A little light in that hallway could solve that problem." He smiled. "What do you have that looks expensive but…"

"Isn't?" Sadie finished for him.

He grinned. "Exactly."

Sadie walked over to one of the huge shelves that lined both sides of the store. What she wanted was out of her reach, so she grabbed her ladder. She pulled it over to a spot right below the lamp she'd had in mind. As she reached for it, the thought occurred to her that Jerry might be able to help her with her questions about the safe. His father, Reuben, had been the manager of the opera house for many years until a few years before his death. Perhaps he had mentioned the safe to Jerry at one point or another.

When she came down the ladder, she carried the lamp over to where Jerry stood talking to Julie. She gingerly handed the lamp to Jerry, who held it in his hands and studied it. "I think it would look lovely on your table. The milk glass will really stand out against the dark green wall."

Jerry looked pleased with her selection. "This is even better than the vase," he said. "How much is it?"

Sadie quoted him a price, and Jerry nodded. "Perfectly reasonable. And Jane will love it. Thanks, Sadie." He carried the lamp over and set it down on the counter next to the cash register. "By the way, Ardis called and told me about the safe he found in the opera house. I'd love to see it."

"Sure, Jerry." Sadie figured, Jerry was the head of the historical committee, so she felt comfortable showing it to him. Plus, if Ardis had called Jerry himself to tell him about the safe, Sadie was more than at liberty.

"Wow, it's really beautiful. How old is it?"

"From my research, I think it was made in the 1870s."

"That's amazing. It's in beautiful condition. Any thoughts as to why someone would put something this nice inside a wall?"

"Besides the obvious answer, that they were trying to hide whatever is inside it, not really," Sadie said. "But it's funny you ask. As I was taking down your lamp I realized you might have some insight into the safe since your father managed the opera house all those years ago. Is there any chance it might have belonged to him?"

He thought for a short moment, then shook his head. "No. I'm afraid not. I'd love to claim it, but we never had anything like this in our family. That I know of anyway."

"Even so, it occurred to me that you might be able to assist me with finding out something about it," Sadie said.

"Oh? I'm not sure how, but I'll do anything I can to help you."

"Do you know where old records from the opera house are kept? Maybe I could find something in them that would point to the owner of the safe."

"That makes sense. I think there are some records in the opera house office," he said. "We haven't done any renovations in there yet, and it's a mess, but you're certainly welcome to look." He frowned. "What time period are you looking for?"

Sadie shrugged. "Ardis says the safe was most likely put in the wall during the renovations in the forties."

"That was before Dad took over," Jerry said thoughtfully. "Franklin Reichert was the manager right up until the time the renovations began in 1943." He frowned. "You know that story, right?"

Sadie nodded. "In doing research about the opera house, I remember reading something about it. Franklin was accused of stealing money from the opera house along with artwork that was on loan, right?"

"Yes, and that's why Dad got the job after he came home from the war. Do you suppose that situation has anything to do with the safe?"

"I have no idea," Sadie said, but she was intrigued by the idea of finding out more about Franklin Reichert. She would have to do some research about him. "If I remember correctly, the theft included two good-size statues. They certainly wouldn't fit into this safe."

"You're right about that," Jerry said with a chuckle. He reached into his pocket and pulled out a large key chain. "Here's an extra key to the opera house office. You're welcome to go there anytime you want and look through things. Just lock up when you're done."

"Thanks, Jerry," Sadie said. "Between the opera house and the library, I hope to find something that will help us determine the rightful owner of this safe." Sadie had spent quite a bit of time at the library doing various kinds of research. There were a lot of copies of the old *Silver Peak Sentinel* on microfilm.

"Good idea."

Sadie rang up Jerry's purchase, and carefully packed his lamp.

"Thanks again, Sadie," he said as he took the package from her. "And good luck. I hope you find what you're looking for."

"Good-bye, Jerry. Say hello to Jane for me." She waved good-bye as he walked out the door.

She turned to Julie. "I'd think now's a good time to run over to the opera house," Sadie said. "Do you mind?"

She shook her head. "We're not busy, and there's still an hour and a half before I have to pick up the boys from school."

Sadie looked at the clock. "I'll be back before then."

She put on her coat and scarf and set out for the opera house. When she stepped outside she could tell the temperature had definitely plummeted, and she saw that the sky had darkened.

When she reached the opera house, the front door was open so she went right in. Before she started her search, she went upstairs and located Ardis so she could tell him she was in the building. She noticed that the wall where the safe was found had already been repaired.

After quickly speaking with Ardis, who was busy instructing some workers, she went back downstairs. She slid the key into the lock that opened the office door. The smell of dust and neglect hit her as soon as she walked into the room. Once the work upstairs was completed, the office would also be renovated, but not as extensively as the main theater.

Sadie flipped on the light switch and looked around. All in all, the room was in pretty good shape. Nothing that some cleaning and a little paint wouldn't fix. She noticed that the large room was being used for storage. Odd chairs, some furniture from the dressing rooms upstairs, and various building supplies were stacked up against the walls. Underneath a row of cabinets mounted on the wall, an ancient desk lay on its side on the floor. Battered filing cabinets covered with dust had been shoved against another wall. Next to them a beat-up safe sat open. This was the safe originally used to collect money from patrons. It was large, bulky, plain, and much more functional than the safe that sat in Sadie's office.

Amid the supplies, she found some cleaning rags. She set the old desk upright, dusted it off, and then pulled a chair over and cleaned it off, as well. Once she was ready, she opened the cabinet doors above the desk.

"Oh my," she said out loud.

The cabinets were crammed full of loose papers, old account books, and tattered files. As she removed the contents from the shelves and started piling everything on the desk, the swirling dust made her sneeze. Once she had all the paperwork out, she was able to go through most of it quickly. She put receipts for goods and services after the last renovations aside. Contracts went into another pile. Account books that had nothing to do with the period she was looking for were put back in the cabinets.

Finally, she found two account books that included information about the renovations in the forties. She put those books into a tote bag she'd brought with her in case she needed to copy any information. When she was done, she placed the papers and books she didn't want back on the shelves. She then opened the filing cabinets. They were empty except for a nest in the bottom of one that must have belonged to a family of mice at one time.

Sadie checked her watch. She only had fifteen minutes before Julie had to leave work to pick up the boys. As she prepared to take off, she noticed that the desk she'd been working on still had one drawer left. The knob was missing, so Sadie fished a nail file from her purse and used it to wriggle the drawer open. It took a few tries since the drawer was stuck, but it finally slipped out. Unfortunately, it was empty. But just as she started to slide the drawer back in, she noticed a word scratched into the wood on the inside bottom of the drawer. She took the rag she'd used for dusting and rubbed at the grime and old furniture oil that had darkened the wood. After a little elbow grease, the letters became readable.

"Livi?" she read, frowning. "Who in the world is Livi?" How odd. She thought for a moment about what "Livi" could mean.

Perhaps this desk had belonged to Franklin Reichert and someone he'd loved was named Livi. Short for Olivia, perhaps? A wife? Maybe a child? But why would someone scratch a name into a desk drawer? Sadie had no idea.

She pushed the drawer back in. Then she grabbed her tote bag and purse, locked the office door, and left. Although she hadn't learned anything helpful yet, Sadie hoped that the account books in the tote bag would bring her one step closer to finding the owner of the safe.

5

When Sadie walked into her shop, she waved at Julie, who began gathering her coat and purse to head home. Sadie was also delighted to discover her grandchildren waiting for her. They sometimes visited her after school, and she was always so happy to see them. Sadie adored both Theo and Sara equally, and had things in common with both of them. Sara and Sadie shared a love of animals. Alice's backyard had become all but a sanctuary for injured and homeless animals. The fourteen-year-old nursed the sick ones back to health and helped homeless dogs and cats find homes. Doctor Ben Armstrong, a kind veterinarian who practiced in Silver Peak, was always willing to help Sara with her patients. Sara wanted to be a veterinarian someday, and Doctor Armstrong not only encouraged her ambition but had told her when she was sixteen she could work part-time in his clinic.

And seventeen-year-old Theo was as curious as Sadie. He loved crime novels and was doing exceptionally well in his history and social studies classes, something in which Sadie, a retired history teacher, felt enormous pride. And he shared Sadie's fascination and enjoyment of old and worn things and loved to discover the stories hidden in them.

Named after T.R., seventeen-year-old Theo constantly reminded her of her late husband. T.R. had been a handsome, steadfast man who'd cared about other people. Theo's similar trait of compassion had been channeled into a desire to be a doctor. He planned to enroll in the University of Colorado's premed program next year.

Sara waved at her grandmother from the Victorian nursing chair where she sat on her phone, likely texting her friends. Sara spent a lot of time on her phone texting and talking to school friends in Silver Peak as well as old friends in Denver. Sadie thought her to be uniquely pretty, with strawberry-blonde hair and bright hazel eyes. But Sara was self-conscious about her braces, sometimes covering her mouth with her hand when she laughed or smiled.

"See you tomorrow, Sadie," Julie called out as she left for the day.

"Sounds good. Thanks, Julie," Sadie said.

"So what do you think is in this safe, Grandma?" Theo asked. He'd come out of the back room just then and Sadie could only assume he'd been studying it with interest. His dark brown hair fell across one eye and he pushed it away.

"I don't know," Sadie said. "But I hope to find out."

"Have you tried to open it?"

"I have. I've tried everything I could think of, but no luck yet. I even tried to figure out the combination, but that didn't work either."

"You'll find a way, Grandma. You could be kind of like...a detective. An antique detective."

Sadie chuckled. "That just makes me sound old. I'm already known as the antique lady. I think I'm happy being only one version of antique."

Theo smiled at her. "Detectives are cool, Grandma. They get criminals off the streets."

"I don't think I'll be putting any criminals away today."

The bell over the doorway jingled and Alice walked in. She greeted the kids as she came over to where Sadie stood behind the front desk. "About ready to leave, Mom? If we're going to your house for dinner, we'd better get on the road." She looked out the large window at the front of the store. "It looks like snow."

Sadie looked around the shop and saw that Julie had done a great job getting everything in order for closing. Not that she'd expected anything different. Julie was a reliable and efficient employee, not to mention a good friend. Sadie felt a wave of gratitude for her, a feeling she'd experienced many times.

"Yep, I'll be ready in just a minute."

Sadie removed the money from the cash register and put it into her bank bag. After putting the bag in her purse, she got her coat and hat and grabbed the tote bag with the account books from the opera house.

"What's that?" Theo asked.

Sadie explained where the books had come from.

Sara frowned. "What are you hoping to find in those old books, Grandma?"

"I'm not sure, but learning more about the opera house might give me some info about the safe."

Sadie closed up the shop, got into her car, and drove home with Alice and the grandkids following behind her.

When they arrived, the aroma of lasagna from Sadie's Crock-Pot greeted them as they stepped inside the house. Sadie could smell the oregano and tomato sauce and could imagine the rich ricotta and mozzarella cheeses bubbling.

Hank bounded toward them and began making the rounds. He loved Theo and Sara and was so excited to see them that Sadie had to tell him several times to calm down.

"Oh boy," Theo said, after saying hello to Hank. "I smell Grandma's lasagna."

Sara smiled. "I love your lasagna, Grandma."

"I know, sweetheart," Sadie said. "That's why I made it."

"We'll set the table," Alice said.

Sadie hung up her coat in the hall closet. "Thanks, honey. While you do that, I'll get the garlic bread in the oven."

"Can I feed Hank?" Theo asked.

Sadie smiled at him. "I know he'd appreciate that."

A short time later, Sadie and her family were gathered around her large kitchen table. Hank had taken his place underneath just in case someone accidentally dropped food. Of course, Sadie and the kids always managed to sneak Hank something while Alice scolded them for feeding him "people food." Sadie didn't take her daughter's admonitions seriously since she'd noticed that Alice had a habit of slipping him tidbits of her dinner when she thought no one was looking.

After Sadie prayed over the food, the family began eating.

"I've been thinking about what might be inside the safe, Grandma," Theo said after stuffing his mouth with lasagna.

"Theo Macomb. We don't talk with our mouth full," Alice said.

"Maybe *we* don't," Sara said grinning, "but Theo does."

"Sorry," he said sheepishly after swallowing.

Sadie resisted the urge to laugh. Alice tried hard to teach her children manners, and Sadie applauded her for it. But for Theo, enthusiasm often overwhelmed his attempts at etiquette, even at seventeen.

"Not sure it will do much good to guess," Sadie said, "although it's hard not to think about the possibilities."

"Maybe it's empty," Theo said.

"Why would someone go to the trouble of hiding an empty safe in a wall?" Sara asked. "Doesn't make any sense."

"I agree with you, Sara," Sadie said. "I think there's likely something in there, but I haven't a clue what it could be. If the safe was in a house, I'd guess someone may have concealed money or jewels. But hiding a safe inside the wall of a public building is a little confusing. And fascinating."

"It could be money, right?" Theo said.

Sadie shrugged. "Maybe, but I tend to doubt it. The opera house has had its glory days, but not in the forties when the building was being restored. The owners would have needed money to pay for the renovations. I suppose someone other than the owner could have hidden the safe in the wall, but it's hard to imagine how they could have pulled that off without anyone knowing. Unless they had permission." Sadie sighed. "At this point, I have very little information to go on. My plan is to search through those account books from the opera house and learn more about its previous owners. I know that for many years the building was owned by a man named Benjamin Wilhite, but I don't know a lot about him. With luck, some research will provide some solid leads." Sadie frowned. "I wish I could remember his wife's name."

"Why is that?" Alice asked.

"I found the name Livi carved into the drawer of a desk in the opera house. I wondered if it might be the name of Benjamin's wife. I'm not certain, but I'm pretty sure Franklin Reichert's wife was named Madeline, and not Olivia."

"And how would you know that, Mom?" Alice asked.

"I read an old article once about a big social event held in Silver Peak's early days. It was a party at the Reicherts' home, and I'm pretty sure her name was Madeline." Sadie shrugged. "I doubt this has anything to do with the safe, but I'd still like to know who Livi was."

"Didn't Jerry Remington's father, Reuben, manage the opera house at one point?" Alice said.

"He did. I actually asked Jerry about the safe earlier today. He said his father never had a safe like the one that was found. Besides, it was most likely put in the wall during the forties, and Reuben started working at the opera house after the work was completed. I don't see how it could have been his."

Sadie missed Reuben Remington. He'd been a close friend of the family. He and T.R. had spent many happy hours fishing and playing chess together. Reuben's death five years ago had been devastating to everyone who loved him, including T.R., who passed away not long after his dear friend. Knowing that they were together again in heaven gave Sadie some comfort.

"You'll figure it out, Grandma," Theo said.

"Theo thinks Grandma should be a detective," Sara told her mother. She giggled as if imagining her grandmother as a hard-boiled private eye. "Like one of those people in mystery books."

Alice smiled. "Well, in a way she is. She researches the past so she can learn about the antiques in her store."

"I'm not a detective," Sadie said grinning. "I'm just nosy."

Theo's eyes darted toward his mother, and he took a deep breath. "Maybe you're not, but I want to be one."

Alice's eyebrows raised as she looked at her son. "One what?"

"A detective," Theo said slowly.

Alice looked confused. "I thought you wanted to be a doctor."

Theo swallowed a little harder than usual and wiped his mouth with his napkin. "Yeah, actually... I've been thinking about this for a while." His eyes darted back and forth between his mother and grandmother. "The University of Colorado also offers a Law and Justice Administration degree. Don't get me wrong, I think doctors are awesome. They save lives. But the police save lives too." He took a deep breath and met his mother's concerned gaze. "I've been praying about it, and I think it's what I'm supposed to do."

Alice was quiet for a moment before finally speaking. "I don't know, Theo. It doesn't sound... safe. I'm not saying I won't support you, but I want to make sure you've really thought this through. Changing your life on a spur-of-the-moment whim isn't smart."

"It's not a whim," he insisted. "I didn't say anything at first because I wanted to be certain about it. I've thought it through very carefully, Mom."

Alice shook her head. "Okay. Let's talk about it later. You caught me off guard. I need to think about it."

Sadie could tell that Alice was concerned. She'd been so excited when Theo had said he wanted to go into medicine. Still, Alice was a great mother who only wanted her children to become what God had created them to be. Sadie was confident Alice would give this her full consideration.

"So you're gonna run around Colorado with a gun?" Sara said with a conspiratorial grin. "That's cool."

Alice shot her daughter a look that quenched future similar comments. Theo just looked at Sara and rolled his eyes.

"Well, whatever you end up doing, I know you'll be brilliant at it, Theo," Sadie said, in part to cut the tension. "Now, who's up for dessert?"

"What are we having?" Sara asked.

"I may or may not have made one of my chocolate cream pies."

"Yum," said Sara.

"Sounds delicious, Mom, thanks," Alice said. "I think we'd better eat quickly though. The weather report is calling for snow tonight."

Alice helped Sadie cut the pie and bring the plates to the table. Theo didn't need any encouragement to eat fast. He gobbled up his chocolate pie before Sadie had a chance to take one bite of hers. Theo asked for another piece and Sadie got it for him. Sara ate her pie quickly too, but only after she took a picture of it with her smartphone and uploaded it to two or three social media sites, a habit Sadie thought was silly. It was one of many social-media-heavy things Sara's generation did that seemed to Sadie to be nothing more than oversharing.

"That was delicious, Mom," Alice said as she took her last bite. "We'll help with the dishes."

"That's okay, sweetheart." Sadie could tell that Alice's motivation for leaving early wasn't only to avoid bad weather; Alice was obviously struggling with Theo's news and clearly wanted time alone to process it. "I can handle it. I'd rather you get on the road before the weather gets bad."

Alice walked over to one of the large picture windows at the front of Sadie's living room. Fat snowflakes had begun to fall.

"Well, I hate to rush off and leave you with the dishes," Alice said. "But I think you're right."

"I know I am. You all need to get going."

Alice smiled at her mother. "Thanks for having us over. We need to plan a movie night soon."

"I'd love that." Sadie and T.R. had long ago started a tradition of movie night with Alice, and when Alice moved back to Silver Peak, they began sharing the tradition with the kids. Her grandchildren had never seen many of the wonderful older movies Sadie and their mother had grown up with. At first Theo and Sara had been certain they wouldn't like them, but after watching classics like *It's a Wonderful Life*, *Mary Poppins*, *To Kill a Mockingbird*, and *The King and I*, they began to get excited about Sadie's movie picks. The next movie on the list was *The Secret Garden* with Margaret O'Brien.

"We'll do it as soon as we can," Alice said. "I'll get back to you."

"Sounds great." Sadie put her arms around her daughter. "Everything will be all right," she said softly. "Theo is a smart young man."

Alice hugged her back. "I know," she whispered.

After saying her good-byes to the kids, Sadie and Hank stood on the porch and watched them as they drove away. When the car's taillights disappeared, they remained outside for a few minutes more, watching the large flakes, illuminated by her front porch light. They looked like small ballerinas dressed in white, dancing in the darkened sky.

Finally, they headed inside. Sadie took care of the dishes while Hank hung around waiting for leftovers. When the kitchen was clean, they headed to bed. Sadie had wanted to go through the books she'd removed from the opera house, but she was too tired and wanted to be sharp as a tack when she looked them over. The books would have to wait until tomorrow.

She'd felt like she'd only been asleep a few hours when the phone next to her bed rang. She glanced at her bedside clock and saw it was a little after two-thirty. Her brain still fuzzy with sleep, she picked up the receiver. It took her a moment or two to hear who was calling. Hank was cuddled up next to her and didn't help by barking loudly at the phone. Once she got him calmed down, she tried again.

"I'm so sorry. Who is this?" she said.

"Sadie, this is Mac Slattery. Can you hear me now?"

"I—I hear you, Sheriff," she said, sitting up in bed, concern washing over her. Was Alice all right? Was something wrong with her grandchildren? "What's going on?"

"It's your store, Sadie. It's been broken into. It seems you've been robbed."

6

————

It took Sadie longer than usual to get to town. She was used to driving in snow, but it was coming down like gangbusters. The road from her house didn't have streetlights, so she had to drive slowly and keep her eyes peeled straight ahead. She was grateful her Tahoe had four-wheel drive.

As she drove, she couldn't help but assume the safe was behind the break into the Antique Mine. True, she had a lot of valuable antiques, but she had always carried valuables, and was rarely concerned about security. But who in their right mind would try to steal a safe that weighed over one hundred and fifty pounds? Anxiety washed over her as she approached the store.

Instead of allowing negative thoughts to invade her mind, she decided to pray. As soon the "amen" left her lips, Sadie felt a release, and peace settled over her. She loved the Antique Mine, but she loved God more. Whatever happened, that love would sustain her. Not taking her attention off the road in front of her, she turned on her CD player. One of her favorite hymns began to play. Sadie sang along. "When peace like a river attendeth my way, when sorrows like sea billows roll; whatever my lot, Thou has taught me to say, it is well, it is well with my soul." By the time she pulled up to her shop, she was ready to face whatever awaited her.

Sheriff Mac Slattery's car was parked in front of the Antique Mine, the flashing lights on the top sending red and blue beams sweeping across the storefronts on Main Street, including her own. She pulled in behind him and got out of her car. When she tried to open the front door, she found it was still locked. She saw no sign of Sheriff Slattery and no indication of broken windows or locks. After sliding in her key, she turned the lock, went inside, and discovered the sheriff standing in the middle of her store. Mac Slattery was a large man with a face that reminded Sadie of a basset hound with a crew cut. His constantly stoic expression made it impossible to tell how serious the situation really was. Sadie's cousin, Laura, stood next to him, covered in a long coat. Her feet were still in slippers and the legs of her pajamas peeked out from beneath the hem of her coat.

"Mac?" she said as she approached him. "What's going on?"

Laura came to Sadie first and hugged her. "Oh, Sadie. I heard the siren and came down to see what was going on."

"Thanks so much, Laura." Sadie hugged her second cousin in return before turning her attention to the sheriff. "I take it the robber came in through the back door? Was anything taken?"

"That's exactly what happened. The back door looks like it was kicked in. But I don't know what he got away with, Sadie. You're gonna have to tell me."

Sadie took a quick look around. As far as she could tell, nothing was missing. She went directly to the back room, where, thankfully, the safe stood in the same place she'd left it.

She returned to the main area of the shop and checked the cash register. It hadn't been opened. "Everything seems to be okay," she said, now even more confused than before.

"Now, how can you possibly know that? This place is packed to the rafters."

"I know my store, Sheriff," Sadie said. "But you're right. I'll look everything over carefully. Still, at first glance, I don't see anything out of place." She shook her head. "How odd. Why would anyone go to the trouble to get inside but not steal anything?"

The sheriff shrugged. "Maybe I got here before the thief could make off with whatever he came here to get. I was only a couple of blocks away when the call came in."

"Who called you?"

"Don't know. The dispatcher said he didn't leave his name." Mac gazed around the room. "Go through your stock with a fine-tooth comb. If you find something missing, write it down and let me know. Of course, if nothing was stolen, there's not much I can do. Regardless, I'll need you to fill out a report. Just stop by the office in the next few days."

"Thank you, Sheriff. I appreciate your help."

A sudden knock on the front door made Sadie jump. She turned to see Edwin standing on the sidewalk. As the sheriff walked out, Edwin came in. Mac and Edwin greeted each other, and then Mac got in his car and drove away.

"Are you all right?" Edwin asked as he approached her. He looked concerned, and his hair, which was usually perfectly combed, was rather unkempt. One tuft of hair in particular stuck out as if standing at attention. He noticed Laura and said hello.

"How did you hear about the break-in?" Sadie asked.

"I have a police scanner. Since I'm running for mayor, I felt I should stay informed about what's going on in Silver Peak. Accidentally fell asleep with it on last night, but I'm glad I did. Heard the call this morning about the break-in. I got here as quickly as I could. Are you all right?"

Sadie smiled. "I'm fine. I wasn't here when it happened."

Relief washed across Edwin's face. "Thank goodness. If anything happened to you..."

Sadie saw something in his expression that made her stumble over her words. "Th—thank you." She suddenly felt warm, but it had nothing to do with the temperature in the room.

"Now that Edwin's here, I think I'll head back to bed," Laura said. "Before I go, is there anything I can do, Sadie?"

Sadie smiled at her. "I'll be fine. Thank you for checking on me. I'm sure waking up to lights and sirens was a little disconcerting."

Laura nodded. "That it was. I'll check back with you a little later. I have a conference call with a client first thing in the morning, but I'll stop by and see you in the afternoon."

Sadie gave Laura another hug. "That sounds fine. Get some sleep."

After Laura left, Edwin walked up and put his hand on Sadie's shoulder. "I'll stay here with you, if you don't mind. I don't think you should be alone."

"It really would make me feel much better if you were here."

Edwin nodded and took his hand from her shoulder. He walked over and pointed at her front counter. "Did you check the register?"

"I did, but it wouldn't have done a thief any good to open it anyway. I removed the money last night."

"I'm so glad." Edwin frowned. "But how did the robber get in here? The front door doesn't look damaged."

Sadie raised her eyebrows. "Mac said the thief came in through the back door. I haven't checked it yet." She hurried to the back of the store. Edwin followed her. Sure enough, the lock was broken.

"How do you know it was a man?" Edwin asked.

"I guess I don't. Not for sure. But the door was forced open. That takes strength." She pushed on the door and then stepped outside into the cold, snowy night. The light over the back entrance revealed exactly what she thought she'd find. The wet snow on the dirty door had created a print. It was large, either made by a large shoe or boot. Since it was wet the print wasn't entirely clear, which made it difficult to tell exactly what kind of shoe the burglar had been wearing. She came back inside the shop and pulled the damaged door shut. "There's a big footprint on the back of the door. Someone kicked it in and broke the lock. Most women don't have feet that large."

"Makes sense," Edwin said. "Well, I'm not sure I'm able to kick down a door, but I'm certainly capable of fixing it."

Sadie smiled at him. "Thank you, Edwin. I think we might need to add a dead bolt, as well."

"Agree. I'll head to Roscoe's first thing in the morning." Edwin retrieved the toolbox Sadie kept in her back room and began to assess the damage to her door. As he worked, Sadie wandered around, carefully checking her inventory. As she'd suspected, nothing was missing.

"Curiouser and curiouser," she mumbled to herself.

"Did you say something?" Edwin asked.

"Nothing important. But I just don't get it. Why would someone break in but not steal something?" She had been sure the safe was what the burglar had been after. If not the safe, then what?

Edwin straightened up and frowned at her. "Maybe Mac got here before the burglar had a chance to finish what he started."

"That's what he said."

"Who called it in?"

"I don't know. Mac said the caller didn't leave his name."

Edwin stared at her for a moment. "Now, that seems odd. I realize we don't know everyone in Silver Peak, but for the most part, people are very friendly. Helping your neighbor is appreciated. Why would anyone want to keep their identity secret when they obviously helped to protect you and your store?"

Sadie sighed, still distracted by thoughts of the safe. "I really don't know. Maybe they just didn't want to get involved? Didn't want to answer questions?"

"What's bothering you, Sadie?"

She sighed again. "Even if Mac arrived before the man could get what he came for, why didn't he grab something? Many of my antiques are small. He could have put something in his pocket so his efforts wouldn't be completely in vain. Unless..."

"Unless what?"

She walked over to the door of the back room and looked in at the safe. "Unless he was after one particular thing and didn't have time to complete his task."

"You mean the safe?" Edwin asked. "But who would try to run out of here with something that heavy? It would take a very strong man to pull that off." Edwin's eyebrows knit together in thought. "Maybe there were two men."

Sadie considered that. "Maybe, but I'm not so sure. The sheriff told me that whoever called in said they only saw one person inside the store. I guess someone else could have been hiding."

"If your intruder didn't bring someone to help him, he must not have been planning to remove the safe."

"I'm thinking the same thing. If he wasn't planning to take it with him, maybe he only wanted to open it." That idea made her all the more curious about what was inside. She walked into the back room and studied the safe.

Edwin put his screwdriver down and came over to where Sadie stood. "But how could he open it without the combination?"

"He couldn't." She turned to stare at Edwin. "Unless he had the combination. I tried to open this on my own, but I couldn't do it. I wrote down all the combinations I tried." She went over to her desk, removed a small pad of paper, and flipped the cover open. Sadie had tried several different numbers when she'd attempted to open the lock. It appeared to be a standard three-number lock so she'd used numbers that pertained to the opera house, including the address, the date it was built, and even the number of rooms in the opera house. She found the last combination noted on her pad and looked closely at the dial. "Yes, it's been moved."

"Maybe the thief tried to open it."

Sadie stared at the number on the dial. "Fifty," she said softly.

"Fifty?" Edwin echoed. "What does that mean?"

"I'm not sure…" Sadie gingerly tried to open the door to the safe in case fifty was the last number in the combination, but it was still locked. Then an idea struck her. She flipped the pages in her notepad until she found what she was looking for, then showed it to Edwin.

"Livi?" Edwin said, confusion in his tone. "Who is Livi?"

"I don't exactly know," Sadie replied. "I found this name carved into a desk in the opera house. I've been trying to figure it out." She rewrote the name. "Now what does this say?" she asked him.

"It looks like Livi in capital letters."

"But if I do this..." She separated the letters to form L IV I.

"Why, it's Roman numerals. Fifty, four, and one." Edwin looked at Sadie, astonished. "Fifty . . ."

Sadie met his gaze, then looked back at the safe. "Here goes nothing." She took a deep breath and turned the dial on the lock all the way around. Then she put in the numbers Edwin had mentioned. Nothing happened.

"Okay, let's try this." As she rewrote the numbers again, Sadie was beginning to wonder if her idea was as silly as it felt to her at that moment. She wrote, L I VI. Then she turned the dial one more time, stopping at fifty, one, and six.

She and Edwin gasped in unison when this time the safe door swung open.

7

———

LATER THAT MORNING, SADIE WAS ON HER SECOND CUP OF coffee from Arbuckle's when she was finally ready to remove the items from the safe. Edwin had gone home to get cleaned up, and Julie had called in to tell Sadie the local schools had taken a snow day, so she had to stay home with the twins. That suited Sadie just fine. Now she could remain at the shop and study the contents of the safe to her heart's content. She and Edwin had already taken a quick peek, enough to see that there weren't any jewels or stacks of currency.

Sadie took a deep breath and pulled the door open. She'd put a small book between the door and the edge of the safe to keep it from locking again. Even though she knew the combination, she didn't want to take any chances. The lock was so old there was a danger of its sticking.

The interior of the safe was lined with crushed red velvet. It contained one drawer that was filled with a couple of smaller things. Larger items lay on top of the drawer. One by one Sadie removed them and placed them on the small table she kept in the back room. So far, there was an aged and worn Bible, a folded army jacket, a green helmet, and a small box. As usual, when she was restoring antiques in the back room, she remained mindful of the front door's bell, in case a customer came in.

She reached in again and pulled out a Colt .45 in an old leather holster. During World War II, many soldiers carried pistols as well as their government-issued rifles. The Colt was the gun that was the most widely used. Sadie had learned a lot about guns from her father, who had collected antique firearms.

Sadie bent down and peered into the safe once again. There was one more thing inside. She reached in and pulled out a large yellowed envelope. There wasn't any writing on the front and the back was sealed shut. It was so old she would probably have to cut the envelope open. The glue on the seal and the paper were probably melded together.

Sadie looked over all the objects lined up in front of her. They told her that the safe had most likely been sealed up during or after World War II. This meant that Ardis was probably right when he said the safe had likely been placed inside the opera house wall during the previous 1940s renovations. The age of the safe had made her wonder if it had actually been hidden during the opera house's original construction, but these artifacts from World War II disproved that theory.

Sadie began to look over each item carefully, starting with the Bible. She opened the front cover, hoping to find the owner's name, but nothing was written there. She started leafing through the pages and found several passages marked with red ink. They all seemed to be about God's forgiveness. One Scripture was underlined and starred: 1 John 1:9: "If we confess our sins, he is faithful and just to forgive us our sins, and to cleanse us from all unrighteousness." There was something scribbled in the margin. Sadie picked up the Bible and moved it closer to her face. *Paul is writing to the church. This means me, doesn't it?* She put the Bible down and stared at it. The owner of the Bible seemed to be wondering if God's forgiveness included him. Sadie felt compassion for him. "He felt guilty about something," she said softly to herself.

Next she picked up the envelope. With a feeling of anticipation, she removed a letter opener from her supply closet. She slowly slid the opener underneath the letter's flap and drew it across the top. The old paper easily shredded. Putting the opener down, Sadie reached inside and pulled out a folded piece of yellowed paper.

She hoped the ink wasn't so faded she wouldn't be able to read it. Thankfully, once she unfolded the ancient paper, she could see that the writing was still legible. But her excitement quickly diminished as she gazed at the words.

The letter was written in German.

With a sigh, Sadie looked down toward the bottom of the page. It was signed, Hans Schweiss. At least she could look him up, but that was all she would learn from the letter until she could get it translated. She wondered if she could use a translator program on her computer to accomplish that.

She put the letter on top of the Bible and continued her search. Next she picked up the small box. She opened it and found a Purple Heart inside. She lifted it carefully from the box and looked on the back of the medal. Unfortunately the name of the recipient wasn't there. During World War II over a million similar medals were made. Sometimes the name was engraved on the back, but most of the time it wasn't. Without the certificate given with the award, there was no way to find out whom it was presented to.

Next Sadie removed the gun. First she checked to see if it was loaded. Thankfully, there were no bullets inside. She looked to see if the owner's name was engraved anywhere, but it wasn't. Still, the gun plus the Purple Heart made her doubt Hans Schweiss was the owner of the safe, since the majority of the items seemed to belong to an American soldier. So who was Hans Schweiss and what did he have to do with this soldier? She had to assume the letter was from Hans *to* the owner. She could barely contain her curiosity about what the letter said.

She put the gun to the side. She would love to add it to the antique gun collection her father had left her, but until she could find the owner, she didn't want to get too attached to the artifact.

She was down to the army coat and helmet. She could tell by the insignia on the coat that it had belonged to a corporal in the army. Again, no labels or tag identifying the owner, but more indicators that the safe's owner had been an American soldier.

"You really worked hard to hide your identity, didn't you?" she said out loud.

"Hello? Sadie?"

Sadie had been concentrating so hard on the safe's belongings that despite her best intentions, she hadn't heard the bell above the front door ring. She gathered the items and put them back in the safe, careful to keep the book in place to keep it from locking. Then she poked her head out of the back room.

Jerry Remington stood on the rug just inside the front door, looking amused. "Talking to yourself again?" Jerry had gotten to know Sadie well enough over the years, and especially over the course of their time together on the Historical Preservation Committee, that he knew her tendency to think out loud.

Sadie laughed. "You got me," she said as she walked toward him.

Jerry began stomping the encrusted snow off his rubber boots onto the snow mat she'd placed at the front of the shop for the winter. "Sorry if I startled you. I guess I should have made more noise when I came in."

Sadie shook her head. "It's not your fault. I was so engrossed in what I was doing, it wouldn't have helped if you'd blown a trumpet."

He laughed. "I heard about the break-in, Sadie. Jane and I were worried about you. Wanted to make sure you were all right."

"Thanks, Jerry, but I'm fine," Sadie said. "Nothing was taken."

Jerry took off his coat and shook the snow off of it. Then he hung it up while he wiped off his boots on the rug. "Jane hates these old things. I know they look terrible, but they keep my feet warm and protect my shoes." He walked over to where Sadie stood. "I'm so glad you're okay. We don't have many robberies in Silver Peak. Odd that nothing was taken."

"Yes, it is. The sheriff was close by, so maybe the thief didn't have time to take anything."

He nodded. "Maybe so." He nodded toward the back room. "Any progress on the safe?"

"You might say that." Sadie smiled. "I got it open."

"You did? How in the world…"

"Believe it or not, I found the combination carved into an old desk in the opera house office. Do you have any idea who it belonged to?"

"Impressive," Jerry said. "But I couldn't tell you about the desk. We've moved so many things around since work started inside, it could have come from anywhere. Dad took his desk out when he left. I have it now. But before that? I'm just not sure. It could have belonged to Franklin Reichert, but there's no way to be sure."

"That's what I thought too. Would you like to see what was inside?"

"I'd love to see them," he said enthusiastically.

He followed Sadie into the back room. Sadie opened the safe's door and put the contents back on the table where she'd had them earlier. Jerry stared wide-eyed at them. "Looks like these things belonged to someone in the military. Anything that points to who owned them?"

Sadie shook her head. "Not yet. I'm hoping that after some research I'll be able to find something that will reveal the owner. I guess it's a mystery waiting to be solved." She ran her hand over the folded jacket. "One question I keep asking myself is why someone would go to such lengths to hide mementos of their service. I would assume that most men and women like to keep their memories close."

"Yes, I guess that's true."

"Your father served in World War II, didn't he?"

Jerry nodded. "He was stationed in England, but he never saw combat. Dad spent his time doing paperwork, I'm afraid."

Sadie smiled at him. "Everything that was done during the war helped the cause, Jerry. From file clerks to generals."

He nodded. "You're right, of course. Dad never talked much about his time in the army. I think he was a little embarrassed because he didn't actually fight on the front lines."

"Reuben was a wonderful man," she said. "I certainly miss him."

"Thank you. I do too."

He pointed at the safe. "It's a little disappointing, isn't it? I was hoping some miner from the early days of Silver Peak buried his silver stash inside the safe."

Sadie smiled. "That would have been fascinating, and we certainly could have used the money for the opera house. But these things were a treasure to someone."

"I'm sure you're right," Jerry said as he made his way back to the front of the shop and she followed. "Now that I know you're okay, I should get back. We've got some guests who aren't too happy about our sudden snowstorm. In fact..."

Before he could finish his thought, the bell over the door rang and to Sadie's surprise, the odd-looking man Edwin had talked to at the rally in Arbuckle's pushed open the front door and came inside.

"How strange to see you here," he said to Jerry curtly. "I thought you were outside shoveling the driveway so the Winstons could get out. They're pitching a fit, you know."

Jerry, ever the patient host, gave a polite nod, despite the man's rudeness. "Yes, I know. Thanks, Barton. They seem to think I caused the storm just so they wouldn't be able to get to Denver today. I'll be happy to shovel, but even if they can make their way off the property, they'll likely get stuck before they get out of town." He shook his head. "It's best if they stay put. The snow will stop before long, and we'll all dig out."

As Jerry spoke, Sadie watched Barton. His coal-black mustache didn't quite match his salt-and-pepper hair. It was obvious he'd dyed it. Sadie found that strange. Although he was wearing a knit cap today, Sadie had seen his bald pate at the meeting. It was surrounded by a ring of hair that made the man look a little like a monk. Still, she didn't want to be rude, so she reached her hand out.

"It's nice to meet you," she said. "I'm Sadie Speers. I remember you from Edwin Marshall's rally."

"Pleased to meet you too," the man said, taking Sadie's hand. His handshake was tepid, and his skin was soft, indicating he didn't do much work with his hands. "I'm Barton Spivey. Here in Silver Peak for some rest and relaxation." He chuckled. "If we get snowed in, I guess I'll get more rest than I bargained for. But that's the benefit of being retired. No real schedule demanding my attention."

His words were friendly, if tinged with an overly formal air, but Sadie was struck by his lack of eye contact. His gaze was not on Sadie but in the direction of the back room.

"I'm glad you're getting some rest, Mr. Spivey," Sadie said in an attempt to be polite. "Is there something I can do for you? Did you come here to find Jerry, or would you like to look around the store?"

"I thought today would be a wonderful opportunity to explore some of the shops on Main Street that are within walking distance of the inn since I can't drive anywhere. Your store looked especially interesting. I love antiques."

"Please, feel free to look around," Sadie said. "If I can answer any questions, just ask."

"Thank you."

"I've got to go, Sadie," Jerry said. "I need to break out my shovel and see if I can help my restless guests get on their way. Again, I'm glad you're okay."

"Thanks, Jerry. Say hello to Jane for me."

"Will do."

After Jerry left, Sadie's focus turned to Barton. He had walked over to some shelves near the door to the back room, which was still open. After casting a perfunctory glance at the collectibles in front of him, his gaze swung toward the open door where the safe was clearly visible.

"Actually, I'm very interested in your safe. Made by Herring and Company, isn't it? Quite rare and valuable. Is it for sale?"

Sadie was surprised. Not many people knew about antique safes.

"No, it's not. Actually, it was discovered in an old building, and we're trying to find the rightful owner. May I ask how you knew what kind of safe this is?"

"Easily explained, dear lady," he said, finally making eye contact. "I own an old Milner and Shaw Cathedral Safe. Not as valuable as this one, but when I was searching for my safe, I saw several pictures of this model. Worth quite a bit, as I remember."

Sadie was impressed by Spivey's knowledge. "I've seen a few cathedral safes," she said. "They're very beautiful. You're fortunate to have one."

He nodded. "Yes, I am. You might be surprised to learn that I also have a Salesman's Sample Key Lock Safe made by Hall's Safe Company. It's quite valuable." He flashed Sadie another smile. "Well, if you don't mind, I'll continue to look around a bit." With that, he turned and began walking slowly around the shop.

"Looks like things have settled down some." Sadie turned to see Laura walking toward her. "How's everything going?" she asked.

"Just fine," she said, although she didn't mention that she'd opened the safe. She glanced over toward Barton, who appeared to be quite interested in an early-nineteenth-century hand-painted Chinese teapot. "Thanks again for being here last night. How are you?"

Laura came up close to her and lowered her voice. "Sadie, I heard a loud noise this morning around two o'clock. I got up and looked out my front window, but I didn't see anything. However, when I went to the back window I saw someone behind the store. He wasn't running, but he was walking quickly. I didn't say anything to the sheriff because I can't be certain he was coming from your store and I really don't want to place blame on someone unless I'm sure."

Sadie frowned. "The sheriff called me about two-thirty this morning, so the time frame is just about right, Laura. Did you see who it was?"

"I—I think so. To be honest, Sadie, I was pretty groggy, and I can't be completely sure. That's why I didn't tell the sheriff. But it looked like Spike. Spike Harris."

8

Spike? Sadie was surprised to hear his name. She knew Spike well and had great affection for him. He ran the Silver Peak Music Emporium and was well known in the region for his music, especially with his band, the Skylarks, whose blend of country, folk, with a hint of rockabilly thrown in for good measure, earned them frequent bookings. Spike, who had sworn Sadie to secrecy when he told her his real name was Wendell, was a widower who'd lost his wife and daughter in a terrible car accident twenty years ago, and an air of tragedy still hung over him. Despite, or perhaps because of, his careworn demeanor, Sadie considered him a friend. So why on earth would he break into her store? It made no sense to her.

"Are you sure?"

"That's just it, Sadie, I'm not." Laura shrugged. "I'm sorry. But I had to tell you."

Sadie sighed. "I understand. Thanks, Laura."

"Well, I'm not sure you should be thanking me, but if the information helps, I'll be glad." She sighed. "I hope I'm wrong about Spike, Sadie. Anyway, I've got to get back to work." She smiled feebly. "No snow days for those of us who spend a lot of time working online."

"How is work?" Sadie asked.

"Pretty good, actually. I'm meeting with Jesse this week. We have an idea for a brochure that will help voters get to know Edwin a little better. I think it will be helpful. Even though I'm not on the campaign anymore officially, I still really believe in Edwin and am happy to help where I can."

"Well, I know Edwin appreciates everything you've done to help him."

"It's a pleasure. He's good for this town." She grinned. "And for you."

Sadie felt herself blush. "Let me know when you have some free time. Maybe we can grab lunch or dinner."

"Would love to."

Laura walked out, leaving Sadie standing alone to wonder why Spike Harris would enter her store early in the morning. It didn't make sense. Was he in some kind of trouble? As far as she knew, giving music lessons and playing in his band provided him steady income. He didn't seem to need money. Besides, how in the world would Spike know the combination to the safe? He was only forty-four. He wasn't even born when it was probably sealed into the wall of the opera house. She supposed he could have been given the combination by someone else, but it seemed entirely unlikely. Sadie considered asking him about it, but she wasn't sure that was the best idea. Laura wasn't sure it was really him, and the last thing she wanted to do was accuse Spike of breaking into her shop unless she had more evidence.

She went into the back room and grabbed a nearby plastic box. After Barton Spivey's interest in the safe, she felt better hiding the items away from prying eyes.

As she exited the back room, she heard the bell ring over the front door. Barton Spivey was leaving just as Roz and Roscoe were on their way in. Although she was happy to see her friends, she'd been looking forward to a little quiet time to process the break-in. Obviously, it would have to wait until later. Roz was encased from head to toe in a long coat with a hood. A wool scarf covered most of her face, and she had on gloves and boots. Although Sadie loved winter, Roz found the cold miserable.

"Come on in," Sadie called to her friends. "What are you doing out in this kind of weather, Roz?"

She pulled her scarf down, uncovering her mouth. "I rode into town with Roscoe. You know our Colorado weather has to work harder than this to keep me down, Sadie." Her eyes widened and she gave Sadie a big hug. "Especially when I heard you were robbed! I just had to make sure you were all right!"

"Oh, Roz," Sadie said with a laugh at Roz's dramatics. "I should have called you. I'm so sorry. I've just been so distracted. Why didn't you just pick up a phone? You didn't need to come down here."

Slowly, Roz began to unwrap herself from her self-made cocoon. "Because if I called you, you'd tell me you were okay. I had to see for myself."

Sadie chuckled. "Come over here by the stove and sit down. You'll be nice and warm in no time."

"Thanks. I think I will."

"Guess what," Sadie said. "I got the safe open."

Roscoe looked surprised. "I thought your special safe guy wasn't coming for several weeks."

Sadie told them about finding the odd carving on the desk at the opera house and figuring out it was actually the combination for the safe after finding that someone had entered one of the correct numbers on the dial.

"So whoever owned the desk knew something about the safe?" Roz said.

Sadie shrugged. "That's my assumption too. But it's not necessarily what happened. Surely a lot of people came in and out of the opera house back then. It could be anyone. I mean, the way everything's been moved around over the years, it could have come from anywhere inside the building." Sadie wiped a rogue strand of hair off her brow. "But I am looking into the management of the opera house, because although anyone could have scratched the combination into the desk, I think someone who worked there is the most likely suspect."

"That makes sense," Roscoe said.

"Perhaps I'll learn something from the account books I found in the office at the opera house. I'm hoping to find something that points to the safe. Since it was found there, maybe someone bought it specifically for the opera house. Or perhaps receipts from the renovations will provide a clue. It's a long shot, but it's worth a try." She had also decided that if she couldn't find anything helpful in the account books, she'd try doing some research at the library. Important events at the opera house were surely chronicled down through the years in the pages of the *Silver Peak Sentinel*. Could there be something in the paper that would point her in the right direction? "What I do know is that the safe can't just sit here forever. Either it needs to be turned over to the family of the owner or it needs to be sold for the benefit of the opera house."

"Well, someone obviously knew at least part of the combination," Roscoe said. "Maybe it's a family member of the owner."

"Could very well be," Sadie replied. "But why wouldn't he just come forward and tell us that the safe belongs to his family? The contents of the safe seem relatively benign."

The bell over the front door rang again and Edwin walked in. Sadie had been expecting him since he said he planned to put a dead bolt on the back door today. Roz and Roscoe greeted him as he walked over to where they stood next to Sadie.

"We were just talking about the safe," Roscoe said.

Edwin shook his head. "A strange turn of events."

"It certainly is," Roscoe agreed. He glanced at his watch. "Well, I hate to rush off, but I've got to get the store opened." He smiled at Sadie. "I'm grateful you're okay."

"Thank you, Roscoe," she said.

"Mind if I join you?" Edwin asked Roscoe. "I want to buy a dead bolt for Sadie's back door."

"Of course." Roscoe kissed Roz's forehead and then he and Edwin left.

"Sadie, do you mind if I hang out here with you for a while?" Roz asked, rubbing her arms with her hands, still trying to chase away the chill.

Sadie smiled. "I wouldn't have it any other way." She grabbed another chair and pulled it up close to where Roz sat.

"So Edwin's buying a dead bolt for your back door?" Roz said with a grin. "Sounds like something a boyfriend would do."

Sadie laughed. "Oh, Roz! I don't know about that," she said, "but it means a lot to me that he's concerned about my safety."

Roz wrinkled her nose. "You see it your way, and I'll see it mine."

"Oh, Roz." Sadie laughed. Roz had a way of making her feel better. But maybe that was what best friends were for. The threatening note crossed her mind, and she decided to confide in Roz about it.

"I've got something to tell you," she said in a low voice. "Actually, I have two things to tell you, but you have to promise to keep them to yourself."

Roz held up her hand, her little finger extended. "Pinkie swear."

Sadie laughed and hooked her little finger with Roz's. "Pinkie swear," she repeated. She scooted a little closer so she could whisper. "Laura told me she thinks she saw Spike Harris behind my shop this morning, right around the time of the break-in."

Roz's eyebrows shot up. "Spike? No way. Why in the world would he do something like that?"

"I don't know. To be honest, I'm not sure it was him. Laura was still sleepy when she spotted this person. She promised to keep it to herself until I have some time to figure out if it really was Spike. At this point I have my doubts. I mean, you know Spike has that craggy, rough-and-tumble look that makes him seem sort of inherently guilty anyway." She raised her eyebrows, knowing Roz would understand. "At least, until you get to know him. But an actual burglar could have been wearing the same kind of clothes as Spike—the man does love wearing black."

"True. And I can't imagine what Spike could want with the safe." Roz appeared to turn the thought over in her mind for a moment, but she didn't come up with any reason to connect Spike and the safe.

Roz's reaction actually added to Sadie's growing suspicion that Laura was mistaken in her identification.

"What's the other thing?" Roz said finally.

Sadie hesitated a moment. Finally she opened the drawer to her cash register, lifted the money drawer, and pulled out the note she'd found stuck on her windshield. She handed it to Roz, who quickly read it.

"Sadie!" Roz's eyes were wide with concern. "You can't keep this a secret. What if the person who wrote this is dangerous? You've got to tell the sheriff."

Sadie sighed. "I promised Alice I would do that if I felt the threat was serious."

Roz peered closely at her friend. "Someone broke into your store, Sadie! I would say that's pretty serious. Maybe you should also say something to the sheriff about Spike."

Sadie grunted. "No. I don't want to raise that flag with the sheriff when even Laura doubts what she saw."

"Why don't you just ask Spike?"

"I considered that, but I don't want him to think I don't trust him. It'd be a pretty serious accusation. Especially when it's doubtful it was actually him."

"I see your point," Roz said. Her thoughtful expression brightened, and she clapped her hands together. "So are you going to tell your very best friend what was in the safe?"

Sadie told her everything she'd found, mentioning the letter last. "I won't know what it says until I get it translated."

"Translated?"

Sadie quickly told Roz about the letter written in German. Then she went to the back room and got the box that contained the items she'd removed from the safe. She opened it up and showed each one to Roz.

"You're right," Roz said with a frown. "Nothing here looks that valuable, but something in here is obviously important to someone. Important enough to write you a threatening note and break in to your shop. I'm really concerned, Sadie."

"Here's why I'm not that worried yet. First of all, the note isn't really all that menacing. I mean, 'Don't open that safe or you'll be sorry?' 'You'll be sorry' doesn't sound like much of a warning. I mean, every time I forget to put my slippers in the bathroom so I can put them on after my shower, I'm sorry. But it doesn't make me violent."

Roz gave Sadie a blank stare. "Not really sure that explanation fits the situation."

"Well, maybe not. But I think you get my point. Also, the person who broke into my shop did minimal damage, didn't steal anything, and he didn't even try to get into the cash register. If this person meant me harm, it seems he would be doing things more specifically threatening to me." Sadie thought for a moment. "It seems clear that whoever wrote this note, and whoever broke in, really wants something from that safe. If I can figure out who that person is, perhaps we can finally sort out the ownership of the safe. Maybe even arrange to have it sold and donated to the opera house, where it was stashed all these years."

"You're trying to appeal to my weakness for that grand old building," Roz said with a small smile. "And it's working. But if you uncover something that concerns me..."

"I know. You'll blow the whistle. Alice has already warned me about the same thing."

Sadie turned her attention back to the items on the table. "I looked inside the Bible. There isn't a name in the front. That would have been helpful. But there are quite a few passages marked inside. And several notes."

Roz frowned. "Notes? What kind of notes?"

Sadie turned the pages of the old Bible until she reached the spot she was looking for. "Reminders about God's forgiveness." She pointed at a spot on the page.

Roz leaned over and read, "If we confess our sins, he is faithful and just to forgive us our sins, and to cleanse us from all unrighteousness." She looked up at Sadie. "Great Scripture. I rely on it quite a bit."

"Me too."

"But if these passages meant so much to him, why would he store his Bible in the safe?" Roz asked. "That doesn't make much sense to me. I'd think he'd want to keep the book close."

"Good question," Sadie said. She looked up at her friend. "Have you ever thrown a Bible away?"

Roz laughed. "No, even though I own about a million of them. It always feels wrong somehow." She gazed down at the old leather-bound edition. "So maybe the owner couldn't bear to dispose of it, yet..." She concentrated for a moment. "Perhaps there is something inside that bothered him so much he had to lock it away. Perhaps he was so convinced about something that these passages began to haunt him."

"That actually makes a lot of sense. Seems he was praying for forgiveness, but, like many people who have done wrong, maybe he wasn't really sure God would cleanse him from whatever sin he felt he'd committed."

Roz nodded vigorously. "It's a good theory, even though it makes me feel sad for him. God is so quick to forgive. As far as the east is from the west..."

"Amen," Sadie said. "So this Bible certainly tells us something *about* the safe owner, but it doesn't tell us who he is or was."

Roz pulled the small box that contained the medal toward them. "What about this Purple Heart?" She opened the box and carefully removed it. "Is there a way to find the owner?"

Sadie shook her head. "I don't think so. Not without a name or the certificate that went with it."

Roz thought a moment. "Okay. Is there some kind of list that names the people from Colorado who were granted this medal during the war? Maybe you could narrow it down."

Sadie sighed. "Unfortunately, no. The National Archive in St. Louis suffered a major fire in 1969 and a lot of records were destroyed. The chance that the information we need survived is minuscule. There's no way I know of for us to find the owner of the safe through this medal."

"How do you know so much about Purple Hearts?"

"They've been through my shop before. Grandchildren bringing in Grandfather's Purple Hearts, hoping to get money for them."

"Are they worth very much?"

"Not monetarily, no. But they are priceless in a more important way," she said. "And I tell them that. Medals awarded to servicemen and women should be passed down in families, along with the stories of their bravery and valor."

"I agree. So you don't buy them?"

Sadie shook her head. "Actually, for one thing, it's illegal. But even if it wasn't, I wouldn't purchase one. It isn't right."

Roz smiled at her friend. "Good for you, Sadie." Roz looked over all the things in the box. "So are there any other clues?"

"Well, we have to assume the owner was in the military, and he either liked antiques or someone in his family owned this safe. Also, I'm guessing that since the letter is in German, he may have been stationed in or near Germany. And by the highlighted passages in the Bible, something happened that he felt guilty about. Perhaps he shot someone?"

Roz looked at her friend in surprise. "And how do you figure that?"

Sadie pointed at the gun. "Why would he put his gun in a safe and hide it? My dad had a gun collection. I mean, he may have sold a gun once in a while, but concealing it behind a wall? Especially one that had some meaning to him? Most military men feel very possessive about weapons they used in the war. But this man apparently wanted it out of his sight. So given the context of the other items, I'm guessing that something happened with his gun that upset him."

"That makes sense," Roz said.

Sadie picked up the letter. "I'll take this letter home and see what I can do about translating it."

The bell above the front door dinged, and Sadie looked up to see Edwin stepping in. "Sorry it took so long," he said. "Roscoe..."

"Jabbered your ear off?" Roz said with a grin. "Sorry about that. Some of my friends say their husbands never talk. That's certainly not Roscoe's problem. Sometimes I'd swear he only opened that hardware store so he can trade stories with whoever stops by."

Edwin smiled. "Well, I enjoy it. He has a lot of good ideas for my campaign." He had a bag in his hand that Sadie assumed contained the new dead bolt. He had some envelopes in his other hand. "Brought in your mail."

"Thanks, Edwin," Sadie said. "Give me a minute to put these things back, and I'll go through it. I've been so distracted, I forgot to bring the mail in."

Sadie put the lid back on the plastic box and quickly carried it to the back room. When she returned, she took the mail from Edwin.

"I noticed the letter on top of the stack," Edwin said, frowning. "It looks unusual."

Edwin took the top envelope off the stack and handed it to her. Her name was written in block letters, but there wasn't an address under it. Nor was there any return address. She shot a quick look at Roz, who scowled at her.

"I think you need to open it, Sadie," she said. "No more secrets."

Edwin studied Sadie through narrowed eyes. "Secrets?"

She wanted to be upset with Roz, but she knew her friend was only looking out for her. She told Edwin about the first note.

"Sadie!" he said, his forehead wrinkled with alarm. "Why didn't you call the authorities? How could you put yourself in danger this way? Whoever wrote that letter probably broke in here. Sounds to me like he's getting desperate."

"Calm down," Sadie said, a little amused at his outburst despite the seriousness of the situation. "If he really wanted to hurt me, he would have waited until I was alone. He didn't do that. Or he could have come to my house. He didn't do that either."

"Like anyone could get past Hank," Roz said. "That dog would protect you with his life."

"That's probably true, but unless the person who is sending me these notes is a close friend, he wouldn't know about Hank at all."

"Have you told the sheriff?" Edwin said.

Sadie shook her head.

"Maybe there's not much he can do at this point, but at least he can keep a closer eye on you. I think you should tell him."

"All right, all right." Sadie shook her head. "But I don't think it will make any difference."

"What do you mean?" Roz asked.

"Sending people letters isn't against the law."

"Threatening people is," Edwin said in a low voice.

"I understand that." She sighed. "I have to go down to the sheriff's office and file a report anyway. I'll tell him about the notes." She swung her gaze back and forth between Roz and Edwin. "Will that satisfy the both of you?"

"I suppose it will have to," Edwin said.

"Well, open this one," Roz said impatiently. "Maybe it will give Mac something he can actually work with."

Sadie sighed again and opened the envelope. Inside was a folded piece of yellow-lined paper, just like the previous note. Roz and Edwin looked over her shoulder as she read:

Please stop looking for answers. You will ruin lives if you proceed.

9

———

"Sadie, I really don't like this," Roz said.

Sadie didn't like it either, but she wasn't afraid. This letter was even less threatening than the first. "It's becoming clearer to me that whoever wrote these notes fears I'll uncover some secret he doesn't want revealed. He's appealing to me, not trying to frighten me."

"I don't suppose this means you'll stop trying to find the owner," Roz said with a sigh.

"I don't think so." To be honest, the pleading tone of the note really bothered Sadie. What in the world could an old Bible, a Purple Heart, clothing from World War II, a letter written in German, and a gun have to do with ruining lives?

"I concede that the person behind this doesn't sound that dangerous," Edwin said. "But I'm still relieved you're going to let Mac know about these notes."

A sudden gust of wind shook the building, and Sadie glanced toward the front window of the store. "It's really starting to snow. We'd better head home."

"I don't know if I like your being home alone," Edwin said, frowning.

Edwin was acting awfully protective, and Sadie couldn't help but notice. She was flattered but unsure how to respond. He was acting like…a boyfriend. And that was a concept Sadie didn't know how to process at this point, so she decided to just focus on the issue at hand. "I'll be fine," she said with a smile. "Like Roz said, I have the best protection any human being could have. Hank takes good care of me. And besides, I can see anyone coming up the road. Tonight everyone will be hunkered down at home anyway. Even our letter writer will be trapped inside."

Edwin stared at the letter and then at Sadie. "All right. But will you stay near your phone? I'll call to check on you. If you don't answer…"

"You can call out the troops."

The front door swung open, and Roscoe came in wearing his thick winter coat and his wool hat. "Ready, Roz?" he said. "It's getting bad out there."

"We were just talking about that." Roz got her coat from the rack in the back room. Before leaving she pointed at Sadie. "You keep your cell phone on. I'll be calling you too."

"Yes, ma'am," Sadie said with a grin. "Sounds like I'm in for a busy night."

Roz nodded. "That's what happens when so many people care about you." With that, she and Roscoe scooted out the door.

Sadie found herself touched by her friend's words. She turned around to find Edwin staring at her strangely. He seemed flustered and quickly turned pink.

"Well, guess I'd better get that dead bolt on," he said gruffly. "You don't have to wait for me. I'll lock up when I'm done."

Sadie smiled. "Don't be silly. I'll get us some coffee. I'm not worried about driving in snow. I've been doing it most of my life."

"I know arguing with you is pointless. When you get your mind made up…" Edwin cleared his throat, then headed toward the back of the store.

Sadie walked over to the door between Arbuckle's and the Antique Mine, hoping Hector and Luz hadn't already left. She was happy to find them still there. When Sadie entered the aromatic coffee shop, Hector was just locking the front door, and Luz was cleaning off the tables.

"Is it too late for coffee?" Sadie asked with a grin.

Even though she was forty years old, Luz sometimes reminded Sadie of a teenager. Her vivacity and enthusiasm matched someone much younger. Luz's silky black hair was piled up on top of her head, and her brown eyes crinkled as she smiled. "Just turned it off, but it's still nice and hot. Want it black?"

"Please. Two cups."

"I heard someone broke in to your shop last night," she said, her dark eyes full of concern. "What did they take?"

"As far as I can tell they didn't steal a thing," Sadie said. "I think they were interested in that old safe that was found in the opera house."

Luz laughed. "They must be pretty strong if they planned to carry off that thing."

Sadie nodded. "I agree. The good news is that everything's okay, I'm okay, and Edwin is putting a new dead bolt on the back door."

"Is that where they came in?"

"Yep. After Edwin's finished, I don't think it will be that easy should they decide to try again."

"I assume you and Edwin need the coffee to keep you going while he works?"

Sadie smiled. "Exactly."

Hector came over and greeted Sadie. Tall and lanky with the same coloring as his wife, he towered above her five-foot-six frame. "I'd head home soon if I were you, Sadie. Forecast says we'll pick up several more inches before this is over."

Luz handed Sadie two cups of steaming coffee. She began to reach for some cash she had in her pocket when Hector waved her comment away. "It's on us. We were going to pour it out anyway."

Sadie gave a grateful nod. "Thanks, Hector."

"You got it," Luz said with a smile. "You're one of the few people I know who can drink coffee this late in the day. I would be up all night, and I own a coffee shop."

Sadie shrugged. "Doesn't seem to bother me. Thanks again. I really appreciate it."

Luz and Hector said good-bye and locked the door behind her as she left.

She carried the cups of coffee to the back of her shop, where Edwin was working on the door.

"Here you go," she said to Edwin.

"Thanks," he said. He had already made some progress on the dead bolt. "So did you find anything in the safe that points to the owner?"

"No, but there's a letter that might reveal something. I'm hoping after it's translated I'll find a clue."

"Translated? It's in another language?"

Sadie nodded. "German. I'm going to use an online translator tonight. See if I can crack it."

Edwin smiled. "I don't think you'll be too happy with the results. I've used them before, and the translations can be a little nonsensical."

"Well, I don't know anyone who speaks German, so my options are limited."

He straightened in mock pride. "Well, milady, you're in luck. I know someone who speaks German, and I'm certain he'd be glad to help."

"Really? That would be wonderful. Who is it?"

"His name is Herman Bruner. He lives just outside of town. He's been out of town looking after his sick mother, but he may be back by now. I'll give him a call and see if he can come by and take a look at the letter. Of course, if it keeps snowing like this, it might be a few days."

"That's fine." Sadie sighed happily. "Actually, getting snowed in might be a blessing. I can spend lots of time doing research. By the time we dig out, maybe I'll have some answers."

Edwin chuckled. "You find the blessing in almost everything, don't you? One of your most endearing qualities, among a great many."

Sadie felt a sudden rush of affection for Edwin. He was a good man, and she was happy to have him back in her life. Unconsciously, she reached up and patted her hair, hoping she looked nice today. Her automatic reaction startled her and she quickly put her hand down.

"Did you hear me, Sadie?"

Edwin's voice jarred her out of her contemplation, and she jumped. "I'm sorry. What did you say?"

Edwin stood up. "The dead bolt is in place. I'd like to work on this door a little more later, but I think we both need to get home. It's certainly stronger than it was. I don't think anyone will be kicking it in again." He handed her a key. "This is the key to the dead bolt. You can still use your other key for the regular lock."

"You know who is really good at cutting off locks?" Sadie asked, trying to keep a straight face.

He shook his head. "Who?"

She grinned. "A barber."

Edwin stared at her for a moment. "Why would a barber..." Suddenly his expression changed, and he burst out laughing. "Sadie, you are a very... singular person."

She winked at him. "I like to think of myself as one-of-a-kind."

"Well, you are that." He smiled at her. "And much more." Sadie felt herself blush. "Thank you so much for putting the dead bolt on. How much do I owe you for it?"

"Not enough to worry about. Roscoe made me a deal."

Sadie laughed again. Roscoe was always giving his friends special prices. Sometimes Sadie wondered how the man made any money at all.

"Thank you again. Let me know when your friend can look at the letter."

Edwin grinned. "I'm glad I can help. It's almost like we're doing research together. Like we're... detectives."

Sadie waved a dismissive hand. "Funny. That's what Theo called me. An *antique* detective." She chuckled. "It just made me feel ancient."

Edwin smiled. "Not even close, Sadie. You're beautiful and vibrant. I remember thinking my dad was an old man when he was only forty. It's all relative."

He put the tools back in the toolbox and carried it to the back room. Knowing she could get snowed in at home for a couple of days, Sadie decided to take the things from the safe with her. Since someone was obviously looking for them, they would be safer with her anyway. She put out the fire in the stove, then went to the back room and grabbed the box.

She and Edwin walked together to the front door, and after Sadie locked up, Edwin walked her to her car.

As she drove away, his words came back to her. Did Edwin really think she was beautiful and vibrant?

10

Saturday dawned with almost ten inches of snow on the ground. Although municipalities in other locations would be shut down from those kinds of accumulations, Silver Peak residents mostly took it in stride. As long as they didn't get much more snow, Campfire Chapel would probably have services on Sunday. Sadie looked forward to church. She loved listening to Pastor Don, and she also enjoyed seeing her friends. Today, however, she was content to stay home, do some research, and spend time with Hank. She felt she'd been neglecting him some. Sadie would call Laura to see if she could put a sign in the window with Sadie's cell phone number to call if someone really wanted her to open, not that she expected Main Street to be awash in shoppers on this cold day.

After a breakfast of pancakes and bacon, Sadie and Hank settled down in the main room of her house. She appreciated how neat and clean her surroundings were, thanks to her weekly housekeeper, Claribel. It was hard for her to enjoy time at home if her house was messy, but running the store, being involved at church, spending time with her family and friends, and being active in her community left very little time for housework. So she'd decided that a splurge on a housekeeper would be worth it. Boy, had it been. Not only had she gained a perpetually clean house, she'd gained a friend in Claribel.

Hank snuggled up even closer to her on the couch, and Sadie covered herself with a thick, soft comforter. On the table she had her coffee, the account books from the opera house, the box with the objects from the safe, and her laptop. Once she was settled, she began working on her laptop. She tried using the online translator she'd used before for smaller foreign words or phrases. Translating marks and hallmarks happened frequently with antiques from foreign countries. But she quickly discovered that trying to translate an entire letter was difficult. As Edwin had anticipated, the results were confusing and Sadie giggled at some of the sentences that made no sense. She became all the more thankful that Edwin had a friend who could help.

Next she went through the books from the opera house. She'd really wanted to go through them last night but was glad she'd waited. She wasn't as tired as she'd been last night after Alice and the kids left. A lot of the entries were faded and hard to read. She found many notes and bills from the renovations, but there wasn't anything that looked odd or pointed toward the safe. She saw the names of the construction company that did most of the work, but a quick Internet search revealed that it had gone out of business twenty-three years ago when the owner died. There didn't seem to be any relatives in Silver Peak. In the end, the books weren't the least bit helpful.

After putting the books aside, Sadie moved on to the coat she'd found inside the safe. She was able to confirm her original suspicion that the coat belonged to a corporal in the army. It had two stripes on the sleeves, but no other identifying marks. If the coat had ever had a name tag, it had been removed. The hat had no markings at all. It was just a soft wool hat with red piping that could be folded. She double-checked the Purple Heart, but as she'd told Roz, there was really no way to track it without a certificate or an inscription. Then, she spent quite a while going through the old Bible, but it didn't yield any new information either. Still, the time she spent paging through the holy book felt sacred to her.

"I feel sorry for the person who owned this Bible," she said to Hank, who cocked his head to one side as if he were really interested. "He certainly was guilt-ridden about something." The handwritten notes scribbled on the margins were hard to read, not only because the ink was faded, but also because the handwriting itself was small and rather messy. "Men," she said, addressing Hank again. "Some of them don't care much about penmanship." She smiled at her faithful friend. "Don't look so innocent. If you could write, I'll bet it would be just as difficult to decipher."

Hank gave her a doggy grin and Sadie laughed. Sometimes she could swear he understood what she was saying although she knew it couldn't be true. Still, it was fun to pretend.

Finally, Sadie began an Internet search using the name *Hans Schweiss*. There was a Hans Schweiss who was a graphic designer in Germany around the time of the war. There was another Hans Schweiss who was currently a musician in Austria and another who served as a Nazi officer in Germany during World War II who was executed for treason. She found one more man who was a journalist for the Russian newspaper *Pravda* from 1920 through 1960. Although there were several other men with the same name, the information on them was sketchy at best. Although Sadie was certain the man who wrote the letter wasn't the musician in Austria since he wasn't old enough, it wasn't possible to narrow the other choices down with confidence. Sadie was even more interested in getting that letter translated than she had been before.

After a couple of cozy hours going through the contents of the safe, she put them all back into the box. She'd thoroughly examined everything, but she had the strangest feeling she was missing something. It reminded her of the times she'd seen an actor or actress in a movie or a TV show and knew she'd seen them before, but she couldn't remember where. Try as she could, she couldn't figure out what it was that bothered her.

Finally, she gave up and checked her watch. It was almost time for lunch. So far Roz had called twice.

She wriggled off the couch, trying not to disturb Hank, and went over to the window. The snow was still falling, but according to the weather reports online, the major storm had moved out. The sun peeked out from behind the clouds and it made the snow sparkle. To Sadie, the world always looked magical after a big snow.

Hank whined and Sadie looked down to see him sitting beside her, staring out the window. She knew him well enough to know what he was thinking.

"Nothing says we can't go outside for a while," she said. "This afternoon I'll bundle up and we'll play in the snow a bit. Would that make you happy?"

Once again, she was greeted with a wide smile. She reached down and patted his head. "I don't know what I would do without you, boy," she said softly. "You're such a good friend."

After a quick lunch of chicken salad and melon, Sadie switched her focus to the safe itself. Some online investigation, along with a few calls to several experts who dealt with safes, helped her to find five Herring and Company safes in the same style as hers that were sold in the last seventy years. Even though her safe might not be among the ones mentioned, she felt it was worth a try. Most dealers kept detailed records, especially with large items like safes.

One of the five safes she found was sold at auction in London in the seventies to a local bank where it was still on display. Another was sold three times, all to collectors in California. One was in an antique store in New York City, and another was purchased just ten years ago in Georgia. That left one safe that was last reported in Reims, France, in the forties. Reims wasn't far from the Belgium border. It was mentioned by an antique safe collector who bought and sold safes. His online site was extensive and he chronicled the sales and purchases of old safes. From her days teaching history, she knew American troops were stationed in France during the war, and Sadie considered it a possibility that this was the same safe sitting in her back room. A chill went through her at the thought that she might have found a trace of where that safe had come from.

Unfortunately, the online trail stopped there. However, she did have one source that might be able to help her. Jean-Pierre was an antique dealer in Paris who was a wonderful source of information for French antiques that came into her shop. She'd met him several years ago when he'd come into the Antique Mine while in Colorado for a skiing vacation. The two had become fast friends, and he had helped her with research when she couldn't find all the information she wanted from books or online. He was the only person she could think of who could locate details she couldn't find online. Not sure she would reach him since it was after ten o'clock in Paris, she was surprised when he actually answered the phone.

"*Bonjour*, Jean-Pierre *ici*."

"Bonjour, Jean-Pierre. It's Sadie Speers from Silver Peak."

"Ah, Sadie! *C'est magnifique* to hear from you." Sadie always loved to listen to the man's charming accent. "I am so glad you caught me. I was just about to leave. How may I help you?"

She quickly gave him the information she had about the safe in Reims, along with the year it might have been sold. He promised to check through his old records. As someone who specialized in antique safes, maybe he could shed some light on what had happened to this particular safe.

"Someone might have bought it in the forties and brought it back to America," she told Jean-Pierre. "It would have been shipped here, but there were so many supplies and possessions being sent back to America after the war, finding anything about this particular safe might be nearly impossible."

"I understand, Sadie," Jean-Pierre said. "I'll see what I can find and call you back."

She thanked him and hung up. Then she looked over at Hank, who was staring at her with his large brown eyes. He whined and she leaned over to pat his head. "You're right, boy. We both need a break." Sadie closed her laptop and stood up. Sitting so long on the couch had made her feel stiff. She walked over to the window and looked out again. "It's pretty deep out there, Hank. But I'm willing to give it a try if you are."

His high-pitched bark made her laugh.

"Okay, okay. Give me a few minutes to get winterized."

Sadie pulled on a pair of rubber boots. She usually put on her leather hiking boots when she and Hank went for a walk, but in bad weather she tended to wear these. After wrapping a wool scarf around her neck, putting on her thermal coat, wool hat, and her thick insulated gloves, she was ready to face the winter weather. She turned to call Hank and found him watching her with a goofy smile on his face.

"So you think I'm funny-looking?" she asked. "I don't have a permanent winter coat like you do, my friend."

Hank barked and jumped up on her.

"I get it. Quit talking and start walking. Okay, okay. Let's go."

Sadie opened the door and Hank bounded outside, full of enthusiasm. Sadie noticed that someone had already cleared her driveway. She wasn't really surprised. Milo was always doing kind things like that for her. Ever since T.R. died, Milo had been watching out for her. Sadie had even given him a key to her back door. She trusted him completely.

She would have to bake him one of her special caramel apple pies. He loved them and she enjoyed making them for him.

She laughed as she watched Hank. Sinking into the snow didn't dampen his spirits a bit. He saw the white cold stuff as nothing more than something exciting to play with. He jumped around and ran through the drifts, biting at the snow as if it were challenging him.

Sadie grabbed a snow shovel she'd put on the front porch before the storm hit and began to shovel off the walk in front of her house. But as soon as she cleared off one spot, Hank would jump through the pile she'd made and push some of the snow back onto the sidewalk. Before long shoveling the sidewalk became a game—one she seemed to be losing.

After finishing her chore the best she could, she spent some time playing in the snow with Hank. He loved to catch snowballs, so she'd toss some to him as he ran around in circles in the yard even though they fell apart when he bit down on them. After about thirty minutes it was starting to get dark. Sadie was exhausted and cold. She walked up to the porch and called to Hank. Although he'd had a great time, he was ready to come in too.

Sadie held on to his collar so she could brush the snow off his coat and feet before he ran inside. Once she'd gotten him fairly clean, she opened the door and let him in. Although she'd wiped her feet off on the mat outside, the moisture made it sound like she was stepping on squeaky mice as she walked to the closet. Hank cocked his head to the side and stared comically at her. He looked so funny, she burst out laughing. She pulled off her boots and was hanging up her coat when the phone rang. She turned on the light and hurried over to pick it up. It was Jean-Pierre. She hadn't expected to hear from him until tomorrow and was glad she hadn't missed his call.

"Sadie," he said, "I looked through some old records I've collected down through the years and discovered a bit more information about your safe. It was sold to an American serviceman right at the end of the war. Unfortunately, I can't give you his name."

"I don't understand," Sadie said. "Why wouldn't the name be mentioned?"

"It was," Jean-Pierre replied. "I have a photocopy of the original receipt, but when it was copied, the ink was already so faded I can't make it out. The person who sold it made a note that the buyer was a corporal from the United States, but that's all I can read."

Disappointment threatened to run through her, but Sadie realized she still knew much more now about the safe than she had yesterday. "I appreciate it, Jean-Pierre," Sadie said. "At least I can be fairly certain this is the same safe, since it belonged to a corporal."

"I am glad to help, my friend. If you decide to sell it, let me know. I might be able to find a buyer for you."

"Thank you. Right now I don't have any claim on it, but if things change I'll definitely contact you."

Sadie hung up and went to the kitchen to put a kettle on for tea. Then she took a quick shower. The hot water warmed her up, and by the time she came out of the bathroom, she was ready for a cup of chamomile tea. She was on her way to the kitchen when the sound of the phone ringing caused her to turn back toward the couch. She was happy to see Edwin's name on her caller ID.

"Hi, Edwin," she said.

"How are you doing, Sadie?"

"I'm fine. You really don't need to worry about me. How are you?"

Edwin laughed. "I'm fine. And I'm not really worried. Just concerned. I called because I have some news."

"What is it?"

"My friend Herman contacted me. He's back in town, and he's willing to look at the letter."

"That's wonderful, Edwin. Thank you. When does he want to get together?"

"He can come by the shop on Monday."

"That's perfect. I'm afraid you were right about the online translator programs. Most of the translation was gobbledygook."

"With luck, Herman will be able to give you something that will help you. Are you staying nice and warm?"

"Sort of. I took Hank outside for a romp in the snow, but that was enough for me. We're back inside and I'm about to warm up with some tea. I'm staying off the main roads today to give the snowplows a chance to do their job. Let's hope we'll be in good shape by tomorrow."

"Then I'll see you at church?"

"I'm planning on it."

"I'm looking forward to lunch at Flap Jack's."

Sadie was too. She always enjoyed lunch out after church with her family and friends, and Flap Jack's was their usual Sunday destination. They made delicious pancakes in all kinds of unique flavors. In the fall, the owner, Jack Wilson, had debuted his tasty pumpkin pancakes. They were a favorite with the residents of Silver Peak, and Sadie could hardly wait to try them.

She said good-bye to Edwin and hung up. Although she knew it'd be an exercise in patience to wait until Monday to find out what was in the letter, she was grateful to know that part of the saga of the safe would soon be revealed.

She hung up the phone and grabbed a new historical fiction novel she'd been looking forward to starting. For a change of pace from the couch, she settled into one of the leather chairs in her living room, propping her feet up on a matching ottoman. She turned on the nearby lamp, set her chamomile tea on the coffee table, and let out a contented sigh. She wasn't used to full days spent lounging around, but she had to admit it was just what the doctor ordered.

She opened to the first page but had only read one word when all the lights in the house went out.

11

———

It was so dark now that Sadie could barely see anything. Although she'd lost power before during storms, she was surprised that it happened now. The snow had almost stopped falling and it wasn't windy outside. She heard Hank whine and reached down to find him standing next to her.

"It's okay, boy," she said. "We've been through this before. We'll be fine."

She got up from the couch and felt her way into the kitchen, where she kept several battery-powered lanterns to use in situations just like this one. She fumbled around until she found the right cabinet and pulled all of them out. A quick *click* of a switch and one by one each lamp came on, filling the room with light. Sadie was very careful to always keep fresh batteries in her lamps and was rewarded with plenty of illumination. Although it was a little silly, she began to whistle, then sing an appropriate song for the situation. "This little light of mine, I'm going to let it shine. Let it shine, let it shine, all the time."

She left one of the lamps in the kitchen and carried the others out into the house. After placing two in the living room, she carried another one to the bedroom. Then she put the last lamp in the bathroom.

Although she hoped it was just a temporary power outage, combined with the notes she had received and the break-in at her store, she couldn't help feeling a little nervous. She went back to the living room, found the plastic box with the things from the safe, and took it into her bedroom, where she slid it under her bed. Hank followed her and sniffed under the bed as if trying to figure out what she was doing.

"I know I'm being paranoid," she said to him, "but it makes me feel better to know it's hidden."

Of course, putting the box under the bed probably wouldn't thwart anyone who was really committed to finding it, but nonetheless, getting it out of sight made her feel better.

She went back to the living room. Since the heat was off, she added wood to the fire in the large fireplace. Within a few minutes it was crackling with gusto, sending welcome heat and a glow of flickering light into the room. She located her battery-powered reading light, grabbed her novel, and settled back in her chair. Within a few minutes she was wrapped up in her book while Hank lay at her feet, enjoying the warmth of the fireplace.

Sadie was on chapter two when she heard a noise that seemed to come from outside. Hank lifted his head, his eyes alert, so she knew she wasn't hearing things.

"Probably just snow falling off the roof," she said, trying not to let her imagination get the best of her. She went back to her story, but a few minutes later, she heard another sound. Hank jumped up and ran over to the door.

"Okay, maybe it's not snow," Sadie said to herself. She got up slowly and went over to one of the front windows. It was impossible to see anything in her front yard. She walked to the end of the room until she could see Milo's brightly lit house off in the distance. In the past, when she'd lost power, Milo had been affected too.

Suddenly, something moved past her window and a high-pitched scream escaped her lips. Hank barked at her, which made her jump and yelp a second time.

"For crying out loud," she said, staring down at him.

Instead of listening, he barked again.

Trying to stay calm, she made her way to the coffee table and picked up her cordless phone. A quick call to Milo would send him over to check things outside. Even though she tried to convince herself her eyes were playing tricks on her, she'd certainly seen something. There were wild animals in the area. Could it have been a deer? A wolf?

She put her home phone to her ear. Dead. She put it back in its charger and then picked it up again. Still dead. Of course, she thought. For some reason, the words from the first note she'd received echoed through her thoughts: *Don't open that safe or you'll be sorry!* Was it possible the note wasn't quite the idle threat she'd believed it to be? Was someone really after her? Someone who meant her harm?

She started to look for her cell phone when she realized she'd left it in the car. Even though her car was in the garage, she didn't feel comfortable going out there right now. The garage had a door that led to the backyard, and she couldn't remember if she'd locked it. She wasn't used to having to take extensive security measures.

Her heart pounding, she sat down on the couch. Hank jumped up next to her again, but it was obvious he was still on guard. His head was up and his ears twitched as if he could hear something she couldn't.

"Dear Lord," she prayed softly. "I'm probably being silly, but right now I'm a little frightened. Your Word talks about angels guarding us, keeping us safe in all our ways. That's what I need right now. Those angels watching over Hank and me, keeping us secure."

Sadie realized she was rocking slightly back and forth and forced herself to stop. "Stop it, Sadie, everything is fine. No one is out there trying to get you. Your imagination is playing tricks on you."

Hank whined again.

"Shh," she whispered gently, in an attempt to calm him. "It's okay."

She didn't hear any other odd noises, so she finally picked up her book again, telling herself everything was all right and there was nothing to worry about. But why was Milo's power still on? She supposed it wasn't out of the realm of possibility.

After a few minutes she realized she was just reading the same page over and over, so she set her book down and decided to go to bed. Thankfully, she had a fireplace in her bedroom so she would stay warm.

As she got up from the couch she heard someone at her front door, wiggling her doorknob. Hank jumped off the couch and lunged for the door, barking and growling wildly. Sadie went to the door and patted Hank on the head, which eventually calmed his barking. She wasn't sure, but, nearly drowned out by Hank's fierce sounds, she thought she'd heard someone knock. However, when she looked through the peephole, she couldn't see anyone. It was too dark. She backed away from the door, wondering if whoever was outside was looking in the windows and could see her. She was thinking about taking Hank, running to the bedroom, and locking the door behind her, when lights flashed across the front of her house.

She ran over to the window. A vehicle was in her driveway. Edwin! She almost cried from relief. She watched as he got out and came toward her front door. He'd kept his headlights on so Sadie was able to see him as he approached the house. Relief coursed through her. She flung the door open, obviously surprising him.

"Are you okay?" he asked, his eyes wide. "I tried to call and your landline wasn't working. Then I tried your cell and you didn't answer."

"Oh, Edwin," she said, her voice trembling. "I left it in my car. I think someone is out there. I saw—"

Before she had a chance to finish her sentence, a loud crash came from her kitchen. Hank turned and ran toward the noise.

"There's someone in the house," she said in a loud whisper. "I saw him outside earlier, and now he's in the kitchen."

Edwin came inside and shut the door behind him. "Stay here," he ordered.

Sadie stood by the door, afraid to follow him and afraid to go outside. Suddenly Hank began to bark and the sound of a scuffle broke out. When she heard another loud clatter, Sadie decided she'd had enough. She grabbed the lantern on the coffee table and ran to the kitchen. She had no intention of letting anyone hurt Edwin.

When she reached the kitchen, she held the light out in front of her, illuminating the room. The other lamp she'd put on the counter earlier lay broken on the floor. A plate she'd left on the counter was in pieces as well.

What she saw make her mouth drop open. Edwin was on the floor with his arms around someone, trying to wrestle him into submission.

"Edwin, stop," she cried out. "That's my neighbor, Milo!"

The struggling ceased and Edwin looked up at Sadie. "Did you say this is your ... neighbor?"

From underneath Edwin came a muffled voice. Although it sounded like, *"Ah mmnnnffuhh tuttle humph,"* Sadie was pretty sure Milo was attempting to say "I tried to tell you."

Edwin slowly got up, putting his hand out and pulling Milo to his feet.

Although it wasn't really funny, Sadie had an almost overwhelming urge to laugh. She bit her lip and forced back a giggle. "Why in the world would you attack Milo?" she asked Edwin.

Edwin adjusted his coat, shrugged his shoulders, and smoothed his hair back into place. It was clear he was trying to restore a semblance of dignity.

"I've never met your neighbor," he said, his words spoken in staccato-like precision. "You told me someone had broken in. I was trying to save your life from an intruder."

Milo, who still looked shell-shocked, shook his head and stared at Sadie, a look of bewilderment on his face.

"I noticed your lights were out, but I saw you outside earlier so I was pretty sure you were home. I wanted to make sure you were okay. You always have your porch lights on at night, and I was worried about you."

"Why didn't you knock on the door?" Sadie asked, confused by his actions.

"I did. I knocked, and I called out your name several times, but Hank here was barking something fierce."

"I thought I heard a knock, but I just wasn't sure."

Milo sighed with exasperation. "I finally decided to go to the back door. I have the key so I let myself in. Funny, but I honestly didn't expect to be thrown to the ground."

"Are you okay?" Sadie asked, biting her lip in an attempt to hold back a nervous giggle.

Milo nodded. "I'm fine. The only bruises I have are to my ego."

Hank chose that moment to bark at Milo and offer him a big grin. It seemed he was extremely amused by the whole situation.

Milo tried to scowl at his canine friend, but Hank looked so comical Milo shook his head and put out his hand. Hank ran to him and leaned against his leg, letting Milo pet him.

"I am so sorry," Edwin said sheepishly. "I thought you were after Sadie."

Milo shook his head. "I don't think Sadie has anything to worry about. Between you, Hank, and me, I would say she is very well protected. Too much so, actually."

The laughter that Sadie was trying to hold back finally burst out. After looking at her as if she'd lost her mind, Edwin and Milo joined in, although Milo's reaction was a little more subdued.

"I—I'm sorry," Sadie said when she finally caught her breath. "But the sight of you two rolling on the floor was…just too funny." She tried to force back another giggle, but in the end, it just sounded like a snort. Hank barked at her, making her laugh even harder.

She sat down on one of the stools in front of her breakfast bar. "Forgive me," she said, still chuckling. "But this has been quite a night. First my electricity goes out and then my phone. Then Edwin shows up and attacks my neighbor." She shook her head. "I think I'm safe in saying it will take a lot to top this evening."

Edwin came over and sat down next to her. "Let's hope you're right. I don't think I could take many more nights like this." He looked over at Milo. "Any idea why Sadie's electricity is out?"

Milo nodded. "The snow made a big tree branch so heavy it fell, knocking out the electric and telephone lines."

"Is it dangerous?" Sadie asked.

"Could be. You need to call the power company right away."

"Is my house safe?"

"Your house is fine," Milo said. "However, the power line is live and could start a fire outside. I don't think it would get far in the snow, but to be safe the electric company needs to cut the power to the line and repair it."

Milo pulled his cell phone out of his pocket. "I'll call and get them out here, okay?"

"Thanks, Milo," Sadie said with a smile.

"Maybe you should stay somewhere else until everything is fixed," Edwin said.

Sadie sighed. "I'm fine. I'll light the fireplace in my bedroom. Hank and I will be nice and cozy."

"Are you sure?" Edwin asked. "I could take you to Alice's. I'd really feel better if you'd leave."

"Thank you, Edwin," Sadie said with a smile, "but I'd really rather stay in my own home."

"What about something hot to eat?" Edwin said. "And remember, you won't be able to take a warm shower."

"Already had a shower, and I don't care about hot food. I'll get coffee on the way to church in the morning."

"Well, all right. I give up." Edwin didn't look happy about Sadie's decision, but she'd been without power before and knew how to get through it. Packing up and going to Alice's was too much trouble. Besides, it would be difficult taking Hank with her, and after all the excitement he was liable to be a little nervous. She didn't want to leave him alone. Right now all she wanted to do was cuddle up with him in bed. She was tired and needed sleep.

A few minutes later Milo came back. "Okay, they're on their way out. Not sure how long it will take them to fix it, but you should have power by tomorrow."

Sadie sighed with relief. "Thank you, Milo. Now, if you two men don't mind, I'd like to get some rest."

"Lock your doggy door," Milo reminded her. "I don't think the guys from the electric company want to be harassed by Hank."

Sadie laughed. "You know he wouldn't do anything more than bark at them, but I'll lock the door anyway. If the power isn't on by the morning…"

"I'll come by and get him," Milo said. "Don't worry."

"You're a good neighbor."

"Yes, I am. But if you don't mind, I'd rather not have to wrestle any more of your boyfriends."

Sadie's was so surprised she couldn't respond. *Boyfriend?* Was that what Milo thought? Before she could correct him, he said good-bye and left.

"I—I'm sorry," she told Edwin, although she wasn't quite sure what she was apologizing for.

He shrugged. "It certainly doesn't bother me, Sadie." He smiled, then leaned closer and said quietly, "I hope someday soon it won't bother you either." He held out his hand. "Give me your keys, and I'll get your cell phone out of your car."

Sadie grabbed her keys from the small table where she kept them. "Thank you. I'm so glad you came over, but in the future I'll try to keep you from having to play the part of my hero."

He smiled. "I don't mind at all. I like being your hero."

Sadie swallowed, but didn't say anything as Edwin headed for her garage. She was touched that he'd rushed over. It really did make her feel protected and cared for.

Edwin was back a few minutes later with her cell phone in his hand.

"Would you feel better if I stayed?" he asked. "At least until the electric company gets here?"

"No, I'm fine. And thank you again, Edwin."

He gave her a small smile. "Anytime...I think. Now, lock the door behind me, okay?"

She nodded, not sure what else to say. After Edwin walked out the door, she locked it and watched through the window as he drove away. She and Hank went upstairs to her bedroom, where Sadie built a nice fire that spread welcome warmth throughout the room. They curled up on the bed, but it was a while before Sadie was able to fall asleep. Edwin's words kept running through her mind. *I hope someday soon it won't bother you either.*

12

As Sadie had hoped, the roads were in pretty good shape by morning. Getting to church wasn't a problem. Not only did the city do a great job of keeping the roads safe, but Silver Peak residents also pitched in to help their neighbors get their driveways cleared.

Before she left, Sadie had checked with the men from the electric company who were working on her line. They assured her the power would be back on by the time she got home. After a quick call from her cell phone to the phone company, Sadie learned workers would be out the next day to restore service. She was relieved to know everything would soon be back to normal.

The parking lot was full when Sadie pulled into Campfire Chapel. The beautiful white clapboard church with its tall steeple had not always looked the way it did now. The aged structure had waited, abandoned and decaying for many years, until Campfire Chapel's congregation purchased it and raised the money for its renovations. Now the restored church stood like a beacon on a hill, overlooking Silver Peak, its simple grandeur preserved for years to come. Sadie not only loved the building that housed Campfire Chapel, she loved the spirit of the church and the wonderful people who made up the congregation. Every week she looked forward to one of Pastor Don Sweeting's sermons. He liked to tell everyone that he wasn't afraid of "getting into their business." Sadie wanted God to be involved in every part of her life and appreciated Pastor Don's down-to-earth messages.

She found a parking space and got out of her car. Roz and Roscoe pulled up next to her, and Roz waved. Sadie waited for her so they could walk in together. Roz was wearing a red wool coat with a wonderful blue vintage hat. The hat had a narrow brim and a red silk flower. Roz was nothing if not colorful. Sadie loved her friend's expressive way of dressing and wished she was a little braver in her clothing selections. Sadie was much more comfortable in earth tones and hiking gear, although with Roz's urging, she'd been known to wear a splash of color from time to time. In fact, she'd added a bright blue scarf to the chinos and brown wool sweater she'd worn to church today.

"Sadie," someone called. She turned to see Edwin striding toward her. Roz, Roscoe, and Sadie waited for him to catch up. He looked especially handsome in a long, black wool coat that highlighted his silver hair.

"Good morning," he said to the three of them as he approached. "A beautiful day, isn't it?"

"Yes, it is," Sadie said. "I love winter. Snow on the mountains. It's what makes Colorado special."

Roz laughed. "And in the fall, the colors of the changing leaves make Colorado special."

"And in the spring," Roscoe chimed in, "the trees and wildflowers make Colorado special."

Sadie laughed. "So basically, Colorado is just all-around special."

The four of them laughed and then walked toward the entrance of the church, greeting others as they headed inside. After hanging up their coats and finding seats together, Sadie looked around for Alice and the kids. She finally spotted them at the back of the sanctuary. She stood up and waved, and the three of them headed toward her. They scooted into the row behind her, and Alice gave her mother a quick hug.

Spike took the stage, along with a young man who played the drums. Sadie couldn't help but wonder again about Laura's comment that she might have seen Spike the night of the break-in. Sadie still didn't know how to be sure it was him, but it bothered her. Although Spike attended Campfire Chapel, Sadie wasn't sure how strong his faith was. Tragedy in his past might have affected his ability to believe in God's love. The idea made her feel sad. But just because his faith was unclear didn't mean he was a burglar.

Paula Deering, the worship leader's wife, took her place at the piano. Her husband, Martin Deering, stood behind the pulpit.

"Will you please stand?" Martin asked. Martin and his wife, Paula, were such blessings to Campfire Chapel. Besides leading worship, they also worked with the youth. The church was blessed to have two such fine young people as members.

As Martin began to lead the congregation in singing, Sadie noticed Barton Spivey two rows up, standing next to Jerry and Jane Remington. She was happy to see him in church, but ever since he'd been in her store, something about him bothered her. She just couldn't put her finger on what it was. Sadie suddenly realized she was thinking about Spivey instead of worshipping God. Forcing herself to turn her attention back to the song Martin was singing, it didn't take long for Sadie to get lost in the wonderful music. Spike's stellar guitar playing added such depth to the music, she thanked God for bringing him to Campfire Chapel.

When the final song ended, Sadie and the congregation sat down. Pastor Don came up and encouraged them to greet each other. This was one of Sadie's favorite parts of the service. She scooted out of her seat and located several friends, including her cousin, Laura, who was sitting next to Fred and Debbie Sunshine, owners of Bless Our Souls, a jewelry store just down the street from the Antique Mine. Debbie asked about the break-in, as did several other people. Sadie ran into a couple of other friends who questioned her about her progress on the safe. She kept her answers brief, because she felt strongly that at this point it was wiser to keep the details to herself.

After several announcements by the one of the church's elders, Pastor Don stepped up to the pulpit. His sermon centered on Matthew 7:1–5. Sadie liked to call these "the judging Scriptures."

"I'm troubled by what I see in the body of Christ," he said. "One church judges another. One teacher tears a different teacher to shreds. A pastor calls another pastor a wolf in sheep's clothing. Seems many in the body are searching for false messiahs instead of following the One True Messiah, Jesus Christ. I've had people tell me that Jesus called out the false teachers. But the truth is, He called out the religious leaders, those who saw themselves above others. I'm concerned that in searching for the wolves, we've become the devourers."

Sadie listened as Pastor Don went on to talk about the body of Christ being one body, not several bodies divided into denominations or defined by certain practices. In Sadie's mind, it was one of his very best sermons. She looked forward to a rousing discussion at Flap Jack's after church.

She and Edwin were on their way to their cars when she heard her name being called. She turned to see Spike Harris walking toward her. Sadie watched the tall, gangly man approach them wearing an old black sheepskin coat with a fuzzy wool collar and cuffs. Sheepskin coats were popular in Colorado, but this one had seen better days. Although his longish dark hair—which was beginning to mix some salt among the pepper—needed a trim, and his craggy face was red from the cold, he didn't look any different than he usually did. His hazel eyes met hers without any hint of guile.

"I just heard that someone broke into the Antique Mine," he said when he reached her. "Are you all right?"

"I'm fine, thanks, Spike," Sadie said, studying him. "And nothing was taken."

He looked genuinely relieved. "I'm happy to hear that."

"I take it your store is okay," Sadie said. "I mean, you're so close to me."

Spike smiled, but Sadie noticed that it was tight and his lips twitched nervously. "My store wasn't touched."

"Good." Sadie realized this was a perfect opportunity to ask him a question about that night. "Someone actually mentioned they thought they saw you downtown the night of the break-in. I'm glad to hear it wasn't because you were robbed."

"N—no. I wasn't even in Silver Peak that night. I had a gig out of town. Probably didn't get home until after four in the morning."

"I see." Sadie smiled. Maybe he really wasn't involved. He certainly seemed relieved that she was okay after the break-in. "By the way, we're going to Flap Jack's. Would you like to come?"

"I'd love to, but I can't. I've got a guitar student coming this afternoon. But thank you for asking. I'm glad you're okay, Sadie."

He turned and walked a little too quickly toward his old truck, got in, and drove away.

"That was a little odd," Edwin said.

"He did seem a little nervous." Even though she was inclined to believe in Spike's innocence, she wondered why he seemed so uneasy.

Deciding to quit thinking about Spike, she turned to see Barton Spivey standing on the other side of the parking lot, talking to Debbie and Fred Sunshine. She wondered how he knew them but remembered that he'd mentioned visiting some of the shops on Main Street. Maybe he was talking to them about buying jewelry.

Edwin and Sadie followed the large group of churchgoers who piled into their cars and headed to Flap Jack's on Main Street. A few minutes later, the whole group descended on one of Sadie's favorite restaurants. Jack Wilson greeted them at the door.

"We've been expecting you," he said with a big smile. He led them to a large table already prepared.

As soon as they walked in the door, Sadie's mouth began to water. Besides the pumpkin pancakes Sadie looked forward to, there were other wonderful choices on the menu including whole wheat, banana, blueberry, and chocolate chip pancakes. Their pure maple syrup was out of this world. They also had great "make-your-own" omelets. Customers could choose almost any kind of filling they desired.

As soon as they were seated, Jack went off to see to other customers, and Diana, a longtime server at the restaurant, came over to take their orders.

"It's so good to see you," she said with a smile. Diana had short red hair and light hazel eyes that shone with enthusiasm. Jack and Diana both had the ability to make their customers feel like family.

Almost everyone ordered pancakes, but Edwin ordered a sausage and cheddar omelet. Jack actually made his own sausage. It was a little spicy for Sadie's tastes, but Edwin thought it was the best sausage he'd ever tasted.

As Diana brought carafes of coffee and glasses of orange juice to the table, Sadie told the group about her exciting evening. She carefully left out any reference to the safe or the letters. Within seconds, everyone was laughing.

"Let me get this straight," Roscoe said. "Edwin Marshall, our esteemed candidate for mayor, was rolling around on the floor last night trying to save you from your neighbor?"

Another round of laughter broke out.

"Just goes to prove that your next mayor isn't above fighting for his constituents," Edwin said, a big grin on his face.

Roz giggled. "I have to wonder if Milo will be voting for you."

Edwin shook his head. "To be honest, I wouldn't blame him if he didn't. It wasn't my best performance to date."

"Well, I thought you were wonderful," Sadie said with a smile. "And you have my vote."

Roscoe snorted. "Guess I'd better vote for you too. I don't want you to beat me up."

When the laughter died down, Julie asked about Sadie's electricity.

"It should be on by the time I get home. The phone company's coming tomorrow."

"If they're late, you can send Edwin after them," Theo said, trying to keep a straight face.

Edwin shook his finger at Sadie and grinned. "See, I've lost all credibility thanks to you."

Sadie grinned back.

The people gathered around them laughed, and soon, the topic changed to Pastor Don's sermon. Each person had an opinion, and Sadie agreed with almost everything her friends and family said. She had decided long ago to leave the judging to God. She might love the kinds of mysteries she read in her books, but understanding the mystery of the human heart was best left up to Him.

Sadie was listening to Laura tell a story about one of her new clients when Sadie noticed Jerry and Jane Remington at a table not far from them. Barton Spivey was still with them. Trying to put Pastor Don's sermon into action, she got up and went over to their table. Jane smiled when she saw Sadie approaching.

"Sadie, I'm so glad to see you. I wanted to tell you how much I love the lamp you suggested for our hallway." She shook her head. "I have no idea who broke the vase that was there before. I found the pieces on the floor after breakfast one morning. No one ever admitted to it."

"Well, it wasn't me," Barton said, his smile reminding Sadie of a picture she'd seen of the Cheshire cat in a very rare first edition of *Alice's Adventures in Wonderland* by Lewis Carroll. The incredible illustrations by John Tenniel had stuck with her ever since.

"We know it wasn't you," Jerry said genially. "You were already up and gone the morning it happened. Besides, you're not the kind of person to break something and not own up to it."

"Really, it's silly," Jane said. "It wasn't expensive. We would never be upset with a guest who accidentally broke an old vase."

"I'm just glad the lamp worked out," Sadie said.

Jane smiled at Sadie. "Jerry tells me you were asking about Franklin Reichert the other day."

Sadie nodded. "I'm wondering if the safe we found might have belonged to him."

"Did you know that Franklin's granddaughter, Marla, just moved to town? She's taken up residence in his old house on Basin Road and is restoring it."

Sadie's ears perked up. "Really? No, I hadn't heard. I love that old house and hated seeing it falling into disrepair."

"You might go by and visit with her. I'm sure she could answer any questions you might have about her grandfather. You know, Jerry and I looked at that beautiful old Victorian when we were searching for a place to open our inn. We loved it, but it just needed too much work for us."

"We stopped by to meet her not long after she moved in," Jerry said. "I have to caution you. She isn't the friendliest person, especially when you bring up the opera house. I think the family harbors some ill will about the scandal. From what I've heard, they felt Franklin was railroaded."

"I really don't know a lot about the scandal," Sadie said. Although she'd already planned to dig around and see what she could find out, she was beginning to feel a sense of urgency. She needed to know more about the scandal and about Franklin Reichert. The scandal might not have anything to do with the safe, but at this point, she had so few leads, she'd follow anything that could possibly take her in the right direction. She couldn't see how the items in the safe belonged to him because he was busy managing the opera house during the war. Maybe they belonged to someone else. Someone he was close to.

"You could check the microfilm at the library," Jane suggested. "They have copies of old newspapers. Maybe there are stories about what happened."

"That's exactly what I'll do, Jane. Thank you." Sadie had spent many hours at the library, scouring through old newspapers in an attempt to learn about Silver Peak's early days. She was certain that a story as big as the scandal at the opera house would be easy to find.

"Who knows?" Jerry said, as if thinking out loud. "Franklin was manager of the opera house around the time renovations were done last. You might be on the right track, researching him."

"I hope so," Sadie said with a sigh.

Barton was leaning forward in what seemed to Sadie like unnecessarily rapt attention. "Well, good luck to you, Mrs. Speers," Spivey said in a high-pitched voice.

"Thank you, Mr. Spivey," she said, trying to be cordial. Sadie said good-bye to the group and went back to her table. She'd only been seated a few minutes when Jane walked over and handed her a small piece of paper.

Can you meet me in the restroom?

Sadie watched Jane walk toward the restroom. Feeling a little concerned, Sadie made a quick excuse and followed her friend, wondering what was so important she needed to talk to her in private.

13

"SORRY TO BE SO CRYPTIC," JANE SAID WHEN SADIE WALKED in. "But I wanted to speak to you about Barton Spivey. I have such a busy schedule the next few days I wasn't sure when I'd get a chance to talk to you again."

"That's okay," Sadie said with a smile, "but I must admit I was a little concerned when you slipped me a note. It seemed so...clandestine."

Jane laughed. "Sorry. I'm just a little concerned about him and felt you should know why."

"What's bothering you?" Sadie asked.

Jane grinned. "Thanks to Pastor Don, this makes what I have to say a lot harder. I don't want you to think I'm trying to judge him."

"I don't understand."

"Spivey is asking a lot of questions about people, Sadie. About Roscoe and the Vidals. He's also very interested in the Sunshines." Although Sadie had known Fred and Debbie for many years, their chosen last name, which they'd taken in the sixties, still amused her.

"I saw him talking to them after church," Sadie said. "But why does that make you uncomfortable?"

"I'm not sure," Jane said with a sigh. "But he's started asking a lot of questions about you too."

"Like what?"

Jane leaned in closer. "Like how successful your shop is. Even how much money you're making. He says it in a way that seems as if he's only curious about Silver Peak because of his banking background, but it's starting to bother me. I just thought you should know."

"I'm glad." Sadie frowned. "If he has any more questions about my business, will you tell him to talk to me personally?"

Jane nodded. "Absolutely. In the meantime, it might be best to keep an eye on him."

"Why do you say that?"

"I can't really explain it. Maybe I'm just rattled by your break-in, but I feel better knowing you're aware of what's going on." She shrugged. "I'm sure it will prove to be nothing."

Sadie wanted to agree with Jane, but she had to admit, she was suspicious of Barton too. Hearing that he was asking about her business and finances added some weight to her thus-far-unsubstantiated suspicions. "Do you know how much longer he'll be in town?"

She shook her head. "I don't. When he first came he said he'd only be with us a few days. Lately, he hasn't mentioned leaving."

Sadie gave Jane a hug. "We'd better get back, or everyone else will start suspecting *us*," Sadie said, hoping to lighten the mood.

"I do feel a little bit like a gossiping high-schooler," Jane admitted. "But I wanted to take the opportunity to chat with you while I had the chance."

"Thanks, Jane. I'm glad you did." Jane walked out then, but Sadie took an extra moment to check her reflection in the mirror over the vanity. As she applied some tinted lip balm, she wondered—*who was Barton Spivey and why was he so interested in her?*

Alice followed Sadie home after lunch. Another reason she loved Sundays was because when her grandchildren weren't spending the weekend with their father, they usually came over after church to spend the afternoon. Sometimes her cousin Laura joined them, but today she had other plans. It wasn't that they did anything special on Sunday, they just hung out and enjoyed each other. As soon as Sadie and Alice pulled in the driveway, Theo jumped out of his mother's car.

"Can Hank come out for a while, Grandma?" he asked.

Sadie smiled. "Of course, he loves to play in the snow. Just don't stay out too long. I don't want either one of you to get frostbite."

Sara was excited to spend some time outside with Hank too, so Sadie let him out. He ran straight to the kids, jumping up and down in the snow, happy to see them. Alice followed her mother inside.

"I remember playing in the snow as a kid," Alice said as they entered the kitchen. "We used to have so much fun. Dad and I would always build a big snowman, and you would try to get him to give you one of his old hats for the snowman's head."

Sadie laughed. "Those silly hats. He only wore a couple of them. The rest sat at the top of the closet. But he protected them. Wouldn't let go of them."

"We always talked him into giving us one for our snowman, though," Alice said. "As long as we promised to give it back when the snowman started to melt." She shook her head. "I wonder where those old hats are now?"

"Why, they're still in the top of our closet," Sadie said with a smile. "I just couldn't get rid of them."

Alice came over and wrapped her arms around her mother. "I miss him, Mom."

Sadie patted her daughter's hands. "I do too, honey." She took a deep breath and the two shared a brief moment of remembrance together. "Now, how about some coffee to warm us up?"

Alice let her go. "Sounds wonderful, and maybe some hot chocolate for the kids? They'll be cold when they come in."

"Good idea."

Alice sat down at one of the stools at the breakfast bar. "Are we still on for a movie night?" she asked.

"Sure, when should we do it?"

"How about a week from tomorrow?" Alice suggested.

"Perfect. I'll get the movie from the library when I go tomorrow."

"Why don't you ask Edwin to join us?"

Sadie, who was getting the ingredients for hot chocolate, turned around to look at her daughter, who was already staring at her. "W-why? I mean, do you really want him to come?"

Alice smiled. "Anyone with eyes can see there is something between the two of you, Mom. I'd like to get to know him better, and so would the kids."

Sadie leaned against the cabinet, letting her guard down a little. "I don't know, Alice. I mean, I do like him, but..."

"But you still feel married to Dad?"

"Yes, in some ways I do."

"But you're not, Mom," Alice said gently. "Dad's gone, and I know he'd want you to be happy. Edwin seems like a very nice man. I assume you've been worried about how I would react, but I want you to know that I would fully support you if you chose to become involved with him."

Sadie smiled at her beautiful daughter, who still, to this day, made her swell with pride. What a tenderhearted soul Alice was. "He is a very nice man, Alice. I—I actually do like him, very much, but you're right, I don't want to make you uncomfortable. I would never try to replace your father."

Alice got up and came over to Sadie, putting her arms around her. "I know that, Mom. If you pursue a relationship with Edwin, it won't hurt my feelings. I mean it."

Sadie was surprised to find herself holding back tears. Were her feelings really so deep? "I really appreciate that, honey." Sadie was touched by her daughter's comments but still wasn't certain what was in her heart. Was she ready to move forward with Edwin? Was Edwin as ready as he thought he was? Even though he'd made several attempts to let her know he was interested in taking their relationship to the next level, she wondered if he really understood how hard it might be for them to put the past behind them and to start a new romance after all their years of married life.

"What was going on with Jane today?" Alice asked, mercifully changing the subject. "I saw you two go to the bathroom together."

Sadie sighed. "I guess we're not very sneaky." While she made a pot of coffee and set milk on the stove for hot chocolate, she filled Alice in on what Jane had shared with her in the bathroom.

"Wow," Alice said when she finished. "Didn't he come into town about the same time you got that first note? Could he be behind it?"

"It's possible, but I don't know what his interest could be in the contents of the safe."

"Could he have some kind of association with Silver Peak?" Alice asked.

"The name Spivey isn't familiar to me, but it wouldn't hurt to do a little poking around. See if I can find a connection."

"Well, maybe he just wants the safe," Alice said thoughtfully.

"He does have a couple of antique safes," Sadie said. "And he did offer to buy the one in my shop."

"So if he has antique safes, then he knows how valuable yours is. Could he be trying to steal it since you wouldn't sell it to him?"

"I suppose, but how would he know the combination? And it seems clear that the person who broke in to my shop is most concerned about what was *in* the safe." She shook her head. "I'm not sure it adds up, but it is something to consider."

"Well, Spivey was already in Silver Peak before the safe was discovered."

"True. Right now, I'm focused on learning details about the scandal that happened at the opera house when Franklin Reichert was the manager. I'm wondering if finding out about Franklin might help me discover who is behind the break-in and the letters."

"What scandal?"

Sadie took a container of cocoa out of one of her cabinets and pointed it at her daughter. "I'm not an expert, but Franklin Reichert, manager of the opera house before Reuben, was accused of stealing money and art in the forties. He was fired right about the time the opera house was undergoing renovations."

"Was there ever any proof?"

"Not that I know of, but that's where my research will come in. I do know that the Reichert family always insisted he was innocent."

Sadie made a paste with the dry cocoa using a small amount of milk, some sugar, and a drop of vanilla. When it was smooth, she slowly added the rest of the milk. The aroma of chocolate filled the room.

"So have you talked to Theo any more about wanting to change his major?"

"Yes. He's convinced he wants to go into law enforcement." Alice sighed. "I have to admit I was excited when he told me he wanted to be a doctor. Law enforcement is a noble profession too, but it sounds so dangerous, Mom."

Sadie concentrated on stirring the cocoa. "I wonder if it has to do with all the mystery novels he's been reading."

"I'm not sure his choice of reading material has anything to do with this. I mean, he likes books about dragons too, but he's never expressed the desire to be one."

Sadie smiled. "So what are you going to do?"

"Just wait a bit. If he doesn't change his mind, we'll pursue a new direction for college."

"What will Cliff say?"

Alice shook her head. "I have no idea. I haven't told him yet. I don't know if Theo has. But if Theo doesn't change his mind, I think Cliff will be willing to listen. We both want him to choose his own course in life."

"So you wait."

"Yes, I guess so. This gives us time to pray for God's will for Theo."

"I'm proud of you, Alice."

Alice smiled. "I remember how you refused to tell me what I should do with my future because you were afraid you'd influence me to choose something that wasn't what God had for me. You were a great example, Mom."

She sighed. "God and Theo will have to figure this one out. I don't want to be responsible for sending him in the wrong direction."

When the cocoa was ready, Alice called the kids inside. Sadie grabbed some towels from her linen closet so they could dust off the snow that covered them before they came in the house.

"If you leave any snow on your clothes it will melt and make a mess, so brush yourself off as well as you can," she warned her grandchildren when she handed them the towels. "And that goes for you too," she said to Hank, whose happy grin and wagging tail made it clear he'd had a wonderful time outside.

"We'll clean him off, Grandma," Sara said, grabbing the extra towel.

As the family gathered in the kitchen for coffee and hot chocolate, Sadie brought them up to date on what she'd learned so far about the safe. Theo looked interested when she mentioned searching through old newspaper stories at the library.

"Can we go with you to the library tomorrow, Grandma?" Theo asked. "I'd really like to help."

She looked at Alice, who nodded, then back to Theo. "Sure, honey. I'll teach you how to use microfilm files to look up things that happened a long time ago in Silver Peak."

She noticed the glint in Theo's eye.

"That's sounds cool," he said.

"I'll come too," Sara said, although she lacked the enthusiasm of her brother. "I've got nothing better to do."

If Sadie hadn't already mothered an adolescent young woman years before, she might have been offended, but this was just Sara being fourteen. She smiled and clapped her hands together. "Now, let's exercise our brains for a while. How about a little Trivial Pursuit?"

Before long they were involved in a stimulating game. Sadie loved playing Trivial Pursuit with Theo and Sara. Not just because she was always impressed with how smart they were, but because the game helped them to learn. Besides, they always had a lot of fun. When Theo didn't know an answer, he'd make up something ludicrous just to make his family laugh. They played until it got dark. When it was over, Alice and the kids helped Sadie clean up. After thanking Sadie once again for offering to watch Theo and Sara, Alice ushered the kids to the car. Sadie and Hank stood on the sidewalk and waved as they drove away.

When she went back inside, Sadie called Julie and told her she planned to close the shop tomorrow.

"That will work out beautifully," she said. "My mom planned to watch the boys the next two days because of the teachers' meetings, but I'll tell her she only needs to watch them on Tuesday."

After saying good-bye to Julie, Sadie made herself a cup of hot cocoa and considered everything that had happened that day. Tomorrow, Edwin's friend was coming to look at the letter, and she was going to the library. Maybe one of those events would move her closer to the truth about the safe. Sadie was excited about that possibility, but as she stirred her hot chocolate, Alice's comments about Edwin came into focus.

Was she ready to move forward with him?

14

MONDAY MORNING, SADIE GOT UP EARLY, FED HANK, AND DROVE to town. It was incredibly cold but Sadie's Tahoe warmed up quickly. She hadn't slept well the night before because of an odd, quirky dream. In the dream, Barton Spivey had appeared in an army uniform at some kind of party where he asked her to dance. T.R. stood off to one side of the room, engaged in a conversation with Edwin. Sadie wanted T.R. to rescue her, but he and Edwin were so involved, neither one of them even noticed her. Finally, Sadie felt compelled to dance with Spivey even though she didn't want to. Halfway through their dance, Spivey turned into a spider and ran away. Sadie woke up from the dream a little upset at T.R. and Edwin until she realized how silly it was.

"Sadie Speers, you are really losing it," she said to herself as she turned onto Main Street. The memory of Spivey turning into a spider made her shiver, but seeing T.R. again, even in a dream, made her heart ache. She wondered sometimes if the pain of losing him would ever dissipate. Although it had become more manageable over time, there was still an empty spot in her heart. "I wish I could sit down and talk to you about Edwin," she said as if T.R. could hear her. "You always gave me wonderful advice. I need some of that now."

She turned on a country CD Theo had given her for her birthday. "I know you love the classics," he'd said, "but here are some contemporary country tunes I think you'll actually really like." He'd been right. She'd especially liked the tracks that featured a bluegrass style, with a driving beat, and a wailing steel guitar or vibrant fiddle.

Sadie sang along, even dancing a little to the beat. If anyone had seen her, they probably would have thought she'd gone batty. But the song encouraged her. Made her feel hopeful and happy. She really didn't care what anyone else thought.

Before going to her store, she drove to the sheriff's office. She'd told Mac she would file a report about the break-in.

The Silver Peak Sheriff's Department was on the eastern edge of downtown Silver Peak, several blocks away from the Antique Mine. It was housed in a small and unassuming industrial-looking brick building. Sadie was sure Mac's office in Denver had been much more impressive, but she doubted he cared much about that. Moving to Silver Peak was a choice he'd made because he didn't want to continue living the big-city life.

She parked in the parking lot and went inside. The sheriff's receptionist, Janet Parks, sat at her desk, riding herd over the sheriff and his deputies. For all intents and purposes, Janet believed herself to be the queen of the sheriff's department. Although her image of herself was somewhat inflated, Sadie knew that if you didn't find a way to get along with Janet, you could find yourself in for trouble. A few unlucky citizens had learned this truth the hard way.

"Well, Sadie Speers," Janet said, peering over her glasses. "Here to respond to a warrant?"

"No, Janet. Just making sure everything's running smoothly. I hear Mac's looking for a new receptionist."

Janet's mouth twitched as she tried to suppress a smile. "I'll keep that in mind."

Sadie and Janet had a long history together. High school friends, they loved to tease each other. But neither woman would admit to their genuine fondness for the other.

"Mac said you might be by to fill out a report," Janet said, "but he's not here. Kyle Kenmore can help you, though. Is that okay?"

"Kyle was one of my former students," Sadie said. "I'd love to see him."

"Yes, I know," Janet said with a sniff. "Thankfully, he overcame that and is doing quite well."

This time it was Sadie's turn to quench her laughter. "Just let him know I'm here, will you?" she said. "If it's not too much trouble."

"It is, but what can I do? It's my job."

She picked up the phone and made a call. About a minute later, Sadie saw Kyle walking toward the door to the front office. A glass wall separated the front area from the larger room where most of the other employees worked. Kyle opened the door and greeted Sadie.

"Hello, Mrs. Speers," he said with a smile. "Come on back and we'll take care of that report. It shouldn't take long."

Sadie followed him back to his desk and with Kyle's help had the report finished a few minutes later. She'd promised Edwin and Roz she would tell Mac about the letters, but since he wasn't around, there was no way she could. As she left, she said good-bye to Janet, who returned her greeting with a grunt. Sadie enjoyed their good-natured banter. There weren't many people in her life she could tease the way she could Janet.

By the time she pulled up in front of the Antique Mine, she was running a little late, but she was ready to face the day. "Please, dear God, lead me in the right direction today," she prayed as she grabbed the plastic box in the backseat that contained the objects from the safe.

The sun was just coming up, bathing Silver Peak in a golden light. Sadie sighed with contentment as she walked into her store. She unlocked the front door but left the sign on the door turned to Closed. Once inside, she checked the back door. It was locked tight, the new dead bolt in place. She was relieved to see that everything was as it should be. She brought some wood in from the back room and started a fire in the potbellied stove. After going next door and getting a cup of coffee from Luz, she sat down in an old wooden rocking chair and spent a few minutes reading the Bible she kept under the counter. She'd done her regular Bible reading before she left home, but the sight of the majestic mountains around Silver Peak reminded her of a favorite psalm. She retrieved her Bible and the pages fell open to the very spot she was looking for, so many times had she read the words on that page. "I will lift up mine eyes unto the hills, from whence cometh my help. My help cometh from the Lord, which made heaven and earth...." The familiar yet always-fresh words filled her with peace and confidence in God's loving care.

When she finished reading Psalm 121, she put the Bible back and carried the large plastic box to the back room. Before starting her day, she turned on her computer. Hearing that Marla Reichert was in town made her curious to know more about her. A quick Internet search didn't bring up anything helpful. If she was to learn more about Marla, and maybe something about Franklin she couldn't discover through her usual research avenues, she might have to talk to Marla in person.

Sadie pulled a notebook out of her desk and started making a list of the tasks she hoped to accomplish that day. She'd just begun to write when the front door opened and Edwin walked in with another man.

"Good morning, Sadie," Edwin called out.

Sadie got up from her desk and smiled at Edwin as he closed the front door. "Good morning to you too," she said.

Edwin motioned toward the man who was with him. "Sadie, this is my friend Herman Bruner," Edwin said. "And Herman, this is Sadie Speers, the woman I was telling you about."

Sadie walked over to the man and shook his hand. "I'm so glad to meet you."

Herman smiled at her. "I'm happy to meet you too. You are as lovely as Edwin said you were."

It had been a long time since anyone had told her she was lovely. Sadie felt her cheeks flush.

"Thank you," she said. "You can hang your coat here," she said, pointing at the hooks near the front door.

Edwin took off his own coat and then took Herman's from him. After hanging up both coats, he motioned to Herman to follow him.

"Wow," Herman exclaimed, "this is a wonderful shop! I love antiques. They remind me of history." He smiled at Sadie. "Edwin tells me you used to teach history."

"Yes, I did, and I loved my job. I'm blessed to be able to still enjoy learning through the items I sell. In essence, I've just changed my path but my course has stayed the same."

"That *is* a blessing. Staying close to our passions keeps us young."

Sadie nodded. "I completely agree. Can I get you a cup of coffee, Herman?" Sadie asked. "We have a wonderful coffee shop right next door."

"No thank you. I can only drink so much coffee, and I have had my limit already."

Sadie could detect a slight German accent when he spoke. "Edwin tells me your mother has been ill?"

Herman nodded. "Unfortunately she can't live alone any longer. Her mind is still sharp, but her body seems to be failing her. She's fallen twice in the last six months. I just moved her into a fine assisted-living facility. It's very nice, but…" His voice trailed off. After clearing his throat he began again. "It's very nice, but it's not home."

"It must be difficult for both of you," Sadie said.

Herman blinked several times. It was obviously hard for him to talk about, and Sadie wondered if she should have even brought the subject up.

"Mom is one of those people who wouldn't complain if her hair was on fire. She did everything she could to make me think she loved the new place, but I know her too well. She really wanted to stay in her home."

"I'm sorry," Sadie said.

He smiled. "Mom and I will be okay. We've been through quite a bit already. She lost her parents in the war and was raised by her grandmother. When Mom was ten, her grandmother died and she was shuffled around with other relatives until her aunt and uncle brought her from Germany to America when she was fifteen. She lived with them until she graduated from college.

Then she met and married my father. She's a tough lady. I admire her more than anyone I've ever known."

"Your mother taught you German?"

He nodded. "She loved her country even though she was ashamed to learn what evil men did during the war. She was always able to separate Germany from their actions. In her mind, they weren't true Germans."

"Your mother sounds very wise," Edwin said.

"She is." He smiled at Sadie. "Now, I'm told you have a letter you want me to translate?"

Sadie retrieved the plastic box and removed the letter, handing it to him. "I tried to translate it using a program on the Internet, but I wasn't successful. Some of it made sense but most of it was gibberish." She smiled. "One passage seemed to say that the letter writer wanted to drown in the ocean. I felt fairly certain that wasn't right."

Herman chuckled. "The German language is made up of words and phrases that mean different things in different contexts. I can understand why the online translator failed." He took a pair of glasses out of his shirt pocket and perched them on the end of his nose. "Would you mind if I took a little time to go through this before I translate it?"

"Of course not," Sadie said.

"I'd really like some coffee," Edwin said. "Why don't we give Herman a few minutes while I fetch us both a cup?"

"That would be wonderful," Sadie said. "Thank you."

At that moment the phone rang and Sadie went to answer it, leaving Herman alone to peruse the letter. After she took care of a customer who was looking for an antique leaded-glass vase, she hung up the phone. Edwin had come back with coffee and handed her a cup.

"I'm ready," Herman said. Sadie and Edwin walked over to where Herman was standing. Sadie could feel a tickle of excitement inside as she waited to hear what the letter really said.

Herman took a deep breath and began to read.

My dear friend,

I write this letter only hours before I face judgment from the world of men. I am ready to embrace their decision, but I feel that first I must seek your forgiveness before I confront judgment from God. When I began this assignment, my goals were clear. As I got to know you, to respect you, those same goals became lost in a sea of confusion. My loyalty has always been for my country. In the past two years my love of country has not waned, but my commitment to the men leading my beloved homeland has been altered by a sad truth. I see now that their decisions are not being made for Germany, but for themselves and out of their own hatred. If I had realized this sooner, perhaps the terrible incident that occurred could have been avoided. Please forgive me for putting you in that situation. This dreadful outcome was not your fault but mine. My lies made you believe you were helping to bring an end to this tragic and useless war. Instead, your information was being used against you. Against your country. But this is at an end. Everything you gave me has been destroyed. I will not betray you again. I am certain the penalty for my perceived betrayal will be my death. Thanks to you and your willingness to share the good news of Christ with me, I am more than ready to face my fate, whatever it may be. You have taught me that even in death there is victory.

My biggest regret at this moment is that I have no idea how you are faring. I wish we could talk just one more time. I would tell you that blame for what happened must be laid at my feet and no one else's. Please do not carry guilt and condemnation because of my poor choices. You must live life for both of us, my friend.

> *May God bless you and keep you.*
> *Hans Schweiss*

Sadie realized she'd been holding her breath since Herman started reading. She let it out with a *swoosh*. "Oh my," she said. "That is so powerful. But I wonder what it has to do with the items in the safe."

"May I see them?" Herman asked.

Sadie hesitated a moment but decided that if Edwin trusted Herman, she could do the same. Sadie brought the box over and took out the other things. "Here they are."

Herman looked carefully through everything. "I would guess these things belong to the person Schweiss wrote to. If you can figure out who he is, you might be able to figure out what 'incident' Schweiss was referring to."

Sadie pondered Herman's words for a moment. "You know," she said finally, "the more I learn about these items, the more of a personal connection I seem to develop for the man who owned the safe. Now, after hearing this letter, I feel like I know Hans Schweiss. I realize it's too late to help him, but part of me wishes I could do something to ease his pain." She looked at Herman. "I'd really like to know happened between this corporal and Hans Schweiss. What was so awful that Hans paid for it with his life while our corporal sealed up his secrets in a wall?"

"I might be able to offer you a possible explanation," Herman said, "although I can't guarantee that I'm right."

"I'm very interested in hearing what you have to say," Sadie said.

"Do you have any idea where your safe was purchased?"

"As a matter of fact I think I do," Sadie said. "I believe it was sold in a small town called Reims."

Herman nodded. "Reims is very close to the border of Belgium. There were Nazi agents in Belgium during the war." He picked up the copy of the letter he'd just read. "I believe your army corporal might have been a spy, Sadie. Perhaps he was passing some kind of information to Schweiss that was meant to help the Nazis win the war."

Sadie nodded. "I'm aware that the Germans worked hard at recruiting American servicemen and women to help them gain intelligence during the war." She'd developed compassion for the man who'd hidden mementos of his life inside the safe. Thinking he might be a traitor made her feelings a little more complicated.

Herman held up his hand. "Before you judge him too harshly, there is no indication that he was being paid for his information. And the tone of the letter leads me to believe this soldier had no idea that what he was doing was detrimental to the United States."

"How could he not know?" Edwin asked. "Anytime you tell the enemy something your side doesn't want shared, you have to realize it's damaging."

Herman shook his head. "Not necessarily. I've spent a lot of time studying the war, and I found that the Nazis were skilled in tricking Americans to help them. Those they couldn't buy off they lied to, trying to convince them their information would bring a quick end to the war, which they believed they were losing." He picked up the letter. "I have to wonder if your soldier is one of these. Listen to this passage again:

> "*'My lies made you believe you were helping to bring an end to this tragic and useless war. Instead, your information was being used against you. Against your country.'*"

"I see what you mean," Edwin said, frowning. "But what was the terrible incident he is referring to?"

Herman shrugged. "I have no idea. That is something you'll have to uncover yourself, I'm afraid."

"Thank you so much, Herman," Sadie said. "You've been so helpful. Edwin told me a little about the letter before I came today, and I did some research on the name Hans Schweiss. I believe I know who he was now. There was a Nazi officer with the same name. He was executed for treason toward the end of the war. I wonder if he is the man who wrote the letter."

Herman nodded. "That would certainly fit." He smiled at her. "If you have any other questions that are war-related, please feel free to contact me any time."

The three of them talked a while longer and then Edwin and Herman left. Sadie made a copy of the letter and Herman took it with him, promising to write it out and send her a copy in English.

Sadie was thinking about Herman's theory concerning the American corporal when she spotted something odd. A tuft of something that looked like dark hair was stuck on a corner of display case near the back room. Sadie wiggled it out from underneath the sharp edge and stared at it. "Now that's interesting," she said to herself. She would have assumed a customer simply got her hair caught, but the hair was unusual-looking. Since she couldn't figure out quite what it was, she put it inside an envelope and put the envelope in the top drawer of her desk so she could look at it later. Could it possibly be a clue to the person who broke in to her shop?

15

Sadie was getting ready to put the items back into the plastic box when she heard the front door open. Alice came in with Theo and Sara following behind.

"Hi, Mom," Alice called out. She smiled at Sadie. "Emmie Barnes called. She asked me to meet her in Silverthorne for lunch. Since I've got the day off, I'm going to drive over and spend some time with her."

Emmie Barnes was a friend of Alice's from Denver. Alice had lost some friends after the divorce, couples who were uncomfortable being around Alice without her ex-husband, but Emmie's friendship had never wavered.

"I'm so glad, Alice," Sadie said. "Please tell her I said hello."

"I will, Mom." She waved at her family and left.

"Hi, Grandma," Theo said. He walked over to where Sadie stood. "Is that the stuff that was in the safe?"

"Yes." Sara came up next to her brother and looked interested in the things Sadie had lined up on the counter.

Sadie showed them each item and explained what it was. Theo was interested in the Purple Heart.

"Don't soldiers get these when they're injured?" he asked.

"Yes. It's awarded to their families posthumously if they're killed."

He gazed at the medal in its box. "Wow. That's really something. So whoever owned this stuff must have been very brave."

Sadie just nodded. After talking to Herman, she wasn't certain the man who owned the things they were looking at was a hero or a traitor. The idea that he might have betrayed his country made her sad for him, but it also explained why he seemed to feel so guilty.

Sadie started to put the lid back on the box, but decided at the last moment to remove the gun from the box. She put the box in the back room, but locked the gun up in a nearby cabinet. Her father had taught her to be careful with firearms, even those that weren't loaded. Seeing the kids looking at the things in the box made her more mindful of the gun and how dangerous it could be in the wrong hands.

The kids grabbed their coats and hats while Sadie bundled up. She was glad she'd worn her warm boots and fleece outfit. The older she got, the more she seemed to feel the cold. Sadie didn't mind getting older. In fact, she enjoyed it. But there were a few things about aging she could do without. Feeling achy in the winter was definitely one of them.

The library was only a short two-block walk away. Anthony Parker was just opening the door when they pulled up. Anthony was a transplant from London. A single man who loved books, he'd first seen Silver Peak as a young man traveling across America with a friend. Anthony had fallen in love with the small town, and ten years later left England to accept a job as assistant to the head librarian, Kimama Temoke, at the Silver Peak library. At first the library committee had questioned why someone with his background would want the job. Anthony had a Master's degree in library science and public administration, and graduate degrees in English and history. The committee was concerned that he was overqualified for the job and probably wouldn't stay in town for long. But Kimama was impressed with the young man and supported his application. Her recommendation, along with a letter Anthony wrote, changed everyone's mind. His love for Silver Peak swayed them, and he was hired. That was almost twenty years ago. Kimama and Anthony became close friends and worked together as a team.

Anthony was a tall man with a broad forehead and straight blond hair that he combed back. He wore glasses that always seemed to rest on the end of his nose, and he had a way of staring at people that made them feel he was seeing straight into their souls. But rather than being judgmental, beneath his formal demeanor, he was one of the kindest men she'd ever met.

"Why, Sadie Speers," Anthony said in his clipped British accent as she approached, "it is so nice to see you. And you've brought your grandchildren."

Sadie reached out and took the hand Anthony extended. He shook her hand and then covered it with his other one, giving it an extra squeeze. Anthony and Kimama both had a way of making people feel as if talking to them was the highlight of their day. And they were that way with everyone. Needless to say, residents of Silver Peak enjoyed going to the library.

Anthony unlocked the massive wooden entrance doors and waved them inside. "What brings you out on such a cold, wintry day?"

"I need to use the microfilm reader," Sadie said. "I'm looking for newspapers around the time the opera house was last revamped. It would have been in the forties."

Anthony pulled the door shut and strode to the front circular desk that sat in the middle of the ground floor room. Sadie stopped and breathed in the smell of old books, lemon polish, and leather. The library had once been an unattractive multiuse building, but after a substantial donation from one of Silver Peak's prominent families, it had been refurbished. It was now one of the most modern-looking buildings in town. Local artwork adorned the walls. There were two stories of books, all accessed from the main floor by a large staircase. The second floor was open, almost like a massive balcony. Sadie found the library breathtaking, and the craftsmanship amazing. The staircase and the shelves were handcrafted with carved finials and other decorative details that couldn't be found in many libraries in the country.

"I know you don't need my help since you've used the machine many times," he said. "I hope you find what you're looking for."

"I do too. Thank you so much, Anthony." Sadie looked around. "Where is Kimama?"

"Away visiting family."

Sadie chuckled. "Seems odd not to see her here."

Kimama was a beautiful Shoshone woman who was an expert on the early history of Colorado. Kindred spirits, Sadie and Kimama could talk for hours about the past.

Anthony smiled. "Getting her to take some time off for herself wasn't easy. I consider it one of my greatest accomplishments."

Sadie laughed. "Good for you. If you can get her to leave her beloved library, you can probably do anything."

"I think you're right." Anthony excused himself and headed toward his desk while Sadie turned and led the way to a long row of small drawers against the far wall.

"These drawers contain film that can be read on the micro-film reader," she explained to Theo and Sara. She looked over the different labels until she found what she was looking for. Reaching into the drawer she removed two boxes. "Somewhere on this film we'll find the story we want."

"I think you're looking for 1943."

Anthony's voice from behind startled her. He was so quiet in his suede shoes she hadn't heard him return. "You're very precise," Sadie said. "Do you know about the scandal?"

"Just a little. I love to read these old newspapers. I remember something that happened not long before the renovations got under way. The opera house closed for two years while the work was being done, and it reopened in 1945. If I recall correctly, the incident that led to the dismissal of the previous manager happened right as the work got underway. That would put the time around 1943."

"Wow, you know a lot of stuff," Sara said. She was obviously impressed with Anthony. She might have also been a little smitten with his accent.

He smiled at her. "I love learning, young lady. Knowing about the past helps us to understand the future."

"'Those who cannot remember the past are condemned to repeat it,'" Theo said softly.

Anthony's expression brightened. "You quoted that correctly, Theo. Very few people do. Now, do you know who said it?"

Theo thought for a moment. "George...something. I can't remember his last name."

Anthony nodded enthusiastically. "Good enough. Many people believe the quote came from Winston Churchill, but its creator was actually George Santayana." He smiled at Sadie. "How nice to find an educated young man."

Sadie nodded. She was pleased about it, as well. Except for his recent declaration about changing his college major, Theo's interests seemed to lie mostly in football and soccer. Lately Sadie was seeing a whole new side of her grandson. His desire to go into law enforcement, his ethical beliefs, and now an interest in literature. He was even more like Sadie than she'd realized.

"Thank you, Anthony," she said. "You've saved me a lot of time."

He gave her a quick nod, turned, and left.

"What an interesting guy," Sara whispered.

Sadie gave her granddaughter a quick hug. "I agree. Now let's go upstairs to the microfilm reader. You'll both get to see something truly amazing."

They tramped up the stairs to the upper balcony. Theo and Sara followed Sadie to a small room in the far corner.

"I didn't even know this was here," Theo said, "and I come to the library a lot."

Sadie opened the door and flipped on the light. The room was chilly, and once again, Sadie was grateful for her warm clothing.

On a table sat the reader. It was a large machine with lots of buttons and knobs. Sadie removed the film from the box and placed it on the spindle on the left side of the reader. Then she pulled the film out and secured it under two rollers. After that she attached the end to the reel on the right. She wound the reel a few times by hand and then pressed the fast-forward button on the main part of the machine. She pushed it a few times until an image appeared on the film, highlighted by a light underneath a glass plate. She gently shoved the entire tray under the microscope until the image appeared on the screen in front of them. She rotated it so it appeared right side up.

"Wow," Sara said. "That's a really old newspaper."

"Yes, it is," Sadie said. "Now we can look back at 1943, many years before you were born, and find out what was going on."

"And you said this was even before you were born, right, Grandma?" Theo said.

Sadie sighed. "Yes, even before I was born. I know that doesn't seem possible…"

"Just kidding, Grandma," Theo said, laughing. "You're not *that* old."

Sara looked at Theo like he'd lost his mind, but she was smart enough to keep her mouth closed.

Sadie shook her head and went back to looking at the screen. "We're searching for a scandal at the opera house," she said softly. "It happened right around the time the work began in the building, so if we find an article about that, we should be close to the story we're trying to locate."

Theo and Sara stopped Sadie many times as she scrolled through the old newspapers. Some of the stories were about the war, and they asked questions about it. They were fascinated with announcements about rationing.

"You mean people weren't allowed to buy some kinds of food?" Sara asked, looking surprised.

"Not just food," Sadie said. "Gasoline, tires, even clothes were rationed."

"Hard to believe," Theo said. "We take all that stuff for granted now."

Sadie smiled at him. "Yes, we do."

Sara pointed at one part of the story. "They rationed sugar?" She shook her head. "I never would have made it."

Theo and Sadie laughed.

As they read on, Theo was excited to see an article about the completion of the Pentagon. Sara was saddened by the number of children who died at young ages. Sadie explained that advances in medicine allowed people to live longer now.

"I guess the good old days weren't so good after all, were they, Grandma?" Sara asked.

Sadie sighed. "That's a good question, Sara. We've advanced in so many areas, but I'm afraid some people have lost their love of God and country. Sometimes I'm not so sure we haven't lost more than we've gained."

Local stories held interest as well. Pictures of downtown Silver Peak sparked a lot of comments. Although most of the same buildings still stood, several were gone or had been changed into something else.

"There's the Antique Mine!" Sara exclaimed, looking over some of the pictures. "I recognize it from the roof. It was a dress shop!"

Sadie nodded. "That's right. Fern's Fine Fashions. It was in business for a long time until Fern Henderson died."

When they had scrolled past September's entries and had entered October, Theo suddenly called out, "There it is!"

Sadie scanned the page and saw the article he was talking about. She focused on it, and then magnified it so it was easier to read.

The headline read: *Manager of Silver Peak Opera House Exposed in Theft*. Sadie went on to read the part that she knew: that Franklin Reichert had been accused of stealing money and property.

The article stated that besides thousands of dollars in cash that had disappeared, two bronze statues by an artist named Lechmere were also taken from the opera house. The pieces were on loan from the Denver Museum. The article had a picture of the statues. They were two angels about four feet tall with wings extended.

"What does this have to do with the safe, Grandma?" Theo asked. "It doesn't seem like the stuff in the safe has much to do with the opera house."

"But maybe the safe belonged to Franklin Reichert," Sadie said. "He could have put the safe in the wall before he left, for safekeeping."

"That makes sense," Sara said. "The Bible had all those things about forgiveness. Maybe he was sorry he stole stuff from the opera house."

"Perhaps," Sadie said slowly. Franklin did seem like the most likely candidate as the owner of the safe—he had the opportunity to hide the safe, he had a German name, and if he really did commit the theft, the notes in the Bible made sense. But what did he have to do with Hans Schweiss?

After making a copy of the article, she scrolled through the following pages until she found this: *Longtime Opera House Manager Leaves Town in Disgrace*. The article stated that since the stolen cash and bronzes were never found, charges couldn't be filed against Reichert. The innuendo in the article made it clear that the writer, Sylvia Carey, believed Reichert was guilty since he was the only person with access to the cash at the time of the theft. The owner of the opera house, Benjamin Wilhite, stated that they'd just purchased a new safe and that Reichert had the only keys.

The article also mentioned Reichert's family. Besides his wife, Madeline, he had two daughters, Edna and Minnie. That meant the items in the safe didn't belong to Reichert's son. Carey also confirmed what Sadie already knew. Franklin Reichert was working at the opera house all during the war. How could the things in the safe belong to him?

"Look, Grandma," Sara said, pointing at the article. "They said something about a safe!"

Sadie was intrigued until she saw what Sara was referring to. "That's a good catch, but it looks like they're talking about a *new* safe, honey," Sadie said. "And I've seen this safe. It's a big metal double-door safe, and it's still in the manager's office."

"Oh," Sara said, sounding disappointed.

"It was a good idea though," Sadie said.

"No wonder this Reichert guy moved away," Theo said, reading over Sadie's shoulder. "People thought he'd done it even though they didn't have any proof. Doesn't seem right."

Sadie patted his arm. "If you decide to become a detective, I know you'll be the kind who will search out the truth, Theo."

"Mom told me it was okay to change my major, but I think she's disappointed I'm not going to medical school," he said with a sigh.

"Well, you're the one who told her you wanted to be a doctor," Sara reminded him.

Theo let out another big sigh. "I know. But I came up with that idea when I was ten. Before the doctor thing, I wanted to be a cowboy. Why doesn't Mom still want me to be a cowboy?"

Sara giggled. "I think you'd make a good cowboy."

"Gee, thanks," Theo said.

Sadie turned to look up into her grandson's face. "Theo, your mom wants you to be whoever God has created you to be. If that isn't a doctor, that's okay with her. All your mom wants is to know that you're absolutely sure this is the right path for you."

Theo nodded. "You're right, Grandma. Thanks."

Sadie turned back to the reader. She made a copy of the second article and then scrolled past it. Nothing else came up about Franklin Reichert although she did find an article about the construction work being done at the opera house.

"Well, I think we've got everything we need for now. Let's get some lunch and then go back to the store. We still have a lot of work to do."

After turning off the machine, the three of them went downstairs. Before leaving, Sadie went to the area where DVDs and CDs were kept. Luckily, *The Secret Garden* was still available, so she took it up to the main desk and checked it out with Anthony. Then the three of them left, first waving good-bye to Anthony, who was busy helping other people. He smiled and returned their waves.

As they left the library, Sadie asked Theo and Sara where they'd like to go for lunch.

"The Depot," Theo and Sara said at the same time.

"The Depot it is."

After a hearty lunch at one of Silver Peak's most popular restaurants, they walked back to the Antique Mine. Sadie saw that the mail had been delivered and took it out of the mailbox next to the front door. As she looked through it, she saw a letter without a return address. Her heart skipped a beat, then began pounding. The writing on the outside looked familiar.

Her anonymous letter writer had struck again.

16

SADIE SLID THE MAIL INTO HER TOP DESK DRAWER WITHOUT mentioning anything to her grandchildren. She had no intention of worrying them. Although she wanted to find out what the letter said, she resisted the urge to peek.

Sadie liked to clean one section of shelves every week. Usually it was on a Monday, like today. Her weekly routine kept her from having to spend an entire day cleaning all her antiques at one time.

Today she'd work on the shelves near the back door. They contained all of her Jadite, depression, and carnival glass. These items were particularly fragile. She took extra care to remove them from the shelves and put them on the counter.

"What are you going to do now, Grandma?" Sara asked.

"I need to do some cleaning," Sadie said. "I don't suppose you two would like help?"

"Sure," Theo said, much to Sadie's surprise.

"We don't have anything else to do," Sara added. "Just tell us what you need help with."

"Wow, thanks, guys. You've proven once again that when I tell people I have the best grandchildren in the world, I'm right."

She put her arm around Sara in a side-hug. "So here's what we'll do. When I hand these things to you, will you carry them carefully over to the counter? Once we get them all down from these shelves, we'll wipe down each shelf. Then we'll wash all these pieces and put them back."

"Wash them? How do we do that?" Sara asked. "You don't have a dishwasher here."

Sadie handed her two Jeanette glass pink tumblers. "By hand in warm, soapy water. You know that utility sink I have in the back room?"

"The big white one?" Sara said, wrinkling her nose. "The one that looks like we could wash Hank in it?"

Sadie laughed. "That's the one. We'll wash each piece carefully and then set them on the big table back there to dry."

"Why don't you just spray them with glass cleaner and use a paper towel?" Theo asked. "That's what Mom does at home."

"That might be fine for newer glass, but these old pieces are too delicate. It's important to treat them carefully."

It was almost three o'clock when Alice pulled up in front of the store and came inside.

"Did you have fun?" Sadie asked.

"I really did," Alice said smiling. "Emmie filled me in on what's happening in Denver, and I told her about life in Silver Peak. She plans to come here in the summer and stay with me for a few days."

"That's wonderful, honey. I'd love to see her."

"Did you have fun?" Alice asked, looking at Theo and Sara.

"We had a wonderful day," Sadie said. "We worked around the store, went to the library, and had lunch at The Depot."

"Oh, great," Alice said. "That means my son is full of spaghetti and my daughter is full of cheeseburger. They won't eat much dinner."

"Which means you don't need to cook," Theo pointed out. "All I want is a sandwich."

"Now that's a good point," Alice said, laughing. "Come on, you two. Thank your grandmother for putting up with you, and let's get going. I want to stop by the store on the way home."

Theo and Sara both gave Sadie a big hug and left with their mother. Sadie sighed with satisfaction. It had been a wonderful day. She watched as Alice's car pulled away. Then she reluctantly went to her desk and removed the new letter from her top drawer. She found her letter opener and slit the top of the envelope open. As she suspected, it was from the same person who had written the other two notes. The writing was exactly the same. The author had a strange way of making the letter *e*. Even when trying to disguise his handwriting, he never changed that one letter. She took a deep breath and started to read.

Dear Sadie,

I have begged you to stop your inquiry into the items you found in the safe. However, you continue. One last time I am pleading with you to let this go. Innocent people will be hurt if you go forward. People you care about. Some things are better left alone. You should know that. Are there things in your past you'd rather no one knew about? If so, you should be able to understand why it is so important for you to stop your investigation.

A friend

Sadie stared down at the paper in her hand. For some reason, this note affected her more than the others. It had a definite tone of desperation. Sadie looked closely at the signature. *A friend.* Was this person really a friend, or was this an attempt to soften and confuse her? She sighed, folded the letter, and slid it back into the envelope.

She finished putting the last of the glassware back on the shelves. She'd been thinking about the information she'd read at the library about Franklin Reichert. She wanted to visit Marla and ask her some questions, but she didn't really want to go alone. She was wondering if Roz or Alice might like to go with her when Edwin walked into the shop.

He greeted Sadie with a big smile. "Was driving past and decided to stop in. Did you get the kind of help you wanted from Herman this morning?"

Sadie smiled. "He not only translated the letter, he is a wealth of information about the war. I'm so glad I got to meet him, Edwin. Thank you so much."

"You're welcome. Are you getting ready to head home?"

"Actually, I was thinking about stopping by to visit Marla Reichert."

Edwin frowned. "I'm not sure I know who that is."

Sadie quickly gave Edwin the condensed version of the Reichert scandal. "Marla is back in Silver Peak to fix up Franklin's old house and sell it. I'd love to ask her some questions. Even though it's looking less and less likely, I'd like to see if the safe could have belonged to Franklin. I'm a little nervous, though, because I heard she's not exactly friendly."

Edwin grinned. "You want me go with you for moral support?"

"Well, if you're not busy…"

"I'm happy to go, Sadie," he said. "Do you need to call her first?"

"I'd rather not. I hate to be sneaky, but calling just gives her an opportunity to tell us not to come." She sighed. "I should warn you that this could be a huge waste of time."

"I get to see you, Sadie. That's never a waste of time."

Sadie smiled but didn't respond. Alice's suggestion that she invite him to their next movie night popped into her head, but for some reason the words just wouldn't come out. There was plenty of time. Right now, she wanted to concentrate on Marla Reichert.

They went out to Edwin's car and drove over to the large Victorian house on the edge of town that used to belong to Franklin Reichert. The beautiful Queen Anne–styled Victorian still needed a lot of work, but Sadie was thrilled to see the work that had already been done. When it was completed, the house would be a fantastic addition to Silver Peak.

Edwin opened her door, and Sadie got out of the car. She felt a little nervous not knowing if they would be welcome. She noticed a tan SUV parked in the driveway. She hoped that meant Marla was home. Sadie took a deep breath as they approached the front door. Edwin, who must have realized she was a little anxious, took her arm.

"Everything will be fine. The worst she can do is tell us to leave. If she does, we'll just go to Arbuckle's. Hector told me they're starting to sell their pumpkin spice lattes this week. That should heal any bruised feelings."

Sadie laughed. Edwin certainly knew how to make her feel better. They walked up the steps, and Sadie rang the bell without hesitation. She squared her shoulders and reminded herself that facing uncomfortable situations head-on was the only way to put them behind you.

About a minute later, the door swung open and Marla Reichert stood staring at them. Her expression was a mixture of surprise and annoyance. She had short hair, dyed coal-black. Her bangs hung down almost to her eyes. Dressed in black slacks and a black blouse, the overall effect was rather depressing. "Yes. What can I do for you?" she asked.

"Marla, I'm Sadie Speers. I own the Antique Mine downtown. Do you have a few minutes?"

Marla looked Edwin up and down. "Is this some kind of appeal for my vote?"

"No," Edwin said. "Sadie has something she wants to talk to you about. It's very cold out here. Mind if we come in? We won't stay long."

Marla glared at both of them, but at least she pushed her front door open.

"Thank you," Sadie said when they got inside. It seemed Marla planned to keep them standing in the hallway. "What a lovely living room," she said, looking past her reluctant hostess. Sadie could tell it had recently been redone. She quickly stepped around Marla and headed for the living room before she could stop her.

"It's very nice," Edwin echoed, following Sadie. "You've done a great job restoring the woodwork."

Looking a little startled and probably wondering how in the world her two guests had made it this far inside her house, Marla followed them.

Sadie was really quite impressed. Marla had not only protected the architectural integrity of the room, she'd actually enhanced it. Ceiling-to-floor windows were bordered by paneled walls painted a rich coffee color. Thick cream-colored and maroon brocade fabric was draped across the top of the windows and down the sides, not blocking the glass. Sadie hated seeing these wonderful old windows covered with drapes. Marla's choice of window dressing was perfect. The oak floors had been brought back to their original beauty. The stone fireplace had been restored, and the room was furnished with pieces that were reminiscent of the early days of Silver Peak.

A large Victorian rug lay in the middle of the floor, with Victorian-styled furniture surrounding it. A couch, a love seat, and an overstuffed chair were covered in cream-colored velvet material with light flowers that pulled in the maroon from the fabric adorning the windows.

"Marla, this is just incredible," Sadie said. "You've brought back the marvelous beauty of this room. If the rest of the house is anywhere close to this, you will have done an awesome job." She turned and smiled at Marla. "I had no idea you were so talented."

Marla's previous scowl slipped a little. Sadie's compliments were an attempt to lighten the mood, but they were absolutely sincere. Marla seemed to realize Sadie's comments were heartfelt.

"Thank you," she said softly. "It's been a real labor of love. I'm so glad someone appreciates the end-result."

"Well, I do," Sadie said. "It's wonderful."

"I'm particularly proud of the fireplace. I only used Colorado rock to rebuild it."

Sadie walked over to the fireplace and studied it closely. The work was beautifully done. She glanced up at the mantle and saw several pictures. Some of them were quite old. She recognized Franklin Reichert in one of them. She'd seen him pictured in the newspaper articles she'd read at the library. He was seated at a desk in an office. Even though the picture had been taken a long time ago, Sadie could tell the photograph was taken at the opera house. Unfortunately, the desk he sat behind wasn't the desk she'd found at the opera house. Obviously, this picture was taken before he lost his job.

"Will you have a seat?" Marla asked.

"Thank you."

Sadie and Edwin sat down on the couch, and Marla sat across from them on the love seat.

"I don't get many visitors," she said. "Is there something I can do for you?"

Sadie hesitated. Marla's disposition had improved since they'd first arrived. She was afraid of offending her and wasn't quite sure how to proceed. She said a silent prayer, took a deep breath, and hoped she wouldn't lose the ground she seemed to have gained with the reclusive woman.

"The men working on the opera house found an old safe inside one of the walls," Sadie said. "I'm wondering if it could have belonged to your grandfather."

Marla frowned and looked confused. "I don't understand. Why would there be a safe inside a wall?"

Sadie shook her head. "I'm not sure, Marla. I'm trying to find out who put it there so we can locate the rightful owner."

"When was it walled up?"

"We can't be completely sure, but according to the contractor, it appears to have been done during a previous restoration. That probably would have been between 1943 and 1945. I believe your grandfather was the opera house manager until sometime in '43. Isn't that right?"

Marla raised one eyebrow, and her previous affable expression changed into something not quite as sociable. "Yes, that's right. But I don't know anything about a safe." She took a deep breath. "I'm not sure what you're trying to do here, but I'm not interested in digging up dirt about my grandfather. He was wrongly accused of theft in the forties and fired under a cloud of suspicion. It affected his life and my family in very negative ways. My grandfather and grandmother had to move, and he wasn't able to find a job for a long time after that because of the situation."

"I'm so sorry to hear that, Marla," Sadie said sympathetically. "We wouldn't think of causing you any further discomfort. We're really just trying to locate the original owner of the safe. If it belonged to your grandfather, we'd like to return it to you."

Marla stared at her for a moment, a look of confusion on her face. "What do you want to know?"

Sadie leaned forward. "Inside the safe we found items that belonged to someone in the military. I know your grandfather was running the opera house during the war, but did he serve in some other capacity? In some way that would have allowed him to stay in Silver Peak and keep his job?"

Marla shook her head. "He was rejected because of his bad back. That was something he kept secret. He didn't want anyone to know about his condition. Years later he was diagnosed with spinal stenosis."

Sadie and Edwin exchanged glances. This information pointed away from Franklin Reichert as the owner of the safe.

"Is there anything valuable in the safe?" Marla asked.

Sadie shook her head. "No, but the safe itself is worth a great deal of money. If we can't find the owner we may be able to sell it and use the funds for improvements at the opera house. That's why it was so important for us to talk to you." She smiled kindly at Marla. "I'm sorry if we touched on a sore subject."

"My grandfather died before he was able to prove his innocence. Of course it's a sore subject, as you say."

"I understand it was Benjamin Wilhite who accused Franklin of the thefts," Sadie said.

"That's right. The Wilhites were a powerful family in Silver Peak back then. Benjamin's father made his money in the silver mines until they began to play out. Then he moved all his money into the banking business and made a fortune. He bought a lot of local property. Benjamin inherited everything when his father died. Ruining my grandfather's reputation meant nothing to him. It was like a giant stepping on a bug." She stood up. "Now, if you don't mind…"

"Certainly," Sadie said. "I'm sorry for what happened to your family. But I'm glad your grandfather left his house to you. It's nice to have a Reichert back in Silver Peak."

Marla shrugged. "We tried to sell the house after Grandfather died so my grandmother would have some money, but no one wanted to pay what it was worth. I decided to fix it up and live in it myself."

Sadie stood up and approached Marla. She took a step back as if she thought Sadie meant to harm her. "I have one more quick question if you don't mind, Marla. I noticed your grandfather's beautiful carved desk in the photograph on the mantel. I know it's an odd question, but do you happen to know if that was the only desk he used when he worked for the opera house?"

"Well, I guess I'm not sure, but I do know that desk was very special to him. He brought it with him when he first took the job, and he removed it when he was fired. It was handcrafted for him by a rather famous furniture maker and was quite valuable. My parents have it now."

"Thanks, Marla," Sadie said. "And thank you for allowing us in your lovely home. I hope to see you again soon."

After Sadie and Edwin had both said good-bye, they stood on Marla's porch and Sadie let out a deep sigh. "Well, that was a little awkward, but certainly illuminating. It of course makes it seem as though the safe didn't belong to Franklin. He wasn't in the service, after all."

Sadie and Edwin walked down the steps toward his car. Before getting in, Sadie turned and stared toward the old Victorian house. "I wonder," she said slowly. "I really wonder."

17

"Are you hungry?" Edwin asked Sadie when she slid into the passenger seat of his car.

"Actually, I'm starving. I had lunch at The Depot today, but I'm definitely ready for dinner."

"How about Los Pollitos?"

"That sounds wonderful," Sadie said.

"Good." Edwin smiled.

Sadie was so busy thinking about her visit with Marla that she didn't even notice when Edwin pulled into the parking lot at Los Pollitos, her favorite restaurant.

"We're here, Sadie," Edwin said gently.

"Oh my." Sadie smiled. "Sorry. Just a little distracted, I guess."

"It's no wonder with everything that's been going on. Let's get some good Mexican food under our belts. Maybe that will help. Brain food."

Sadie laughed. "I think that's fish, but I bet you were just baiting me, weren't you?"

It was Edwin's turn to laugh. "And you took the bait, hook, line, and sinker."

Sadie shook her head. "Very punny."

Edwin snorted, got out of his car, and then came around and opened her door. They walked quickly into Los Pollitos since the night air was growing colder.

Gloria Garza, one of the owners, greeted them when they came inside and led them to a table in the corner. A candle flickered in a red glass candle holder, giving the table a romantic aura.

"It is so good to see you both," Gloria said with a smile. Gloria had long brown hair and dark brown eyes that shone with enthusiasm. It wasn't just the food at Los Pollitos that Sadie looked forward to, it was also the welcoming atmosphere the Garzas had created.

The food at Los Pollitos was wonderful. Sadie loved their enchiladas and homemade tamales. They started their meal with warm tortilla chips and tangy salsa, and perused the menu.

"I think I'm going to try the steak quesadilla today. You?"

Sadie chuckled. "I was just thinking of ordering the chicken quesadilla. Believe it or not, even after coming here probably a hundred times, I've never actually tried it."

"Well, then you must. Maybe I'll order the steak and you can order the chicken so we can try both dishes."

Sadie nodded but didn't say anything. T.R. used to do the same thing. Sadie would tease him about eating her food. "If you want something, order your own," she would say. "Quit eating mine." He'd always laughed, but he kept sampling her food. She smiled at the memory.

Someone called out her name, and she looked across the room to see Pastor Don and Jeanne sitting at a table with Doc Conroy. She waved at them and then noticed Ardis and Mabel Fleagle sitting nearby. When Ardis saw Sadie, he got up and came over to the table.

"Good to see you both," Ardis said to Sadie. He shook hands with Edwin.

"Good to see you too," Sadie said with a smile. "How are things going at the opera house?"

"We're making a lot of progress, but there is more work than we originally anticipated." Ardis shook his head. "These old buildings can hide surprises. Some good and some bad."

"I understand," Sadie said.

"Speaking of surprises, I'm glad I ran into you. Have been meaning to ask if you've been able to get that old safe open?"

"Yes, actually, to my surprise, I was. There wasn't anything of apparent monetary value inside, but there were some things that might mean something to the family of the person who owned the safe. Unfortunately, we haven't located them yet."

"Well, I hope you find them, Sadie. Let me know when you do." He turned to look back at Mabel, who was staring at him. "Guess I'd better get back to my table while my food's still hot." He sighed. "Mabel gets worried if I let food get cold. I can't figure out why. It might not taste as good, but cold food hasn't killed me yet."

"She's your wife," Edwin said with a smile. "She's probably just trying to take care of you."

Ardis laughed. "I guess you're right. Sometimes I wish she's take a little less care, though."

He turned and went back to his table just as Elena Garza, Ramon and Gloria's daughter, came up to them. "Good evening, Sadie, Edwin."

"Hi, Elena. How are you?" Sadie said.

"I'm okay. A lot of homework." She sighed. "Sometimes I'm not sure I'll ever get it all done." Elena was sixteen years old, tall and slender, and very popular in school. She looked like a younger version of her mother.

"My students used to say the same thing," Sadie said with a smile.

"And what advice did you have for them?"

"Turn off the TV, and hang up the phone. As far as today's generation goes, I'd add, quit playing on the computer. Or your phone."

Elena laughed. "Are you spying on me?"

Sadie shook her head and grinned. "No. Getting rid of distractions has helped almost every student I've even known. I'm sure things haven't changed that much since I retired."

"Thanks, Sadie. I'll take your advice." She smiled at Sadie and Edwin. "What can I get you to drink?"

Sadie ordered coffee and Edwin ordered a soft drink.

"Do you know what you want to eat?"

Edwin looked at Sadie. "Do we?"

Sadie laughed. "Yes, I think we want a steak quesadilla and a chicken quesadilla."

"Great choice." She wrote down their order and hurried off to turn it in.

Sadie took a deep breath. "My, it certainly smells good in here."

"Yes, it does," Edwin said.

"So how is your campaign going?"

"Seems to be chugging along. I feel I'm building support. It's hard to tell, though, Sadie. James has some very loyal followers, and he's a good man. This race may come down to the wire."

"It's good that we have two qualified candidates."

"Yes, it is," Edwin agreed.

"Well, many of us in town are very excited about your ideas and enthusiasm."

"I hope so. I would really like to serve Silver Peak. Find a way to give back to this wonderful community."

"We would be blessed as well." Sadie sighed and reached for her purse. "By the way, I got another letter."

Edwin grunted. "I'm getting tired of these letters. I'd like to spend a few moments alone with the person writing them."

Sadie grinned as she took the envelope from her purse. "After the incident with Milo, I'm no longer sure you're joking."

Edwin laughed. "That was out of character for me, I'm afraid. Usually anyone who upsets me will only face a vigorous discussion."

She smiled and handed him the envelope. As he read, his forehead furrowed. By the time he finished, he was frowning deeply. "I'm not sure what to make of this," he said. "It sounds so…"

"Personal?" Sadie said. "That's what I thought. It's as if I know him."

"Is he implying that he intends to release some deep, dark secret about you into the public eye?"

Sadie shook her head. "I don't know. It almost comes across that way. Maybe he was trying to make me feel empathy for him. I know this makes me sound incredibly boring, but I really don't have any deep, dark secrets." She grinned. "I did use bottled spaghetti sauce once and didn't tell anyone. If that's the big secret he wants to spread around, I think I can live with that."

"Speaking of the public eye," Edwin said. "Have you read the *Chatterbox* lately?"

The *Chatterbox* was an anonymous blog that posted commentaries about the residents and goings-on of Silver Peak. No one seemed to know who was behind it, but somehow the writer seemed to have his or her finger directly on the pulse of the town. More than once, Sadie had been impressed, amused, and sometimes admittedly dismayed by the writer's ability to ferret out the truth.

"I've been so busy I haven't checked the blog for days." Sadie frowned. "What does it say?"

"You'll have to read it to get the exact wording, but the current post is about you."

Sadie's eyebrows shot up. "About me? What about me?"

Edwin shook his head. "Well, let's see. Part of it was about the safe being found in the opera house. Then there was something about the break-in. The writer wonders why nothing was taken. Then there's some kind of hint about who broke in, and finally, there was a comment about your running around town acting like Sherlock Holmes." He smiled. "That was my very favorite part."

Sadie laughed. "I wish I were Sherlock Holmes. I'd probably be able to know everything about the safe just by looking at it."

"Well, may I say that I'm certainly glad you're not Sherlock? You're much prettier than he was."

Sadie could feel herself blush. "Well, thank you. I'm not sure how much of a compliment that is though."

Edwin grinned. "Maybe not. But trust me, it was meant as a sincere compliment. As far as the *Chatterbox* is concerned, there's nothing there to be worried about." He handed the letter back to her.

She held the letter up. "Just like I don't think there's anything to worry about in connection to this last letter. But I certainly would like to find the link the letter writer has to the owner of the safe. The original owner couldn't possibly still be alive. Or if he is, he's very, very old. Too old to kick open the back door of the

Antique Mine. And this handwriting doesn't look like it belongs to an elderly person."

Edwin shook his head. "Whatever happened was obviously traumatic. Whoever is writing these letters must have a very close connection to the situation."

"But who would go to these lengths? And why wouldn't they just come to me and explain? People know me well enough to know I would never spread a story that would hurt someone." She shook the letter in her hand. "I haven't considered this, but perhaps this person isn't a real friend. If he was, surely he would trust me to keep his secret."

"Good point," Edwin said. "So why do you think they're sending these letters?"

"There's something else going on here. Something that puts our letter writer at risk. But for the life of me, I can't figure out what it could be."

"Speaking of letters," Edwin said and reached into the pocket of his coat that was draped over his chair and took out an envelope. "Here's the written translation of your letter. Herman dropped it off and asked me to give it to you."

Sadie took it from him. "Oh, thank you. Please give me his address so I can write him a note of appreciation for his help."

"I'll e-mail it to you. I'm sure he'd enjoy hearing from you."

Elena arrived with their quesadillas. They thanked her, and she left.

"Shall I say grace?" Edwin asked.

"Please," Sadie said, grateful for his leadership.

Edwin blessed the food and asked God to give them wisdom about how to deal with the situation Sadie faced.

"Thank you," Sadie said after Edwin closed the prayer. "That's exactly what I need. Wisdom."

Edwin took a bite of his steak quesadilla. "Delicious," he said.

"The chicken is wonderful too," Sadie said. "Just the right amount of spice. I'm glad I decided to try something new."

"Sometimes you just have to take a chance," Edwin said, looking into Sadie's eyes. "Jump in with both feet. No one can promise it will work, but if you don't try, you could lose out on something wonderful."

Sadie didn't know how to respond so she just said, "I'm glad we came here tonight."

"Me too," Edwin said. He wiped his mouth with his napkin, then spoke again. "Sadie, I want to tell you something. The last thing I ever want to do is hurt our…friendship. And I know I've said this before, but I want to make my feelings clear. My feelings for you go beyond friendship."

He gazed into her eyes, and Sadie felt as if she couldn't catch her breath.

"I'm not asking you to make any kind of commitment. Not until you're ready." He took a deep breath and slowly let it out. "When Rose died, I was convinced I could never love anyone again. But in the last few months, I've started to see myself moving on with my life. I will always love Rose, but that doesn't mean I can't make room for someone else." He reached across the table, put his hand over Sadie's, and before thinking, wrapped his hand around hers. "All I'm asking is for you to think about it. Will you do that?"

Sadie gulped and tried to figure out what to say. In the end, the only words that came out were, "I will think about it, Edwin. I promise."

He squeezed her hand one more time before slowly pulling away. "That's all I can ask. Thank you."

He took another bite of his quesadilla. "So what now? What's your next step regarding the safe?"

It took Sadie a few seconds to refocus her thoughts back to the safe. "I don't exactly know. I suspected that the safe had belonged to Franklin Reichert, but since he didn't serve in the military, and Marla had no knowledge of the safe, I'm tempted to rule him out. And as far as who broke in... I'm not sure. There is something I have to follow up with. It's too soon to tell exactly what will come out of it."

Edwin looked intently at Sadie. "Just be careful."

She smiled. "I will. Edwin, can I ask you a question about someone I saw you talking to at your campaign meeting?"

"Shoot."

"It's a man who is visiting Silver Peak. His name is Barton Spivey."

Edwin's forehead wrinkled in thought for a moment until realization dawned. "Are you talking about the man who's staying at Jane and Jerry's B and B?"

"Yes, that's him," Sadie said.

Edwin nodded. "Yes, I remember him."

"Can I ask what you were chatting about?"

"Sure. He wanted to talk about Silver Peak. Told me he was thinking about moving here. Asked to meet with me. But as much as I wish I could meet with everyone in town, and every prospective new citizen one-on-one, it's just not feasible, especially right now during campaign season."

Sadie gave him a sympathetic look. "Everyone understands, Edwin. You're a busy and popular man right now."

"I wish Barton had been that perceptive. He was rather insistent about meeting. I told him I might be able to carve out some time after the campaign was over, but until then, I suggested he stop by City Hall and pick up some brochures. Visit some of the sites, go by the library and read about our history."

"And what did he say to that?"

"He still wanted a meeting." Edwin paused and fiddled with the salt shaker for a moment. Then, he looked up at Sadie. "I got the strangest feeling that he had another agenda."

Sadie wasn't surprised. She'd gotten the same impression. "Interesting."

Edwin laughed. "What does '*interesting*' mean?"

"It's just funny because I've felt the same thing. I'm going to do a little poking around. See what I can find out about Mr. Spivey."

That night when Sadie got home, she pulled up the *Chatterbox* blog on her laptop and read the latest entry:

Silver Peak's Sadie Speers has been a busy lady lately. Besides trying to find out who owns an antique safe discovered during renovations at the Silver Peak Opera House, like Sherlock Holmes, she's also on the trail of a burglar who broke into the Antique Mine and for some strange reason didn't take anything. What's that about, dear readers? Someone in town knows who is behind it. When will the truth come out?

Yours truly,
Chatterbox

Sadie laughed and wondered as she frequently did just who the *Chatterbox* writer was. She really had no idea, but she found the blog entertaining. Before she logged off she glanced at the place on the page for posting comments or sending a message to the blog writer. She'd wondered sometimes if some of the information the Chatterbox received was sent by readers who were availing themselves of the comment section. It would certainly explain where all the information came from. How could one person know so much? She shrugged and logged off the Internet.

Tomorrow was another day, and she had something important to do. Something more important than thinking about who was behind the *Chatterbox*.

18

TUESDAY DAWNED COLD, BUT AT LEAST THE SUN WAS SHINING. Sadie took Hank for a walk. The mountains glittered with snow, and Sadie paused more than once to drink in their beauty. When they got back to the house, she fed Hank and spent some time reading her Bible and praying. By the time she left the house, she felt prepared to enjoy the day God had given her.

When she arrived at the Antique Mine, she found Julie already there. "Did you have fun with the boys yesterday?" Sadie asked.

Julie laughed. "I love them to pieces, but to be honest, getting away sometimes is great too. They're with Mom today, and she loves having them. I think one day is just perfect for her, but two days can begin to take a toll. They're pretty rambunctious at this age."

After putting the box with the things from the safe in the back room, Sadie started the fire in the stove while Julie added change to the cash register. Once they were ready, Julie unlocked the front door. The weather forecast had promised more snow. The promise of fresh snowpack beckoned visitors to nearby ski resorts. Would-be skiers invaded Silver Peak with money in their pockets and time on their hands, so Sadie and Julie were busy all morning. Although

Sadie was grateful for the business, her mind kept drifting back to the safe and to Marla Reichert. She couldn't shake something Marla had said. When things slowed down around lunchtime, Sadie told Julie she had an errand to run. She called Theo, who was still home because of the two-day teachers' meetings. She told him she was making a quick trip to the library to do some additional research. "It could prove to be very interesting," she told him. "I thought you might like to be in on it."

"Sure, Grandma," he said. "It's boring around here. Sara's at a friend's house. Besides, I really like looking up things with you."

After saying good-bye, Sadie jumped into her car and drove straight to the library. Once she arrived, she parked and then hurried inside. She'd just said hello to Anthony when Theo came in the front door behind her.

Theo came over to his grandmother. "I'm really curious. You said you'd discovered something interesting. I can't wait to see what it is."

"I need to use the microfilm reader again," she told Anthony.

He nodded. "You're in luck. No one's up there now."

"Thanks."

Sadie went over to the drawers that held the microfilm, searched for what she wanted, and hiked upstairs, Theo following behind her. After loading the film up in the reader, she scrolled to an article and stopped.

"Well, what do you know?"

"What, Grandma?" Theo asked.

Sadie pointed to the article she was reading. "The name of the sheriff who investigated the theft at the opera house was Anderson."

"Why is that important?"

Sadie scrolled to another page. "It mentions here that Sheriff Anderson was Benjamin Wilhite's cousin. Very convenient, isn't it? Seems they were keeping things in the family." She moved the film through several issues until she found what she wanted. "A few months after the theft, Sheriff Anderson moved away."

Theo frowned. "Sounds very suspicious."

"To say the least," Sadie said. After reading the article very carefully, she went back to the story she and the kids had looked at previously. "Now, let's look at this article again with fresh eyes."

"What is it about this story that makes it important?" Theo asked. "We read it the other day."

"You're right. But sometimes we have to look at things a second, third, or even a fourth time before we see what's really essential. Since you want to be a detective, I thought you might like to see why that could be critical to a case you're working on."

Theo leaned over his grandmother's shoulder and stared at the article. Then he shook his head. "It looks the same to me."

"That's because you don't have the information I do." Sadie told him about her meeting with Marla, specifically repeating something she had said about her grandfather. "Now do you see it?"

Theo sighed as he peered again at the article. "No, nothing different. I don't…" Suddenly, he stopped. "Wait a minute."

Sadie smiled up at him. "We're getting ready to solve a mystery, Theo. One that should have been cracked a long time ago. But first, we need to find something else. Unless I miss my guess, it will be here somewhere." She scrolled past several issues of the *Silver Peak Sentinel*. Finally, she stopped and read one particular announcement. "There it is!" she exclaimed.

"What does that mean?" Theo asked.

"It means we've caught a thief. Unfortunately, it's too late to turn him over to the authorities, but thankfully, it's not too late to right a wrong. Maybe it's not all about catching the bad guys. Maybe, in this case, it's about proving who's innocent."

He smiled. "I like that."

Sadie stood up and patted her grandson on the back. "Since you're off today, how about some hot chocolate at Arbuckle's before you head home?"

Theo smiled. "I'd love that, Grandma. I'll meet you over there."

Sadie said good-bye to Theo and quickly made some copies. Then she turned off the microfilm reader.

When she returned to her shop, there were only a couple of customers. She told Julie she would be having hot chocolate with Theo next door.

"If it gets busy again, feel free to come and get me," she said.

"I'm sure I'll be fine," Julie said with a smile. "Have fun."

Sadie went next door and found Theo waiting for her with two cups of hot chocolate on the table, whipped cream forming a peak that extended over the rims.

"Thank you for ordering," Sadie said as she sat down. She saw Luz behind the counter and waved at her. Luz smiled and waved back.

"I was wondering if that friend of Edwin's translated the letter," Theo said after they'd each sipped some of Arbuckle's delicious hot chocolate. "Can I read it?"

Sadie reached into her purse and took out the copy of the letter Edwin had given her. "Here it is," she said, handing it to him.

Theo was silent as he read. "Wow," he said finally. "That's really something."

"Yes, it is," Sadie agreed, "but what does it mean to you?"

"Well, this Hans obviously did something that caused trouble for the guy he sent this letter to," he said. The deep creases in his forehead made it clear he was trying to understand the letter. "I mean, Hans is saying he's going to die because of what happened." He looked up at Sadie. "What did you say happened to Hans, Grandma?"

"If it's the same man I researched, and I think it is, he was executed for treason not long before World War II ended."

"This guy, this American soldier Hans was writing to, whoever he was, must have been passing secrets or something. He thought he was helping to end the war, but Hans was using the information to help Germany. Then something terrible happened. Hans felt bad about it, realized it was his fault, and he decided not to help Germany anymore. They decided he was a traitor and killed him."

"That's exactly what Mr. Bruner said, Theo," Sadie said. "And I agree with him."

"But what was the 'terrible incident'?"

"The passages underlined in the Bible make it clear that whatever it was, the American corporal felt responsible even though his friend shouldered the blame."

"So the corporal actually caused this terrible thing?"

"That's what I'm thinking," Sadie said. "But what do you think he did? What's the terrible thing?"

"He killed someone," Theo said, his voice low. "That's why there was a gun in the safe."

"That makes the most sense to me too." Sadie had also been thinking that way and was impressed to see her seventeen-year-old grandson come to the same conclusion. "But why would he keep a weapon he used to end someone's life?" Sadie already had a theory, but she wanted Theo to draw his own conclusions. If he saw the same thing she did, it could help to confirm her suspicions. Besides, a little deductive reasoning was a good thing for someone who wanted to be a detective someday.

"A reminder of his crime?" Theo said slowly. "I mean, if he felt guilty about what he'd done, maybe he'd keep something that would help him to remember it, but he wouldn't want to see it every day. You know, because he felt responsible."

In the light of Theo's revelation and everything Herman had told her, all the pieces seemed to fit.

"But this is the thing I'm struggling with the most, Theo. This crime happened almost seventy years ago. Who would be concerned that the truth would come out now?"

Theo thought for a moment. "A relative," he then said emphatically. "I bet we're looking for a relative who knows what happened. He or she is trying to stop the truth from coming out. It's the only thing that makes sense."

"Good thought. But even if their family member was involved in something dishonorable, even if he killed someone, why take it so personally?"

"Hmm. That's a good question," Theo said. "I think it's one you'll have to answer, Grandma. But you'll do it. I have complete faith in you."

Sadie smiled at him. "Thank you. I'm afraid you have more confidence in me than I do at this point." She downed the rest of her cocoa. "You know what? You're going to make a great detective, honey. You just took several pieces of a puzzle and really helped cement some of my suspicions. You helped me a lot, Theo."

Theo's shy smile told her he was pleased by her encouragement. He handed her the letter and she slid it into her purse.

"Now you should get going. Since this is your last day off from school, I'm sure your mom would like to spend some time with you."

Theo grunted. "By if *spending time with me*, you mean she wants me to clean my room, you're right."

Sadie laughed. "If you get it done today, you'll get to come to my house Monday for movie night."

Theo perked up. "We haven't done that for a while. What's the movie this time?"

"It's called *The Secret Garden*."

Theo frowned. "I'm not sure about the 'garden' part, but I like that there's a secret. Sounds mysterious."

Sadie smiled at him. "It is. I think you'll like it."

After Theo said good-bye, Sadie headed back to the shop. Business was slow but steady. Several customers came in looking for specific things, and three people approached Sadie with items they wanted to sell. Sadie picked up a set of rare Jadite Fire King salt and pepper shakers, an old Bakelite radio, and a Steiff bear in fairly good condition.

Around three o'clock, things slowed down quite a bit. While Julie took care of their only customer, Sadie took out her laptop and set it up on her desk. She put in the name *Barton Spivey* but nothing came up. She thought for a moment, recalling the things she'd learned about Barton since she'd seen him at the campaign meeting. Thoughts swirled in her mind until something curious came into focus.

On a hunch she picked up the phone and called a friend who owned an antique store in Denver. After speaking with him a few minutes, she went back to the computer and did another search. She clicked a few more links and made a few more calls.

"Eureka!" she said after a few minutes.

"Something interesting?" Julie asked.

"Something very interesting," Sadie said, closing her laptop.

She stared at the laptop for a moment, debating what to do. Then, she picked up the phone and called Edwin. "You know that meeting Barton Spivey asked for?" she said when he picked up.

"Yes," he said.

"I know you're busy, but I think I might be on to something. Could you call him and ask him to meet you here later this afternoon?"

"I suppose so," Edwin said, sounding amused. "What are you up to, Sadie?"

"You'll just have to trust me. Will you do it?"

"Yes. I'll call the B and B and then call you back."

Sadie said good-bye and hung up. She was a little concerned Barton would find it odd that Edwin was requesting a meeting at her antique shop of all places, but it was a risk she was willing to take. A few minutes later, Edwin phoned and told her that he and Barton would be at the Antique Mine around five.

"That sounds perfect," Sadie said. "I'll see you then."

After making one more phone call, she went back to her computer, pulled up a few things, wrote them down, and then quickly typed up a message and sent it.

The rest of the day stayed slow. When the last customer left and the store was finally quiet, Sadie told Julie she could leave.

"Thanks, Sadie. I'm sure Mom is ready for a break."

While Sadie waited for Edwin and Barton, she made some notes from the information she'd found on the computer. At precisely five o'clock, the bell tinkled over the front door and Edwin walked in.

"Am I early?" he asked.

"No, right on time. Barton isn't here yet."

The words had no sooner left her mouth when the front door opened again and Barton Spivey walked in. Sadie greeted him and then walked over and closed the front door behind him. Then she turned the Open sign to Closed.

Spivey spied Edwin standing by the front counter. "Thank you for meeting with me, Edwin," he said. "Could we go to the coffee shop next door and talk?"

"I'm sorry, Mr. Spivey," Edwin said, "but I'm not the one who invited you here."

"It was me," Sadie said. She motioned to a chair near her desk.

Spivey's expression showed his confusion, but he sat down in the chair Sadie indicated. "What did you want to talk to me about?"

"Something you said the other day stuck in my mind," Sadie said. "At first it slipped by me, but later when I thought about it, I realized why it was significant."

Spivey shook his head. "I'm sorry, but I'm confused. What was it I said?"

"You told me that you had a Salesman's Sample Key Lock Safe made by Hall's Safe Company."

"Yes, that's true. I'm not sure why you find that so important."

Sadie came over and sat down in her desk chair. "That's a very rare safe, Mr. Spivey. I had to look it up to be sure exactly how rare it is. I have an antique dealer friend in Denver who mentioned selling a safe like that about a year ago. I called him to check. He sold it to a man who collects rare safes. His name is Alex Grimes. Do you know him?"

Spivey's face went white, and his eyes grew wide. "I—I have no idea what you're talking about."

Sadie flipped open her laptop and turned it toward Spivey. "Maybe this will jog your memory. Here is the Web site for a company called Colorado Resorts, Inc. A little research and a couple of calls revealed that this company has a habit of sending one of their employees ahead to scout out a town, look for available land, or for business owners they can manipulate. They offer to 'invest' in these businesses and offer contracts that are written very deceptively. Colorado Resorts ends up owning the businesses they've *invested* in. Then they tear them down and build a resort."

"That sounds highly illegal," Edwin said gruffly.

"It is," Sadie agreed. "That's why they're currently under investigation. But unfortunately, they're still out trying to finagle land away from unsuspecting business owners." She looked at Barton. "This is why you've been asking so many questions about some of our residents. I know you had me on your list as well." Jane had confirmed as much at Flap Jack's the other day.

Edwin looked confused. "How is Mr. Spivey connected to Colorado Resorts?"

Sadie clicked a link on the home page. "Here are their employees. You might recognize one of their salespeople." She pointed to a picture of Spivey. Under his picture was the name *Alex Grimes*.

"Hmm," Edwin said. "I'd say it was nice to meet you, Mr. Grimes, but I'd be lying." He scowled at the man sitting in the chair. "You were at my campaign meeting. We talked about how we weren't interested in developers that wanted to change us. What didn't you understand about what we said?"

"You can't speak for the entire town," the man Sadie now knew was Alex Grimes said, his mouth twisted. "It's up to them to decide what they want to do."

"That's true," Sadie said. "But what your company does is lie to them. You tell them you're just trying to help them. You don't inform them you intend to run them out of business with your tricky contract."

"Obviously you don't realize how much revenue a ski resort would bring to this town," Grimes snapped.

"We realize it would change Silver Peak forever," Sadie said. "And that's not what we want."

"So you're saying you can speak for everyone who lives here?"

Sadie smiled. "Once they know the truth about you, I can say without reservation that no one will be interested in your offer."

"I think it would be best if you cleared out of Silver Peak, Mr. Grimes," Edwin said.

Edwin's grim demeanor seemed to frighten the diminutive man for a moment. Then anger flashed across his features. "You all are a bunch of losers. Our company pays business owners a lot of money. More than they'll ever make in this two-bit town. You are only hurting yourselves," he sputtered, "but you hicks are too dumb to know it." He pointed his finger at Edwin. "And no one tells me when to leave. I'll get out of here when I'm good and ready."

"I called Jerry Remington over at the Silver Peak Bed and Breakfast before you got here," Sadie said. "He asked me to tell you that all your belongings will be out on his front porch when you return. And there's no reason to look for another place to stay. We're not looking for your 'business,' Mr. Grimes."

"You can't call everyone in town you know," Grimes said.

"Well, Jerry knows almost everyone who owns an inn or motel in Silver Peak. But we have another way to get a message out. Actually, it's pretty efficient."

Sadie brought up the page for the *Chatterbox*. "I sent a note to our town's blog and told them all about you. Almost everyone in Silver Peak checks the *Chatterbox* daily. Let me read it to you:

The Chatterbox has learned that a man posing as Barton Spivey, a retired banker from Denver, is in fact Alex Grimes, a salesman from a company called Colorado Resorts. This company is under investigation for deceptive business practices. Mr. Grimes is seeking unsuspecting business owners who will give him control of their properties so he can demolish them and put in a ski resort!

Silver Peak's Sadie Speers uncovered this plot and passed this information on to the Chatterbox.

Silver Peak residents need to be on guard against this underhanded plot. However, it sounds as if Mr. Grimes is packing his bags and will be heading out of town as you read this blog. If he attempts to return, we will certainly spread the word!

Yours truly,
Chatterbox

Sadie addressed the crimson-faced Alex Grimes. "I want you to know that we will pray for you, Mr. Grimes. Surely you don't actually enjoy hurting good people just to make a few bucks. That would make you a very sad person. I will pray God will help you to change your life."

Grimes stood up and glared at her. "I'm not interested in your prayers. You can forget that."

"Good-bye, Mr. Grimes," Edwin said with a tight smile.

With one last angry look, Alex Grimes walked out the door.

"Well, that was quite a surprise," Edwin said. "I guess that answers one question. But that means Mr. Grimes definitely wasn't in town because of the safe."

"Actually, at first I started to wonder if I'd made a mistake. He collects antique safes. Maybe the break-in had nothing to do with the letters. Maybe he did try to steal it."

"What made you change your mind?"

"Mr. Grimes has small feet. And he only wears loafers. When I talked to Jerry, I asked him to check Mr. Grimes's closet and let me know if he had any boots. Whoever kicked in my back door either had very large feet or they were wearing boots."

"And no boots?"

Sadie nodded. "No boots."

"Amazing."

"Well, is there anything else you need me for?" Edwin asked. "I have a meeting with Jesse tonight. It seems the *Silver Peak Sentinel* wants an interview. He's going to help me prepare."

"An interview, huh? That sounds exciting."

"It could be. They're interviewing both me and James."

"I'm sure you'll be great."

"Thanks, Sadie. I hope to see you soon."

"Me too." Sadie hesitated a moment.

"Was there something else?" Edwin asked.

"Uh…no. I guess not." She smiled at him. "Thanks again for your help."

He returned her smile. "Anytime."

Sadie watched as he left. She'd come close to asking him about movie night. Should she invite him? Would he come? What would that mean?

As the questions swirled around in her head, she got her coat and hat. Then she locked up and headed home. She spent the rest of the night trying to listen to the voice of her heart. Was she ready to move forward, or was she still too tied to the past?

19

WEDNESDAY WAS A SLOW DAY AT THE SHOP, AND SADIE used the extra time to catch up on the receipts from the day before and reorganize her shelves.

As soon as she locked the doors at five, she drove over to Marla's house. She was excited to share what she'd found out at the library and prayed the woman would be receptive.

When Marla answered the door, she didn't look happy to see Sadie.

"Hi, Marla," she said. "I have something important to talk to you about," Sadie said. "May I come in for just a few minutes?"

"I don't know. I'm very busy..."

"I really think you'll want to hear this."

Although she looked reluctant, Marla pulled the door open and ushered Sadie inside. She went straight to the living room and sat down.

Marla stood with her arms folded and glared at her. "I'll give you five minutes. That's it."

"That should be enough time," Sadie said with a smile. She opened her purse and pulled out an envelope. Then she opened the envelope and removed some copies she'd made from the microfilm at the library.

"What's that?" Marla asked.

"This is proof that your grandfather, Franklin Reichert, was innocent. He didn't steal anything from the museum, and I can prove it. I can also prove who did."

"I—I don't understand."

"Your grandfather was accused of stealing over two thousand dollars in cash, along with two bronze statues by Lechmere on loan to the opera house from the Denver Art Museum. Are my facts correct?"

Marla nodded.

Sadie nodded. "But your grandfather had spinal stenosis, Marla. How could he possibly have lifted those statues?"

"He brought that up at the time, but no one would listen to him. The sheriff said he probably had an accomplice."

Sadie nodded. "There was an accomplice, all right, but it wasn't your grandfather he was helping."

Marla frowned. "What do you mean?"

Sadie pulled some of the papers out of the envelope she had in her hands and put them on the coffee table in front of her. "Did you know that the sheriff who investigated the theft was the cousin of the opera house's owner, Benjamin Wilhite?"

Marla's eyebrows peaked in surprise. "No, I had no idea."

"I doubt your grandfather did either. I did some research about Sheriff Anderson. He left town not long after the opera house incident. Moved to Denver and bought a very nice house."

"What are you saying?"

"I'm saying that the sheriff and his cousin, Benjamin Wilhite, and most probably someone at the museum in Denver, conspired to steal those valuable statues."

"But they couldn't have sold them. They were famous pieces, and the theft was in almost all the newspapers."

"They didn't have to, although selling them wasn't as impossible as you might think. Unfortunately, there are private collectors who will pay top dollar for stolen art. They don't care how they get it. They just want to own it."

"But what do you mean, they didn't have to sell them?"

"The Denver Museum was small back then. In fact, their exhibits were displayed in a large home they bought and fixed up. What they really wanted was a big commercial building so they could expand. But they couldn't afford it." Sadie smiled. "They did find enough money to insure some of their art, though."

"The statues were insured?" Marla asked, realization dawning on her face.

"Yes," Sadie said. "For fifty thousand dollars. Not a lot for famous artwork in today's market, but a fortune back then."

"So Wilhite, Anderson, and someone from the museum split the insurance money?"

"I'm not sure how the money was split, but I suspect it was enough to pay for his new house. Wilhite probably took most of it. I don't think Lechmere saw a penny. The only reason I found out about the insurance money was because I called someone at the Denver Museum. I knew there had to be money involved somehow, and the only thing that made sense was that the statues were insured. My contact at the museum went through some old records and was very surprised to learn about the insurance. She couldn't find any record that they'd received anything. They're doing some investigating of their own. Not that there's much they can do after all these years. The museum employee who most probably funneled the insurance money to Wilhite died a long time ago."

"But what happened to the statues?" Marla asked.

"I found them," Sadie said. "Benjamin Wilhite settled in England. I have a friend who located the statues in a small museum on the outskirts of the city. Martin and I went to college together, and he runs an art auction house in London. He was able to trace the statues back to Wilhite. According to the records from the museum, Wilhite held on to them for a long time—until he was certain no one was looking for them any longer."

"I can't believe you found them."

"You might like to know that a lot of artwork increases in value, but some decreases," Sadie continued. "Seems that Lechmere was upset that these statues were stolen so he made more. A lot more. Because they were no longer unique, the value plummeted. At least Wilhite didn't make much when he finally sold them."

"But how can you prove my grandfather wasn't involved in this plot?"

"Besides being able to link Wilhite to the statues, it's obvious your grandfather wasn't involved. He lost everything. His job, his home, his reputation. He didn't profit from this theft, but all the other men did."

"I—I don't know how to thank you. This really does prove that my grandfather was innocent." She sighed. "My parents will be thrilled to hear this. It's too late for Grandfather, though."

Sadie nodded. "I know, and I'm sorry about that."

"Still, this will mean a lot to my family, Sadie. Thank you."

Sadie smiled. "It's my honor to have been able to help." She stood up. "I should go." Marla walked her toward the front door. When she turned around to say good-bye, Marla gave her a quick hug. Sadie returned the hug, then stepped out onto Marla's front porch. It was cold outside, but she felt warm inside. Helping bring closure to Marla and her family's history brought her great contentment.

Sadie got into her car and sat there for a moment. She wanted to tell someone about her meeting with Marla, share her happiness about the way things had turned out. She used to tell T.R. everything. He'd always listened to her, making her feel as if he was interested in whatever she had to say. She missed that. She could always share things with Alice and Roz, but it wasn't the same. She suddenly realized that more than anyone, she wanted to tell Edwin about her visit. He'd been with her when she first talked to Marla. He'd want to know how things turned out.

Sadie checked her watch. If she hurried, she could still make it to the worship service Campfire Chapel was holding tonight. Sporadically, the church held a praise and worship night, and she always found the services to be reviving.

She drove to the church, hoping Edwin would be there. Sure enough, when she pulled into the parking lot she saw his car. She hurried toward the building, realizing the service was getting ready to start. Martin, the church's song leader, was just walking up to the podium when she stepped inside the sanctuary. It took a moment for her to see Edwin. She walked up the aisle hoping there would be a seat near him. Surprisingly, the chair next to him was empty. As Edwin rose to join the singing, she caught his eye and pointed at the chair. Edwin smiled and motioned to her. She scooted past several people and made her way over to him.

"Were you saving this?" she whispered.

He nodded. "For you."

Sadie smiled. As she took off her coat and put it on the back of her chair, she felt a sense of belonging, as if her coat was supposed to be next to Edwin's. As if it was perfectly natural for him to save her a seat. As she tried to concentrate on the music and on praising God, she couldn't get rid of a warm feeling that wrapped itself around her.

After the service, Edwin walked her to her car. She told him all about her meeting with Marla.

"I'm thrilled to hear that, Sadie," he said with a smile. "What a wonderful gift you gave her and her family." He gazed into her eyes. "You're a remarkable woman."

"I don't know about that, but I really appreciate everything you did to help me," she said. "You're a big part of what happened."

"I'm here whenever you need me," he said. The look on his face made Sadie's heart skip a beat.

After they said good-bye, Sadie got into her car and headed home. She was so busy thinking about Edwin and her visit with Marla that she was pulling into her driveway before she realized she'd left the box with the artifacts from the safe in the back room at the shop. She'd meant to grab it as she left, but the anticipation of her meeting had made her forget all about it. She thought about driving back to the store and retrieving the box, but in the end she decided it should be safe for just one night. By the time she sat down to eat her dinner, she'd forgotten all about it.

20

As Sadie drove in to work the next morning, she was still flying high over the events of the night before. Of course, she was painfully aware she still had another mystery to solve. Try as she might, she hadn't linked anyone to the safe. She was turning over in her mind all the pieces to the puzzle she had gathered when she pulled up in front of her shop. She was surprised to see Mac Slattery's car out front. She parked, got out, and approached his car. When he saw her, he got out and greeted her.

Before Sadie could say anything to him, Julie came rushing out the front door. "Oh, Sadie," she said. "We've been robbed again."

Sadie knew without asking what had been stolen. She hurried inside and checked the back room where she'd left the box the day before. It was gone. She was grateful she'd locked the gun up in a different place. At least she could be assured it wouldn't be used for nefarious reasons.

"Is anything missing this time, Sadie?" Sheriff Slattery asked.

She nodded. "They took a box with the things from the safe."

"Oh, Sadie," Julie said. "I thought you were taking the box home at night."

"I was. Last night I forgot." She shook her head. "I knew I should have come back to get them."

"How would anyone know you'd left them here?" the sheriff asked. Sadie thought he cast a suspicious glance toward Julie.

"I have no idea, Sheriff. How did they get in this time?"

"I don't know. I just got here myself."

Sadie looked at Julie for help.

"I haven't checked the doors," she said. "When I saw the door to the back room open, and things tossed about, I called the sheriff right away. I guess I should have looked around more."

"Well, let me check the entrances," the sheriff said. He pointed at Sadie. "You know the drill. Write down everything you believe is missing, and check the rest of your inventory in case the thief took something else."

Sadie nodded, but she knew in her heart that just as it had happened the first time, none of her other property had been touched. This thief had only one objective. A quick look around confirmed her suspicions. She had just finished making a list of the stolen items when the sheriff came back, a look of confusion on his face.

"The building seems to be secure," he said. He looked at Julie. "How did you get in this morning, young lady?"

"I unlocked the front door like I always do," she said. "I didn't notice anything strange until I saw the open desk drawer."

"The back door is still locked tight," Mac said, "and the dead bolt is in place." He motioned toward the door between her shop and Arbuckle's. "Is there any way in or out of that room from the outside?"

Sadie shook her head. "Luz secures it every night," Sadie said. "Then Hector locks their front door. If he got in that way, he would have to come through the coffee shop's main entrance. The Vidals would have noticed."

The sheriff walked toward the connecting door and checked the handle. "What if Luz forgot to lock it some night? Anyone could get inside here from the coffee shop."

"I suppose it's possible. But again, a thief would still have to access the front door of the coffee shop to get to this door," Sadie said as she walked toward the sheriff. "I guess we need to check with the Vidals to see if…"

Sadie stopped and stared down at the floor.

"What's wrong?"

Sadie picked up a small piece of folded cardboard. She held it up so that sheriff could see it.

"I don't understand," he said.

"Just a minute." Sadie went into the coffee shop and found Luz talking to a customer. She waited until she was finished, and then asked her to get the key to the door. "Can you spare a couple of minutes? I want to try something," she said.

"Of course," Luz replied. "Is anything wrong?"

"Someone broke into my store again. This time he took something."

"Oh, Sadie. I'm so sorry." She frowned. "Why do you want me to get my key? Do you think he came in through here?"

"I don't know. That's what I'm trying to find out. Was anything wrong with your front door this morning? Any signs that someone had tried to get in?"

"No. Everything was fine. Our entrance is very secure. We're especially careful because we're connected to you."

"I know that, and I appreciate it," Sadie said with a smile.

"I'll be right back." Luz went over to the counter and got her set of keys out of a drawer before rejoining Sadie. "What do you want me to do?"

"When I tell you to, I need you to lock the door. I'll be on the other side."

"And then what?"

"First of all, don't look at the door until I tell you to. When I call out, lock it. I'll tell you what to do after that, okay?"

"Okay," Luz said slowly.

Sadie reentered the Antique Mine. After a few seconds she called out, "Okay, Luz. You can look at the door. And go ahead and lock it just like you always do, okay? Don't do anything different."

Mac, Sadie, and Julie, who had come over to see what was happening, waited until they heard a *click*.

"The door is locked," Luz called out.

"Let's see if my theory is correct," Sadie said. She put her hand on the doorknob, turned the knob, and the door swung open.

"But...but that's impossible," Luz said. "I locked it. How in the world..."

Sadie bent down and picked up the same piece of folded cardboard she'd found earlier. "Someone slipped this into the doorjamb when you weren't looking." She put the paper between the latch and the strike plate. "This keeps the latch from connecting all the way." She took out the cardboard. "He taped it down so you wouldn't see it. You closed the door and turned the key. The latch clicked, but it didn't actually lock."

Luz shook her head. "I just assumed it was locked. But why didn't I notice this?"

Sadie studied the cardboard. "I think because the person who did this was very careful and also very determined to get what they took from the store. It seems crazy, but I suspect he must have been here every day, removing an old piece of cardboard and taping down another. Luz, can you think of anyone who came here every day this week?"

"I can think of at least a dozen people, Sadie, probably more. I have more regulars than first-timers."

Sadie had expected that to be Luz's answer, but it wasn't exactly what she wanted to hear. There was little chance of narrowing down the culprit by listing all the regulars in Luz's shop.

"Why do you think he did this from Arbuckle's?" Julie asked. "Why not in our store?"

"I suppose because Arbuckle's gets much busier than we usually do. It would be easy to quickly tape something on the door during the morning rush without anyone noticing. I open later so by the time you or I came in, the deed was already done."

"And then after checking your shop for what he wanted, he threw the old cardboard away," Mac said. "This is one determined fellow."

Julie still looked confused. "But even if the Arbuckle's door was accessible, the front door of the coffee shop wasn't. How did he get in?"

Sadie nodded. "Again, I'm guessing, but since I always close before Arbuckle's, I think he slipped inside my store and hid until the coffee shop closed. Then he looked around for what he wanted. After that he could easily leave by my front door. This time he was careful not to make the same mistakes he made when he broke in the first time. No one saw him."

Julie looked like she was trying to put the pieces together. "Why didn't the thief leave the same piece of cardboard there all the time? Wouldn't that have been easier?"

"Someone might have noticed it," Mac said.

"Yes, and also because the tape probably wouldn't have held for several days."

"Still, I should have seen it," Luz said. "I'm sorry, Sadie."

"It's not your fault. Whoever did this has been patiently waiting for me to make a mistake. I finally accommodated them. I'm the only one to blame."

"No," Mac said gruffly. "The fault belongs to the person behind this."

"Why didn't he carry away the evidence?" Julie asked. She pointed at the cardboard square. "If he'd taken this with him, we wouldn't have known how he got in."

Sadie shrugged. "He probably didn't care—or he just forgot. Most likely he was so happy about finally getting what he was after, he took off without thinking about the evidence he left behind."

Mac sighed. "Well, we'd better get started on filling out another report."

"Wait a minute," Sadie said.

"Is there something else I need to know?" the sheriff asked, his tone somber.

Sadie shook her head. "Uh, no. But now I want a cup of coffee."

Luz and Julie laughed. The sheriff shook his head, but couldn't hold back a chuckle.

"I'll get your coffee, and then we'll sit down with the sheriff," Luz said, still smiling.

"Thanks, Luz." Sadie was a little embarrassed, but talking about coffee, smelling coffee, and thinking about coffee only made her want coffee more.

Luz handed Sadie a cup, and then they sat down at a table to discuss the details of the break-in.

"So now what?" Julie asked as they finally went back into the store.

"I have no idea. To be honest, there's nothing more I could have learned anyway. It just grieves me to know that this man finally succeeded."

"I know," Julie said sympathetically.

Sadie sighed. "To be honest, I don't have anywhere else to go at this point. I'm at a complete dead end."

"Something will pop up, Sadie. You'll see."

"I hope you're right, but unless it does, I may have to give up."

21

With reports of fresh powder on the slopes, the day was much slower than the previous couple of days, but the Antique Mine still had a good morning.

Sadie was on her ladder putting a new acquisition on one of the higher shelves when Roz came in.

"Oh, Sadie. Please be careful," Roz said, her tone worried.

Sadie made a clucking sound. "You're something else, you know that? You've seen me on this ladder many times, but you've never scolded me before. What's going on?"

Roz sighed. "I guess I've been concerned about you lately. Don't get offended. Just come down here. I came to take you to lunch."

"Well, in that case…" Sadie turned back to the old oil lamp she'd just placed on the shelf, adjusted it, and then started slowly down the ladder.

"Another new treasure?" Roz asked.

"Yes. Jay Beecham is selling his mother's things. This is the second piece I've bought from him. Henrietta especially loved that lamp. A sweet reminder of her childhood. All of the children in her family had a special job. Lighting this lamp every evening was her responsibility."

"Goodness. Henrietta's only been gone a week, and he's already clearing out her house?"

"I'm afraid preserving family heritage isn't important to everyone." Sadie sighed. "It's sad, but if people didn't sell their family treasures, I'd be out of business, I guess. Henrietta was such a sweet soul. I'll miss her."

"I will too."

"I'm glad you came by, Roz. I need someone with a fresh perspective. Besides, all kinds of things have been happening that I want to tell you about."

"Well, I read the *Chatterbox* this morning. Looks like you've already solved one mystery. Glad Mr. Spivey, or should I say, Mr. Grimes, is on his way out of Silver Peak."

Sadie sighed. "I told him we'd pray for him."

Roz wrinkled her nose. "I'm sure he took that well."

"Nope," Sadie said. "But I'm still going to keep him in prayer. But I have more than just my run-in with Mr. Grimes to share with you."

Roz smiled. "I've already heard some of it, I'll bet. I ran into Troy Haggerty from the *Sentinel*. He told me you'd solved that old case from the opera house."

"With some help from my grandson."

"Theo?"

"Yes. He's decided he wants to go into law enforcement." Sadie shook her head. "I have to admit I was a little concerned when he first brought it up, but he really has a knack for detection, Roz. It's impressive."

Roz chuckled. "I guess the apple doesn't fall far from the tree."

"Well, according to some people, you should probably substitute that apple for a nut."

Roz laughed. "Hey, I think you have a lot to tell me. When can you leave?"

Sadie checked with Julie, who'd brought her lunch.

"Go ahead," she said. "We're not that busy anyway."

"So where do you want to go?" Roz asked.

"How about Sophia's?" Sadie suggested.

Sophia's was a rustic pizza place that served pizza and calzones. Many people in Silver Peak felt they made the best pizza in Colorado.

"I could go for a ham and pineapple pizza," Roz said. "How does that sound?"

Sadie smiled. "Perfect."

After telling Julie they were leaving, Roz and Sadie got their coats and walked to Sophia's. As they came in the door, the aroma of Italian spices greeted them. Sophia's had all the ambience of a real Italian restaurant. Empty bottles of wine with candles decorated the handcrafted wood tables. There were only twelve tables since a lot of the restaurant's business was take-out. Near the wood-burning oven in the back of the restaurant was a large marble-topped table covered with mounds of rising dough, fresh cheeses, and various seasonings. It was fun to watch the chef assemble the pizzas, toss them, and then put them on a wide wooden paddle and slide them into the oven.

Roz and Sadie found a table and sat down.

"Boy, I'm hungrier than I realized," Roz said as she took off her coat. "I think I'm in hibernation mode for the winter, and I'm ready to add a layer of fat to protect myself."

Sadie giggled. "Oh, Roz. Like you've ever had a layer of fat."

Roz snorted. "You'd be surprised. Once you get to a certain age, things that were once tight... aren't anymore. It's discouraging."

"Well, whatever your size, Roscoe still has that look in his eyes when he looks at you."

"I think that look is an astigmatism," Roz said, rolling her eyes.

Sadie laughed again. She'd really missed spending some time with her best friend. No one could make her laugh like Roz could.

"Speaking of someone having a look in their eye," Roz said, "what's going on with you and Edwin?"

Just then a waitress came up to take their order. Roz and Sadie asked for a large Hawaiian special.

"We're sharing it," Roz said. "And I'll take iced tea." She looked at Sadie.

"Iced tea sounds good," she said.

The waitress left and Roz pointed at Sadie. "I didn't forget my question. Has anything happened between you and Edwin?"

"Oh, Roz. He's told me cares for me, and I like him too. I'm just…"

"Afraid?"

"I guess so. I mean, T.R. and I were together for so long. I'm not sure I want to get involved again."

"Is that really it, or are you worried about Alice?"

Sadie sighed. "Believe it or not, she suggested I ask Edwin to come to our movie night on Monday."

"Why, Sadie, that's great. Why don't you do that?"

Sadie shook her head. "I don't know."

Roz frowned at her. "So Edwin is ready. Alice is ready. That just leaves you."

"I know."

Roz reached over and covered Sadie's hand with hers. "Honey, T.R. is gone, but if he could talk to you, I know he'd tell you that more than anything he wants you to be happy. You know that, don't you?"

Sadie nodded. She was certain Roz was right, but it wasn't as easy as she made it out to be. She would never be able to let go of T.R.

As if reading her mind, Roz said, "Moving forward with Edwin doesn't mean turning your back on everything you and T.R. had, Sadie. That will never go away. You're not choosing Edwin over T.R. You're just starting a new phase of your life."

"I understand that. Maybe I just need some time to think about it."

Roz patted Sadie's hand and pulled her own back. "Okay, but if you need to talk, I'm here."

"I know that. Thank you." She smiled at Roz, thankful to have a friend like her to share her thoughts with.

"So now bring me up-to-date on all the other exciting happenings in your world," Roz said. "Spill the beans, girl."

Sadie started off with the break-in that morning. Roz listened with her mouth hanging open.

"So almost everything is gone? But why? If there's nothing more to learn about that stuff, why would anyone want it?"

"That's the sixty-four-thousand-dollar question. It was obviously important enough for someone to figure out a way to gain access to the Antique Mine from Arbuckle's." She sighed. "There's something I'm just not seeing, Roz. I'm trying to put the pieces together, but they just don't seem to form a picture I can understand. I keep thinking I've missed something. Like I heard something important, but it didn't register."

"Maybe you're just missing a piece or two. When you find them, everything will make sense."

"I hope you're right." Sadie grinned. "You know what happens if you work too hard on a puzzle, don't you?"

Roz sighed. "No, but I'm sure you're going to tell me."

"Well, you can just go to pieces."

In spite of her friend's bad pun, Roz laughed. "You're too much, Sadie." She shook her head. "Did you finally get the letter translated? What did it say?"

Sadie took the letter out of her purse and handed it to Roz. She read it and handed it back.

"Wow," Roz said. "But having the letter translated still hasn't given you the information you've been searching for, has it?"

"Well, actually it's starting to create a clearer picture of the situation. I have a better understanding of *what* was going on, but I still don't know *who* was involved."

"Okay, so now tell me about Marla Reichert," Roz said. "How in the world did you figure that whole thing out? For crying out loud, it happened so many years ago."

Sadie explained how her research had uncovered the truth about the theft at the opera house.

"So all those men conspired together to steal those statues and the money? And they had no problem allowing Marla's grandfather to pay the price for their actions?"

Before Sadie could respond, the waitress came with their drinks and a basket of breadsticks. After they prayed, Roz grabbed a breadstick. "So go on," she said.

"I guess so. Franklin didn't go to jail, but his life was ruined anyway."

"That's awful," Roz said. "I feel sorry for him and his family. Good people care about their legacy. No one wants to be ashamed of their ancestors."

Sadie paused, a breadstick in her hand.

"Uh-oh. I know that look. What are you thinking?"

"Reputation, legacies, and family."

"What?"

Sadie shook her head. "Nothing. You just got me to thinking. It might not mean anything."

Roz laughed. "When you start thinking, it almost always means something."

Sadie stared thoughtfully at her friend. "You reminded me of something Theo said." She smiled at her friend. "I'm sure the missing piece of the puzzle has to do with family. But whose family? If I could just answer that question, the secret of the safe would finally be solved."

Roz stared at Sadie through narrowed eyes. "You know, I can appreciate how you're using your head to figure out what to do in this case, but when it comes to Edwin, I think you need to turn off your head and listen to your heart, my friend. That's where you'll find your answer."

Sadie sighed. "I'm sure you're right, but turning off my head is harder than I thought it would be."

"I know," Roz said gently.

Just then their waitress brought their pizza. As she and Roz ate and chatted, Sadie pondered her friend's words. Although she didn't say anything to Roz, by the time they'd eaten their delicious ham and pineapple pizza, Sadie had made a decision. It was one that lined up with her heart—and her head.

She got back to the Antique Mine around one. A little after two, Josh Ralston walked through the door. "Hello, ladies. Did you miss me?" he called out. His blue eyes twinkled with humor.

"I don't know. Who are you?" Julie said innocently. "You look slightly familiar…"

"Very funny," Josh said, laughing. "I was busy hawking my wares in Denver. I'm sure the whole town was talking about my absence."

"Yes, we were at a standstill awaiting your return," Sadie said smiling. "What wares did you hawk?"

"I'll have you know that I'll be spending the winter building ten chairs."

Sadie shook her head. "You'll be spending the winter building thirteen chairs." She pulled open her desk drawer and pulled out three invoices, orders for Josh's Adirondack chairs.

"Well, there goes the ski trip I'd planned," he said. "Guess I'll spend the winter months being a hermit."

"We also sold the child's rocking horse and two jewelry boxes," Sadie said. "So we have some money to ease your suffering."

Josh sauntered up to Sadie's desk. "All joking aside, this helps a ton." He studied Sadie for a moment. "I managed to catch Spike Harris at his store. He told me you had a break-in but that nothing was stolen. Weird. Are you two all right?"

"We're fine, Josh, thanks." Sadie appreciated Josh's concern but didn't see a reason to explain the details of the robbery to him.

Sadie handed him a check to cover his sales. "Great work, Josh. So any dates lined up?"

"No, not yet. I just got back, ladies. Give me time." He laughed. He waved his check. "I need to get going, but it was great to see you both."

"Great coat, by the way," Julie said. "New?"

Josh looked down at his brown suede jacket with fuzzy wool cuffs around the bottom of the sleeves and the lapel. "Yep. A good old Colorado-style coat. Keeps me warm even though I feel like I should open a sheep ranch."

Sadie eyes widened as she stared at him. "A coat," she said softly.

"What did you say, Sadie?" Julie asked.

Josh laughed. "I think she wants my coat."

Sadie shook her head, trying to clear her thoughts. "As much as I like it, I think it'd be big on me." She smiled. "But I'm sure glad you wore it today. Josh, do you know how long Spike will be in his store today?"

He looked at Sadie curiously. "As a matter of fact, he told me he's giving lessons all day."

Sadie smiled. "Thanks. Glad you're back."

"Yeah, me too. See ya later, ladies."

After Josh left, Sadie told Julie she needed to run a quick errand. She had a task she didn't look forward to, but it had to be done. Before she walked out the door, she took something out of her desk drawer. As she put on her coat, she prayed that God would give her the wisdom to handle a situation that could cost her a friend if she wasn't careful.

22

A BRISK WINTER WIND PUSHED SADIE DOWN THE STREET A little faster than she wanted to go. She pulled her collar up as she made her way to the Silver Peak Music Emporium. Before opening the front door she gazed in through the front window. It looked like Spike was just wrapping up a lesson. Sadie recognized the son of one of her former students.

"Hello, Michael," she said with a smile.

"Hi, Mrs. Speers," he said.

"How are your lessons coming?"

Michael looked at Spike. "I'm not sure. I keep putting my fingers on the wrong strings."

Spike grinned at him. "You're doing fine, Michael. It takes a while to get it right."

A car honked outside and Sadie turned around to see Michael's mother, Sue, parked in front of the store. She waved to Sue as Michael grabbed his coat and ran out.

"It's good to see you, Sadie," Spike said, putting his guitar back in its case. "Did you just stop by to visit, or can I do something for you?"

Sadie sat down in one of the chairs Spike had lined up against the wall. "I need to ask you something, Spike."

He sat down on the stool where Michael had been only seconds before. "Sure."

"Were you in the Antique Mine the night of the break-in?"

Spike's face flushed. "I—I don't know what you mean."

"Laura saw someone run away that night. She thought it was you, but she wasn't certain. That's why I didn't say anything. Then I found this. It was stuck in a corner of a display case." Sadie took a small envelope out of her purse. She pulled it open and took out a small tuft of black fur. "At first I didn't know what this meant. I thought it was hair. But the closer I looked at it, the less it looked like hair. It wasn't until I was talking to Josh that I realized it wasn't hair at all. It's wool, from a coat." Sadie studied him for a moment before saying, "I believe it came off your coat, Spike." She pointed to Spike's coat, which had been tossed on top of a piano near the wall. "I could match this torn piece to your sleeve, but I don't think I need to do that, do I?"

Spike looked dumbstruck for a moment, then shook his shaggy head. "I'm sorry, Sadie. I should have told you what happened right away, but I was afraid you'd think I was the one who broke in."

"Why don't you tell me what happened?" Sadie asked gently.

Spike took a deep breath. "I was passing by the store that night after playing at a club on the edge of town, and I saw a light in your store. Not like a regular light. It was moving. Like a flashlight. I drove around to the rear of the store and parked. The back door was open. I went inside to see what was going on, and I guess I frightened your intruder away. He ran past me, almost knocking me down. I tried to chase him, but he got away." Spike shook his head. "I called the sheriff and then I took off." He ran his hand through his hair. "I should have waited. I should have told the sheriff what I saw. But I've never been in a situation like that before. I panicked. Last thing I wanted was for you to think I was guilty, and since I didn't get a good look at the intruder, I wouldn't have been any help to you anyway. I guess I just thought it best to...to stay out of the way." He looked down. "But what I did was cowardly. Can you ever forgive me?"

Sadie smiled. "Of course. But you should have known I wouldn't have accused you, Spike."

"I know. I realized that later. But I worried it was too late. If I delayed telling you about the break-in, I worried you and Mac would wonder *why* I'd delayed telling you. Avoiding telling you in the first place made me look even guiltier."

"I get it, Spike," Sadie said, gazing warmly at the forty-four-year-old man who in that moment looked more like a contrite child. "Anyway, you probably frightened the burglar away. Most likely you're the reason nothing was stolen that night."

The tightness in Spike's face relaxed, and a small, tentative smile flitted across his face.

"I know you didn't get a good look at him, Spike, but was there anything about the intruder that happens to stick in your mind? A sound? A smell? Anything?"

Spike shook his head slowly. "No. I don't think so." Suddenly his eyes widened. "Wait a minute. This is going to sound weird..."

"Anything could help. What is it?"

"He squeaked."

Sadie's eyebrows shot up in surprise. "He squeaked?"

Spike nodded. "I heard a strange squeaking sound when he ran past me."

Sadie had a mental picture of herself following people around Silver Peak, trying to find out if they squeaked. "Well, maybe that's just the thing that will help me figure out who it was. Thank you, Spike." She got up to leave. "I'll see you at church this Sunday."

Spike nodded. "See you then. And thanks again, Sadie."

She smiled at him and left the music store. On her way back to her shop, she contemplated the tip he'd given her. Why would a man squeak? Sadie's grandmother had squeaked because of her old-fashioned hearing aid, but today's hearing aids were much more advanced. Sometimes her bones creaked too. Could that have been what Spike heard? But anyone who made that much noise when they moved probably wouldn't be capable of running away from anyone.

Since they weren't busy, Sadie sent Julie home around four-thirty. Sadie was ready to close up and take off herself, but as she started making preparations to leave, the front door opened and Jane Remington came in.

"Jane, hello," Sadie said warmly. "I'm happy to see you. How can I help you?"

"Nice to see you too, Sadie. Thanks again for getting rid of that creepy Barton Spivey. I mean, Alex Grimes. I know it's crazy, but I swear the aura of the B and B feels lighter without him around."

"I believe it." Sadie pointed at the box Jane held in her hands. "What have you got there?"

"These are some old books that belonged to my father. I found them when I was cleaning up the attic. When we bought the B and B, we stored a lot of things away. We've been so busy I haven't had time to go through all of it yet, but I did find these. I thought you might be interested in them. They contain some intriguing history about Silver Peak."

Sadie smiled. "You know how much I love books like that. Let's see what you've got."

Jane pulled the books out of the box and put them on the counter. "As you can see, these are about the early days of Silver Peak." She pointed to the book on top of the stack. "This one is especially interesting. It's about one of the early mine owners. There was a story back then that he'd discovered another vein of silver but covered the entrance so no one would find it. According to gossip, he died before the silver was ever found. Some people think it's still out there somewhere."

Sadie chuckled. "I've heard the story."

Jane smiled. "There are also a couple of early schoolbooks. And here is an old yearbook. I wish I had time to look through it more thoroughly, but I just don't think I'll be able to. I have pictures of my father, so I don't really need his yearbook. It occurred to me that someone in town would love to have it. Maybe someone with a family member who attended Silver Peak High School."

"I'm sure you're right," Sadie said. She flipped open one of the books. The name *Edgar Kendall* was written inside the front cover. Sadie frowned. "Who is Edgar Kendall?"

"My father."

"But I met your father and mother once. I thought their name was Meyer."

Jane nodded. "Gareth Meyer was my stepfather. I called him my father because that's who he was to me. My biological father died before I was born."

"Oh, Jane. I didn't know that. I'm so sorry."

Jane waved her hand dismissively. "Thank you. I'm very grateful to have been raised by a wonderful man. I couldn't have had a better father than my stepfather."

"How did your father die?"

"In the war." Jane put her hand on one of the books as if it might give her a connection to the man she never knew. "Actually, it was really sad. The war was almost over. Soldiers were already coming home. My mother was told they found his body in a field outside of the town where he was stationed. The army assumed he'd been shot by German sympathizers since there wasn't a battle that day. I guess he was just in the wrong place at the wrong time."

Sadie sighed. "Your mother must have been devastated. Raising a baby alone must have been very hard."

Jane smiled. "She was blessed to have support from family. And from our angel."

"Your angel?"

Jane laughed. "It's a story I don't tell very often."

Sadie grinned at her. "Well, now you're committed. You can't leave me hanging!"

"Fair enough," Jane laughed. "I suppose I shouldn't tease a history buff!"

"Most certainly not," Sadie said playfully. "Out with it."

"Well," Jane began, "not long after my father was killed, Mom started receiving money from someone who wrote a letter telling us that he wanted to help us. That he knew my biological dad, and that they were friends. He never identified himself, but the gifts came for many years. Even for a while after my mother remarried."

"That's incredible. Did you ever learn who your angel was?"

Jane stared wistfully at the pile of books. "I know this sounds silly, but I've always felt…" She sighed. "Don't think I'm crazy, but I like to think that somehow my biological father was behind it. I know that's impossible, but it makes me feel good." She shook her head. "Now you really think I'm crazy."

Sadie chuckled. "No, I don't. It's a lovely thought. And who knows? Maybe he did have something to do with it." She pointed at the books. "Are you sure you want to get rid of all of these, Jane?"

She nodded. "I have other things that belonged to my dad. These books should be read and appreciated, not stuck away in a box in my attic."

"What do you want for them?"

"Nothing."

When Sadie started to protest, Jane held her hand up. "If you want them, Sadie, I'd like you to have them." She chuckled. "Besides, you gave us such a great deal on that lamp we probably owe you money."

"Well, you don't owe me anything, but I understand. You're not the first person to refuse money for something that's been in their family." She smiled at Jane. "I'm honored to accept them. I promise you they will be read and appreciated."

"I'm so glad. That makes me very happy." Jane glanced at her watch. "Well, I'd better get going. Let's get together for lunch soon."

"You've got a date. Just call me."

Jane smiled. "I look forward to it."

After Jane left, Sadie locked up. She started to put the books away, but decided at the last moment to take them with her. She loved Silver Peak history. Poring through the books would be fun.

She went next door to tell Luz and Hector she was leaving. Luz carefully locked their connecting door. Sadie knew she would be vigilant. No one would be able to fool with that door again. Of course, the thief had already gotten what he wanted, so it didn't really matter.

Sadie walked out into the cold, clear afternoon. The trees were still adorned with fall colors: reds, oranges, yellows, and gold, and the ground was covered with snow. Colorado was breathtaking this time of year. Sadie never grew tired of it. She put the books in the passenger seat and got in. On the way home, she stopped at the pet store and got a new toy for Hank. He loved his squeaky toys, often piling them up together as if he were counting his stash. He also loved playing fetch with anything he could find. It didn't have to be a ball, any of his toys would do. Since their walks had grown shorter due to the winter weather, Sadie planned to play catch with him after dinner.

When she got home, she carried Jane's books inside, put them on the coffee table, and made a quick dinner. Alice was always bringing her storage containers of leftover stew, soups, or whatever she'd recently made. Sadie stacked them up in the freezer and took them out on nights just like this. She found a container with chili and stuck it in the microwave. Before long, the spicy aroma of Alice's wonderful chili filled the kitchen.

After dinner, she and Hank played for almost an hour. By the end of it they were both tired and happy. Hank snuggled up next to her on the couch and within minutes was snoring peacefully, smiling in his sleep at whatever it was that made dogs smile.

Sadie had made a cup of chamomile tea and set it next to her on the coffee table, along with Jane's books. She started reading the book about the miner who had supposedly hidden a vein of silver that had never been mined. It was interesting, but Sadie was tired and kept drifting off to sleep. She put that book down and picked up the yearbook. She loved looking at pictures from long ago. The yearbook was over ninety years old, and it made Sadie sad to realize that every fresh face she looked at was long gone. She scanned the pictures of different classes, searching for Jane's father. She finally found him. Edgar Kendall was a handsome boy whose features reminded her of Jane. It was clear they were related. Then she glanced at the picture next to Edgar and what she saw made her almost drop the yearbook.

Thinking she must have read the name wrong, she checked again. Sure enough, she was right the first time. As Sadie sat on her couch, pieces of the puzzle she'd been thinking about for so long began to fall into place. After contemplating the situation for a while, she picked up her phone, dialed a number, and asked a question. The person on the other end promised to get back to her with the answer. Sadie put the phone down and stared into the crackling fire in her fireplace. About thirty minutes later, the phone rang, and by the time Sadie hung up, she knew who the items in the safe belonged to, and she was pretty certain she knew why they were so important.

Friday morning Sadie arrived at the Antique Mine around nine. She'd called Julie and given her the morning off. Then she made another phone call, arranging a meeting at her shop. The sign on the door was turned to Closed.

Around nine-fifteen there was a knock on the door. Sadie went over, opened it, and let her visitor in. "Have a seat," she said, pointing toward a chair that sat next to her desk. She was going to offer him coffee, but he already had his usual cup from Arbuckle's. She'd gotten hers, as well. She took a sip as she stared at the man sitting so close to her.

"I knew it was over when you called last night," Jerry Remington said.

23

"OH?" SADIE SAID, ALTHOUGH SHE WASN'T SURPRISED.

"It was the only reason you'd ask that particular question."

"You didn't explain to Jane why I asked, did you?"

"Actually, yes. I told her you'd called and why. I had to. She was sitting right there with me. I couldn't lie my way out of it this time. She looked through an old diary of her mother's and found the answer. Then she called you back. But I still didn't tell her the whole truth." He shook his head. "I've been keeping this secret so long the idea of finally facing the consequences terrifies me. If I'd just been honest when I found out, we could have been past this by now."

"You're right, but I truly believe you both can recover."

He took a sip of coffee, then put the cup down. Sadie could see the lines of worry on his face and felt sorry for him.

"When did you start to suspect?" Jerry asked.

"I couldn't put my finger on it right away. After Jane called me back last night, I realized what had been bothering me. When you first saw the things from inside the safe, you mentioned that they belonged to a 'corporal.' But the jacket was turned over. The insignia wasn't showing. There was no way you could have known that."

"I—I didn't realize I'd said it."

"Then there are your boots. Your rubber boots."

He frowned. "My boots? I don't understand."

"When they're wet they squeak when you walk, Jerry. Mine do the same thing. Spike heard a squeaking sound the night of the break-in. I should have realized it sooner."

He shook his head. "Undone by a pair of boots. How ridiculous."

"That was just one small part of the puzzle, believe me. I began to realize a few days ago that no one would go to such lengths for items that seemed to have such limited monetary value. There had to be another reason. The only thing important enough to cause someone to react so strongly was love. Then Jane brought those books in. I was looking through the yearbook she gave me and I saw..."

"You saw my father's picture."

She nodded. "Reuben King. Right next to Edgar Kendall."

Jerry frowned. "But there must be more."

Sadie nodded. "There is. You told me your father hadn't lived in Silver Peak before coming here to manage the opera house. You also told me he came after the renovations in the late forties. That's why I never thought seriously about Reuben being the owner of the safe. But once I discovered that your father had lived here as a boy, I began to realize I couldn't believe anything else you'd said. I'm sure a little checking will prove Reuben was in town well before the work on the opera house was completed. He had plenty of time to put the safe he purchased in France inside that wall." She shook her head. "And then, of course, there was the vase."

"The vase?"

"You broke it so you'd have an excuse to come here and get a look at the safe. But you made a mistake. When I got in this morning I looked closely at the credit card receipt you signed when you bought the lamp. You have an odd way of writing the letter *E*. It looks like a *C*. The person who sent the letters wrote exactly the same way."

"I tried to disguise my handwriting."

"If you had just changed that one letter I might not have tied the receipt and the notes together."

Jerry's sigh was full of resignation. "That stupid safe. My father loved it when he bought it, but later, after what happened, everything that came from overseas became a curse to him. That's why he put those things inside that safe. They reminded him of that awful day."

"What have you been hiding, Jerry? What happened on that day? Why couldn't you have just claimed ownership of the safe from the beginning? I'm sure Ardis would have given it to you, no questions asked."

Jerry stared at Sadie, anguish written clearly on his face. "I hid the truth because I was afraid I would lose my wife. How do you tell someone you love something like this, Sadie? Something so terrible?"

"Why don't you practice with me, Jerry? Tell me the whole story."

Jerry took a deep, trembling breath. After staring off in the distance for several seconds, he finally began to talk. "All I can do is tell you what my father told me on his deathbed. His father, my grandfather, was a traveling salesman for a vacuum sweeper company. As the title implies, he traveled a lot. My father rarely stayed in one place for long. When he was fifteen, they came to Silver Peak. My grandfather was in charge of all the territory in and around this town. Dad was enrolled in school here, and he made friends with Jane's father, Edgar Kendall. In fact, they were best friends. Although Dad had learned not to get too close to people in case he had to pull up stakes and move again, Grandfather told him they would be staying in Silver Peak for a long time. Dad believed him. Unfortunately, six months later, they left for Chicago. Dad didn't see Edgar again until they ran into each other in the army. They were both stationed in a small town in France, near the Belgium border. They were even in the same company. Dad was thrilled to see his old friend, and Edgar felt the same way." Jerry paused as if continuing with his story was too difficult.

"But something happened," Sadie said gently, trying to urge him on. "There was a man named Hans Schweiss. Who was he?"

"Hans Schweiss was a Nazi officer stationed in Belgium," Jerry said softly. "Dad was an assistant to a high-ranking army officer, someone who was involved in the movement of troops and was privy to information the army wanted to keep secret. Somehow Schweiss convinced Dad that he believed Germany was on the wrong side of the war. He insisted that if Dad gave him certain information, it would bring a quicker end to the fighting. That American lives would be saved."

"Isn't that naive?" Sadie asked gently.

Jerry shrugged. "Probably. But Dad believed him." He looked at Sadie, his eyes welling with tears. Sadie assumed it was from the stress of holding this story in for so long. "No matter what he did, he was my father. I have to believe he was trying to help our country."

Sadie nodded. She understood and had no desire to pursue Reuben's guilt or innocence. That wasn't her business. It was something better left to God.

"Anyway, Edgar found out about it. He confronted Dad and Hans, demanding that they stop what they were doing or he'd turn them both in. There was a struggle. Dad's gun went off, and Edgar was killed. Dad felt terrible, obviously. At that point, he thought about going to the army and telling them the truth. But he didn't. He was afraid."

"And what about Hans Schweiss?"

"Now, that was really interesting. He knew my father was a Christian. He'd been asking Dad a lot of questions about God. Somehow, after Edgar was killed, Schweiss felt convicted of his part in his death. He asked Dad to pray for him, and he accepted Christ. Then he went back to his superiors. He refused to give them any more information gathered from my father. He also told them of his conversion."

"And they executed him."

Jerry nodded. "Sadly, yes. After that, Dad felt as if he had the blood of two friends on his hands. He came back to the States, determined to take care of Edgar's wife and child. While he was checking on their welfare, he found out about the job at the opera house. He applied for it and got it. During the construction, he hid the safe in the wall, along with personal belongings that reminded him of his time in the army. I can't explain exactly why he didn't just dispose of them. He said it had something to do with not being able to throw away his sins."

Sadie nodded. Reuben couldn't forgive himself enough to let go of the past. Instead, he concealed it, not really understanding why.

"He met and married my mother, and he never told anyone he'd lived here for a few months as a child. He didn't want to be connected to Edgar. It was so long ago, and he was here such a short time, no one remembered him. Then he worked on building a life here even though he never forgot what happened. Down through the years he kept an eye on Jane's mom and on Jane. Sent them money."

"Jane's angel."

He nodded. "Yes, Jane's angel."

"You grew up and then the unthinkable happened."

"The kind of thing that should only occur in the movies, I guess. I fell in love with Jane. Dad was so conflicted. Although it would help him to keep an eye on her, at the same time, would Jane really want to marry the son of the man who killed her father? In the end, he decided not to do anything to stop it, and we were married. Not only was he a wonderful father, he was an incredible father-in-law. Jane loved him very much."

"You must have been shocked when Reuben told you the truth. How could you bear it for so long, Jerry?"

A sigh escaped him that seemed to come from somewhere deep inside. "It's been awful. But how could I tell her? How could I hurt her? Jane is the love of my life. I would never do anything to cause her pain."

"I know that, but keeping secrets hurt your father. Now you're paying the price too. If only you'd gone to Jane at the beginning…"

"It's too late for that now." He gazed at Sadie, and she was struck by the sadness in his eyes. "I broke into your store, Sadie. I'm sorry. I was so desperate to protect Jane, to keep this secret."

"But none of your father's possessions pointed to him," Sadie said.

"How could I know that? He told me about the letter. And the Bible. I was afraid there was a link there. Something that would lead you to Dad. I thought about trying to grab the entire safe before you got it open, but how could I explain that to Jane? Or anyone else? Word would have gotten around that the safe was my father's, and in a small community like ours, people would have wanted to know what was inside it. I'd have to explain everything. It was too risky." He took a deep breath. "The night before I broke in the first time, I suddenly remembered a notation inside one of Dad's old phone books. Numbers. I realized they could be the combination to the safe. I had to try them. If I could open the safe, I could grab whatever was inside, and no one would ever know the truth. But Spike Harris came in and caught me before I could finish dialing the entire combination. I was determined to get my dad's things so I waited day after day until one night when you finally forgot them. I went into the back room and finally found the box. I'm sorry I made such a mess. I was afraid to turn on the light and it was difficult to see. I'm afraid I knocked several things over."

"You're the one who actually led me to him." She sighed. "You and Reuben gave me what I needed to figure out the secret of the safe. That was his desk at the opera house, wasn't it?"

"Yes. His first desk. I had no idea he carved the safe's combination into the wood until you told me. If I'd known I would have gotten rid of it." Jerry rubbed his eyes. He looked tired. "My goal was to take away anything that might lead you to Dad. I want you to know that I never intended to hurt you, Sadie."

"I understand that. But how could you send me those letters? Didn't you realize they would cause me concern? Frighten people who care about me?"

He hung his head for a moment. "I was just so desperate to stop you. It was so hard writing those notes. You've always been a good friend. I honestly didn't want to scare you."

"I know. You never suggested you would actually harm me."

"Still, I shouldn't have written them. I've had two chances to be honest about the past. Once when Dad told me the truth, and the other when the safe was discovered. I'm just sorry you've had to force me to finally confess." He shook his head. "I've been such a fool, and because of it I'll probably lose my wife."

Sadie took his hand. "Jerry, Jane will be shocked. And she will be hurt. But in the end, she will understand and forgive you. Jane loves you. Truly loves you."

"I pray you're right. I'm not so sure Sheriff Slattery will understand though."

Sadie frowned at him. "Why are you concerned about the sheriff?"

"I broke into your store, Sadie. I stole from you. Unless I'm mistaken, that's against the law."

Sadie squeezed his hand and let it go. "First of all, I have no intention of filing charges against you for the break-ins, and as far as stealing from me, that's not true. What you took belongs to you, not to me. You didn't remove anything from my store that wasn't yours. Mac won't hear about any of this from me. Nor will anyone else."

Jerry wiped his eyes with the back of his hand. "Thank you, Sadie. It's much more than I deserve."

"You're wrong, Jerry. Please don't internalize this. Your father caused this situation whether he meant to or not. The only thing you did was to keep his secret because you didn't want to hurt your wife. What you did to me, you did out of desperation. That's understandable."

Jerry sighed again. "So now what do I do?"

Sadie stood up. "You go home and talk to your wife."

"And what will you do?"

Sadie pondered his question. "I don't intend to do anything. Telling the truth is up to you, Jerry."

"I can live with that," Jerry said, standing to his feet.

Sadie knew Jerry was afraid to talk to Jane, and she felt bad for him, but telling her everything was the only way the couple could be free. This secret had been hidden for too long. The truth, just like the safe, had finally been revealed.

Sadie walked Jerry to the door and after giving him a hug, said good-bye. As he walked away, she leaned against the door and prayed that God would guide Jerry and Jane through the valley they were about to walk through.

Then she walked over to her phone and made a call that she suspected might send her life in a brand-new direction.

"Edwin? Hi, it's Sadie. I was wondering if you'd like to join my family and me for a home viewing of *The Secret Garden*?"

24

"So what did you think about the movie?" Sadie asked her grandkids after *The Secret Garden*'s credits began to roll.

"It was pretty good," Sara said. "At first I thought that boy was kind of weird, but then I started feeling sorry for him."

"I liked it," Theo said, "but next time can we get something a little more..."

"Manly?" Sadie said, grinning.

"You might like *The Maltese Falcon*," Edwin said. "Good story about a detective."

"Now we're talkin'."

Sadie laughed. "We'll put it on the list."

"Mom, let me help clean up," Alice said. She got up and started picking up their empty plates.

"Thank you, honey."

"Can I help?" Edwin asked.

"No, you stay here. Maybe you and the kids can write down some ideas for future movies." Sadie got up and went over to a small lamp table. She opened the drawer and took out a small pad of paper and a pen. She took it back and handed it to Edwin. "Movies for all of us, please. Even the unmanly ones."

Edwin laughed. "You might be surprised to hear that *Little Women* is one of my favorite movies."

"Oh no," Theo said, looking dismayed.

Edwin winked at him. "Hey, we haven't talked about Sherlock Holmes, Charlie Chan, and Nick Charles."

Theo perked up. "Sounds promising."

"Maybe we could add a couple of those movies...once in a while," Sadie said.

"That sounds fair," Edwin replied, smiling at Theo and Sara.

Sadie and Alice carried the dishes into the kitchen and put them on the counter next to the sink.

"Great enchiladas, Mom," Alice said. "They reminded me of the enchiladas at Los Pollitos."

Sadie started scraping the dishes. "Doesn't surprise me. Gloria Garza gave me the recipe after making me promise I wouldn't share it with anyone else."

Alice leaned against the counter and waited for her mother to hand her the dishes that were ready to go in the dishwasher. "Not even with your own daughter?"

"No, not even with you, dear."

Alice laughed. "Well, I guess I'll have to be content to come over here and eat them."

Sadie handed her a plate. "That sounds wonderful to me." She paused in her dish-scraping duties. "So what do you think?"

Alice straightened up after placing the plate in the dishwasher.

"About what?" she asked innocently.

Sadie sighed. "You're teasing me. About Edwin, of course."

Alice put her hand on her mother's arm. "I think he's marvelous. I already liked him, you know. But seeing the way the kids react to him made me like him even more."

Sadie nodded and went back to the dishes.

"So what now, Mom?"

"I don't know. We're good friends. If something else happens…"

Alice grinned. "I think something else has already happened as far as Edwin is concerned. But he seems to be the kind of man who will allow you all the time you need to…feel something else, if that's what you need."

Sadie handed Alice the next plate. She wasn't ready to talk about her feelings for Edwin yet. In her mind, that conversation should be between them first. Tonight had been wonderful. Having him with her family had felt so right.

"Thank you for being so kind to him," she said. "And for allowing me to…"

"It's not up to me to allow you to do anything, Mom," Alice said. "And as far as Dad goes, I know how much you loved him. And still do. Having Edwin in your life doesn't change what you had with Dad."

Her eye wandered to the beautiful vase of flowers Edwin had brought to her tonight. Wildflowers and roses. It had been a long time since someone had brought her flowers. She couldn't help but smile.

"Do you mind if I change the subject for a minute? I'm wondering about Jerry and Jane. What's going on with them? They've closed the B and B for a couple of weeks, and they're not talking to anyone. Is something wrong?"

Sadie shrugged. "I think they're just trying to work out some things between themselves. I do have some good news that concerns them though."

"What's that?" Alice asked.

"The Historic Preservation Council has approved their idea for the dinner theater in the opera house, as long as she and Jerry run it. They seem to be genuinely excited."

"And how did you swing that?"

Sadie smiled. "Edwin was able to prove to Luz that using local talent is usually more successful than bringing in the kind of celebrities we could afford. Luz is a reasonable woman. Once she was faced with the facts, she quickly changed her mind."

"That's great news."

"I have some other good news." She smiled at her daughter. "The safe is going to auction and the proceeds will be given to help finish the work on the opera house."

"Mom! Really?" Alice laughed. "Who's the owner of the safe?"

Sadie shook her head. "It's not for me to tell. But let's just say that everything's turned out okay and leave it at that."

Alice frowned. "But what about the break-ins and the threatening letters?"

"I know who was behind it and because of the circumstances, I'm not pressing charges."

Alice started to say something else, but Sadie hushed her. "You'll just have to trust me when I ask you to let it go."

Alice sighed. "Okay, Mom. I trust you, but I'm still curious."

"I don't blame you, honey."

"I can't believe you not only figured out the secret of the safe, but you also unraveled a seventy-year-old crime involving the opera house," Alice said, shaking her head.

Sadie smiled. "I had help. Theo has quite a head for figuring out puzzles—and people."

Alice nodded and she took another dish to put in the dishwasher. "That's one of the reasons that after his senior year, he'll be going to college to work on a degree in criminology. With my blessing."

"I'm so glad, honey. I know he'll be wonderful."

"I'm really excited to hear about the dinner theater. It sounds like so much fun."

"I think it will be. Jerry has asked me to help contribute some writing for plays about the early days of Silver Peak."

"Sounds like fun. You'll do a super job."

Laughter from the living room made it clear Edwin and the grandkids were having a good time. Hearing their joyful voices made Sadie feel happy.

After she and Alice finished the dishes, they cut pieces of caramel apple pie for everyone and carried them into the living room.

About an hour later, Sadie's family left for home. Even though it was cold outside, Sadie and Edwin decided to sit outside on the porch swing for a while. Away from the lights of town, the sky looked like a glittering blanket of stars. Gazing up at a Colorado night sky always filled Sadie with awe.

"I had a wonderful time tonight, Sadie," Edwin said. "Thank you so much for inviting me over. I hope you'll ask me again sometime."

Sadie chuckled. "Sounds like you've got the kids all excited about upcoming movie choices. Seems to me you should be here to take responsibility for your suggestions."

"I'd like that."

"I have deep feelings for you, Sadie. You know that, don't you?"

"Yes," she said quietly. And although she didn't tell him she felt the same way, she reached over and took his hand. They sat there together for quite a while, enjoying the beauty of God's creation and anticipating the future.

About the Author

CAROLE JEFFERSON IS THE PEN NAME FOR A TEAM OF WRITERS who have come together to create the series Mysteries of Silver Peak. *Nobody's Safe* was written by Nancy Mehl. Nancy is the author of eighteen books in the mystery and suspense genre. She won the Carol Award for mystery in 2009 and was a Romantic Times Reviewer's Choice nominee for 2013. Nancy lives with her husband, Norman, and her very active puggle, Watson, in Festus, Missouri.

Read on for a sneak peek of another exciting book in Mysteries of Silver Peak!

Silver Surprise

"Sadie, hi!" Luz Vidal said with a welcoming grin when she saw Sadie appear in the small doorway that connected Sadie's antique shop, The Antique Mine, with Arbuckle's, the charming coffee shop that Luz ran with her husband, Hector. "Just popping in for your regular?"

Sadie gave a rueful smile. It was bad enough to have a coffee shop next door, especially one with treats as tempting as the ones at Arbuckle's, the delectable baked goods created by Maggie Price. Before she met her husband, Lou, Maggie had been a big-time pastry chef in New York City before moving to Silver Peak to enjoy some of life's simpler pleasures, but she hadn't lost her touch: both the Market and Luz's pastry cabinet at Arbuckle's were always full with a rotating selection of inventive, and delicious, temptations, like maple blondie brownies, grasshopper cookie sandwiches with mint butter cream smoothed between chocolate cookies, and red velvet bar cookies frosted with the best cream cheese frosting Sadie had ever tasted. But to have a door directly between her shop and Arbuckle's, with the delicious scent of coffee and hints of sweet things pouring through it all day, was too much for Sadie to resist. She tried to go light on the treats, although she didn't always succeed. And anyway, she figured all her long walks with Hank helped ward off the calories. But she did love her coffee, and Luz usually started to set up Sadie's standard order the instant she saw Sadie come through the door.

Today, however, Sadie shook her head.

Luz, who had already bent down to pull a clean coffee cup, looked up in surprise, a questioning look in her eyes.

"I'm meeting a friend," Sadie explained. Even as she said the word, she felt a little pang. Edwin Marshall was one of her oldest friends. She'd known him even longer than she'd known T.R., her husband, before she was widowed. In fact, she couldn't remember the first time she had met Edwin, who sometimes liked to joke that they might have made their first acquaintance as babies in the Silver Peak maternity ward, although that was a stretch—they'd been born in the same year, but not the same month. But they'd both grown up in Silver Peak, and Edwin had been such a familiar part of life there that he seemed like part of the town itself, just like the streets Sadie knew so well, or the peaks of the mountains outside of town, which Sadie had memorized without trying, simply from gazing up at them so many times over so many years.

But Edwin had never really been only a friend, not since the romance they had shared as teenagers. They'd been young, of course, and they'd had lots of fun together—but neither of them were flighty, even as teenagers, and the feelings they'd had for each other then had been more serious than a fleeting teenage crush. That romance had ended when Edwin went off to college. Their feelings had been serious, but both of them were also sensible, even as kids, and they'd agreed that it made sense to let their relationship end when Edwin left Silver Peak. Of course, part of Sadie had hoped that Edwin might come swooping back to claim her—and maybe part of Edwin had secretly hoped to do that as well. But that wasn't where life had taken them. When Sadie had gone off to college, she'd met T.R., and Edwin had married and moved to Chicago, and their paths hadn't crossed for decades, until Edwin moved back to town, a widower, after his retirement.

He'd already made it clear that he would like to rekindle their own romance, but Sadie still wasn't entirely sure she was ready for that. She'd spent most of her life believing she would never love anybody but T.R., and for a while after he passed away, she hadn't even wanted to live without him. But Edwin had continued to be a good friend to her since he moved back, always there for her, but never too insistent—and a few times, more and more recently, she'd wondered if the little thrill of pleasure she sometimes felt when he stepped into the Antique Mine, or called her on the phone, was more than just friendship itself.

"How are you doing today, Luz?" Sadie asked, to cover the uncertainty she felt.

Luz smiled again. "It's been a good day so far," she said. "Marisol called from school last night. It's always so good to hear from her."

Marisol was Luz's daughter, who Sadie had gotten to know during her visits home from college. She shared her mother's thick brown hair, dark eyes, and beauty, and to Sadie, it was obvious that she had a crush on Josh, a handsome young man who was gaining a national reputation for his innovative woodwork. Sadie had gotten to know him when he started supplying interesting pieces of his carpentry to her shop, and she liked him. He was unfailingly kind, and patient, but not because he didn't have any spirit. He could also get incredibly excited about the intricacies of his work. And at twenty-six, he was really only a few years older than Marisol, who was twenty. Sadie had always liked the idea of Marisol's crush turning into an actual romance, but for now, Josh just seemed to think of Marisol as a college kid.

"Any big news?" Sadie asked.

Luz's eyes lit up. But as she began to speak, she hesitated. After a minute, a smile spread over her face again. "I guess not," she said. "Not really. I mean, not anything that would really be news to anyone who's not her mother. She's doing well in classes. She seems happy."

"That's great," Sadie said. "If you ask me, that sounds like news. Just good news. And there's not always enough of that."

"I guess to me," Luz said, "the biggest news is that she still wants to talk with her mother, even though she's all grown up. I'll tell you, there were years when she was a teenager when that was the last thing I'd ever have expected."

"Well, that's how you know she's growing up," Sadie said, and winked.

As she did, the chime above the front door from the street rang merrily, and Edwin stepped into the shop, leaving a swirl of wind and aspen leaves on the sidewalk behind him. After a cold snap that had brought a fair amount of snow, the capricious Colorado autumn had brought back bright sun and warm, crisp air that had many of the locals trading winter coats for shirtsleeves.

Edwin glanced around for a moment, dressed as always a bit more formally than other Silver Peak natives, in a collared shirt, vest, and neat khakis: a formality that was probably a remnant of the decades he'd spent as a Chicago judge. His salt and pepper hair glowed briefly in the sun that fell through the window. Then he caught sight of Sadie, and his face lit up.

This time, the little thrill Sadie had gotten used to feeling when she saw him was tinged with nervousness. The conversation she had had with Edwin, where she told him that she wasn't ready for anything more than friendship, had been coming back to her more and more frequently recently. She'd started to wonder if she had said the right thing—and if she hadn't, what she ought to say to him, and when. But she still wasn't sure how she felt. And it could have been her imagination, but something had seemed different to her about the way that Edwin had asked her to meet him today. Usually, he was more casual, dropping into her store, or calling to ask her advice on his never-ending restoration of his father's house, which was a source of many of both his joys and frustrations.

But this time, he had called her a few days before, and asked if she would be willing to meet him at Arbuckle's. He'd sounded a little nervous himself—almost the way he had decades ago, when they had first started to go out. Sadie had told herself time and time again over the past few days that it wasn't a date. Edwin knew better. But she couldn't help realizing that, along with her nervousness, there was a growing hope that it might be one.

It didn't help that, as soon as Edwin came in the door, Luz turned away like a knowing mother, trying to give two awkward kids the space to work things out among themselves.

Feeling for all the world like a gawky teenager, she somehow managed to cross the store to greet Edwin.

"How are you?" she asked.

"I'm happy to see you," Edwin told her, and gave her a quick kiss on the cheek.

Sadie tried to remember whether he had done this before or not in the past, but for some reason she had trouble organizing her thoughts. Hoping to collect them, she started to sit down at the nearest table.

"Don't you want anything?" Edwin asked.

Despite that fact that Sadie couldn't usually resist Luz's coffee, she had completely forgotten about ordering a drink.

Sadie pushed her chair back to stand again, but Edwin gestured for her to stay put.

"I'll get it," he said with the same tone of generosity and confidence that Sadie had always liked about him.

"Your regular?" Luz asked from the nearby counter.

Sadie nodded, then offered up a quick prayer while Edwin placed his own order, and paid for the two of them.

Lord, she prayed. I have no idea what I'm doing. That's probably true more often than I know, but I sure know it right now. Please guide me. I don't want to try to live in the past, but I don't want to miss whatever you have for me in the future.

A moment later, Edwin was back with both drinks, and a fruit bar balanced on top of his own: pale yellow, with ribbons of deep red.

"Lemon with raspberry," he told Sadie with a quick smile. "Luz assured me it's the best."

"I think they're all the best," Sadie said.

Edwin's smile broadened at her joke. "You might be right about that," he said. He took the cup in his hands, leaned back in his chair, took a sip, and looked across the table at her.

Sadie held his gaze for a moment, but it seemed to last so long that she became embarrassed and looked down. "What?" she said.

"Pardon me," Edwin said, with his slight courtroom formality. "I just like to look at you."

"Oh, there's not much to look at," Sadie said.

"The two of us are just going to have to disagree on that," Edwin said, and took another sip of his drink.

Then he put it down on the table between them. "Sadie," he said. "I wanted to talk to you about this race for Silver Peak mayor."

A wave of—was it relief or disappointment?—washed over Sadie. So that was why he'd made a special appointment with her—the Silver Peak mayoral election, in which he was running as a candidate. Edwin had put himself forward for the position.

Just like Sadie, Edwin cared deeply about history and restoration, while James Morgan, his opponent, seemed more interested in leading Silver Peak forward into some kind of progressive future that even he didn't seem quite clear on. Both Sadie and Edwin liked James, who had graduated from school in Silver Peak several years before they had. And everyone else in town seemed to like him too. But Edwin was worried that, without strong leadership, much of Silver Peak's history could be lost or tainted—and with tourists and new residents pouring into town, if growth wasn't managed carefully, it could compromise Silver Peak's future.

"I'm up for anything," Sadie said. "You just let me know, and I'll do it."

Edwin gave her a wry smile. "Well, you might want to hear what I'm asking, first."

"It doesn't matter," Sadie said. "Whatever you need, you've got it."

"I'm not going to hold you to that," Edwin said. "But I want you to remember you said it."

He pushed the lemon bar across the table. "Try a bite?" he said.

Looking down at the delectable treat, Sadie realized that her usually reliable appetite had also fled. But she took a bite anyway, to give her a chance to clear her head.

Edwin stared down at the confection thoughtfully. The campaign hadn't seemed to worry him much before: like everything, he just seemed willing to give it his best, and let the chips fall where they may. But now his face had turned serious, and he seemed to be choosing and weighing his words.

"We have our first events for the campaign starting this week," he said.

Sadie already knew this, and not just from talking with Edwin. Just about everybody in town followed the brief season of the mayoral election. It only lasted a few weeks, but between the debates between the candidates, the ensuing debates among Silver Peak's citizenry, and the whirl of barbecues and stump speeches each candidate was expected to offer, election season was always some of the best entertainment Silver Peak had seen since Sarah Bernhardt, Collin Malloy, and Mark Twain had graced their historic opera house's stage.

But there was no point in interrupting Edwin, Sadie knew, or in trying to get him to cut to the bottom line. Edwin had a lawyer's patient, logical mind, and nothing would stop him from starting at the beginning, and carrying it through, point by point, to whatever he thought of as the end.

"The campaign is going to take a lot of my time," he said. "And if I win, being mayor may take even more. It'll take a significant commitment."

Sadie nodded, still uncertain what all of this had to do with her.

"But seeing you is important to me too," Edwin said. He looked up as he said it, and his eyes locked with hers for a moment before he glanced away. "I probably won't have the time to call you up for advice on the house in the near future. Or to drop by the store and find you there."

"I'll be there anytime you stop by," Sadie offered.

Edwin grinned. "I know you think that," he said. "But it's not really true. You spend a lot of time out and about, Sadie Speers. Believe it or not, I only catch you about every other time I come by."

Sadie felt a flush come up in her face. Did Edwin really come by to see her twice as often as she knew?

"Sadie," Edwin said. "You know how I feel about you."

"Well," Sadie said, "I know what you said before."

"I still feel that way," Edwin said. "I've been trying to take it slow. We've got time, and I don't want to push you. But I don't want to have to pretend I'm always just dropping by or stopping in. I'd like to be able to call you up and hear how your day went, and know that I'm going to get to see you sometime soon. I know what you said the last time I brought this up, and I respect that. Nothing's changed for me since then. But I can't help hoping that something might have changed for you. What do you think, Sadie. Is there any chance you'd ever consider…" He locked eyes with her again, uncertainty playing with a certain mischievous look on his distinguished features.

"…going steady with me again?"

The last time Edwin had asked her, Sadie has known her answer immediately. This time, she felt even more uncertain than he. She still felt a strong sense of loyalty to T.R. and their life together. She still couldn't imagine what a future with Edwin might look like. But under it all, she felt a deep happiness. Why, she wasn't sure. And she was even less sure about what to say.

She reached for her coffee and took a sip, then looked over her cup at Edwin.

He looked back at her, waiting. Once he'd said his piece, Edwin was a man who knew how to bide his time. But he would want an answer eventually. And Sadie couldn't even begin to put all of her thoughts, let alone her feelings, into words.

A footstep fell behind her. Sadie started, suddenly mortified at the idea that Luz had been nearby, listening to all of this. But before she could turn, a familiar voice called out.

"Grandma!" her grandson Theo cried. "Wait'll you see what I found!"

Sadie twisted in her seat to smile at Theo. He was seventeen, lanky, with thick dark hair that tended to fall into his eyes, especially when he was excited. It was drooping so far down over his eyebrows right now that she could barely believe he could see through it, which must mean he'd found something he was pretty excited about.

But then she remembered Edwin, and glanced back at him. Instead of the frustration she'd been afraid she might find on his face, she saw amusement.

"I'm sorry," she mouthed.

Edwin shrugged. "It's been decades," he said. "I can wait another day."

By this time, Theo had reached their table, breathless with excitement. "You're going to love this," he said, pulling up an empty seat from a nearby table and sitting down. "I was just at a yard sale in Denver. I wasn't actually looking for antiques. I was hoping to get a bike to use in Silver Peak, since I keep my good one at Dad's so he and I can go biking on the weekends we're together. They had a bunch of them advertised, but by the time I got there they were all gone."

"You have to get there early," Sadie told him.

Theo nodded, somewhat impatiently. "I know," he said. "I've staked out plenty of early-morning yard sales with you before. But I hit rush-hour traffic, and got there ten minutes after it opened, and –" he made a noise like a rushing wind.

"Sounds like bikers are about as enthusiastic as antiquers," Sadie said.

"I guess I wasn't the only one," Theo admitted. "But then I'd already driven all the way out there, so I decided to poke around. They didn't have much that was too interesting to me, just a lot of kids' clothes, and some power tools. But then, in with the knick-knacks, I found this."

He pulled a slim green bank ledger out of his pocket, slightly larger than a piece of standard letter paper.

Sadie couldn't help eyeing it appraisingly. Paper ephemera—books, ledgers, notebooks, and photograph, were some of her favorite antiques. They weren't as highly prized by decorators, who tended to gravitate toward furniture and other large elements that could be used in design, but Sadie loved antiques not just for their beauty, but for their history, and ephemera tended to offer a wealth of details that the mysterious initials cut into a desk, or the wear patterns on an antique chair, simply couldn't give. In terms of history, ephemera was often a gold mine.

"I know how you like paper ephemera," Theo rattled on. "And I thought there might be some interesting Colorado history in it, probably something about Denver..."

As he spoke, Sadie took in the details of the cover. She'd spent an interesting day a few years ago, in a pole barn on the property of an avid ephemera collector who had converted it into a personal library for his cache of antique bank ledgers. They weren't just full of out-of-date numbers, he'd taught her. They were a fascinating glimpse into changes in accounting practices, but also into the stories the numbers themselves told: like the patients recorded carefully in a doctor's ledger, which held stories of suffering and hope, or the decades represented by the careful columns of names and payments for a local bank's mortgage holders. And the ledgers reflected changes in the business of printing itself—more lush during times the American economy was flush, more Spartan when times were hard.

This one was so simple that Sadie suspected it might even be Depression era, and the simple design on the cover seemed to match the austerity of that time as well.

"But then," Theo said, breaking into her thoughts, "I looked at the frontispiece of this ledger, and it said Silver Peak!"

Even Edwin leaned forward at this. Excitedly, Theo opened the ledger, and pointed to the front page, where "Silver Peak Bank" was carefully printed. He pushed it toward Sadie, who stared down at it in fascination.

"Well," she said. "I wonder how this wound up at a yard sale in Denver. And I wonder what kind of stories the numbers will tell us."

"Well, that's the thing," Theo said.

"What?" Sadie asked.

Theo caught the upper corner of a page, and turned it for her. "There are no numbers," he said. Across the neat columns, ribbons of text ran, the neat lines of a standard diary entry. Sadie had seen ledger-keepers take notes in the margins before—sometimes impassioned or hilarious ones. But it was uncommon to see a ledger used as a diary.

"Well, I wonder who…" Sadie began.

"I searched through it pretty well. There might be clues in the entries, but I couldn't find a name or any identifying information for the author," Theo said.

At this, Edwin, who had crowded around to get a better look at the page, jabbed his finger at an entry, which contained a name in the course of the description.

"The writer mentions a 'Jules M,' " he read.

Sadie met his gaze, recognition in her eyes.

"Do you think that..., " Edwin began.

"I don't know who else it could be," Sadie said.

"Jules Morgan," Edwin said, finishing her thought for her.

"Who's that?" Theo asked.

Edwin let the ledger fall closed on the table between them. "The father of my opponent in the mayoral election."

A Note from the Editors

We hope you enjoy Mysteries of Silver Peak, created by the Books and Inspirational Media Division of Guideposts, a nonprofit organization that touches millions of lives every day through products and services that inspire, encourage, help you grow in your faith, and celebrate God's love in every aspect of your daily life.

Thank you for making a difference with your purchase of this book, which helps fund our many outreach programs to military personnel, prisons, hospitals, nursing homes, and educational institutions. To learn more, visit GuidepostsFoundation.org.

We also maintain many useful and uplifting online resources. Visit Guideposts.org to read true stories of hope and inspiration, access OurPrayer network, sign up for free newsletters, download free e-books, join our Facebook community, and follow our stimulating blogs.

To learn about other Guideposts publications, including the best-selling devotional *Daily Guideposts*, go to ShopGuideposts .org, call (800) 932-2145, or write to Guideposts, PO Box 5815, Harlan, Iowa 51593.